Jim Crace is the prize-winning author of eleven books, including *Quarantine* (winner of the 1998 Whitbread Novel of the Year and shortlisted for the Booker Prize) and *Harvest* (shortlisted for the 2013 Booker Prize). He was elected to the Royal Society of Literature in 1999; he has also received the E.M. Forster Award and the Guardian Fiction Prize. He lives in Birmingham, England, with his wife, Lauren Rose Crace, who played Danielle Jones in *EastEnders*.

HARVEST

As late summer steals in and the final pearls of barley are gleaned, a village comes under threat. A trio of outsiders — two men and a dangerously magnetic woman — arrive on the woodland borders and put up a makeshift camp. That same night, the local manor house is set on fire. Over the course of seven days, Walter Thirsk sees his hamlet unmade: the harvest blackened by smoke and fear, the new arrivals cruelly punished, and his neighbours held captive on suspicion of witchcraft. But something even darker is at the heart of his story, and he will be the only man left to tell it . . . Timeless yet singular, mythical yet deeply personal, this beautiful novel of one man and his unnamed village speaks for a way of life lost for ever.

Books by Jim Crace
Published by The House of Ulverscroft:

ALL THAT FOLLOWS

JIM CRACE

◆

HARVEST

Complete and Unabridged

CHARNWOOD
Leicester

First published in Great Britain in 2013 by
Picador
an imprint of
Pan Macmillan
London

First Charnwood Edition
published 2014
by arrangement with
Pan Macmillan
a division of
Macmillan Publishers Limited
London

A catalogue record for this book is available
from the British Library.

ISBN 978–1–4448–2017–1

Published by
F. A. Thorpe (Publishing)
Anstey, Leicestershire

Set by Words & Graphics Ltd.
Anstey, Leicestershire
Printed and bound in Great Britain by
T. J. International Ltd., Padstow, Cornwall

This book is printed on acid-free paper

Happy the man, whose wish and care
A few paternal acres bound,
Content to breathe his native air
In his own ground.

'Ode on Solitude', Alexander Pope

1

Two twists of smoke at a time of year too warm for cottage fires surprise us at first light, or they at least surprise those of us who've not been up to mischief in the dark. Our land is topped and tailed with flames. Beyond the frontier ditches of our fields and in the shelter of our woods, on common ground, where yesterday there wasn't anyone who could give rise to smoke, some newcomers, by the lustre of an obliging reapers' moon, have put up their hut — four rough and ready walls, a bit of roof — and lit the more outlying of these fires. Their fire is damp. They will have thrown on wet greenery in order to procure the blackest plume, and thereby not be missed by us. It rises in a column that hardly bends or thins until it clears the canopies. It says, new neighbours have arrived; they've built a place; they've laid a hearth; they know the custom and the law. This first smoke has given them the right to stay. We'll see.

But it is the second twist of grey that calls us close, that has us rushing early from our homes on this rest day towards Master Kent's house. From a distance this smoke is pale. No one has added greenery to darken it. But the blaze itself is less faint-hearted. It is rackety. It is a timber fire, for sure. But ancient wood. Long-felled. The years are in its smell. We fear it is the manor house that burns and that we will be blamed for sleeping through. We'd best prepare excuses now. So, if we heard the cracking of its rafters and its beams in our slumbers this morning, we must have mistaken it for the usual busying of trees and wind, or for the toiling of dreams, or for the groaning of our bones. Yesterday was harvest end, the final sheaf. We were expecting to sleep long and late this morning, with heavy shoulders naturally but with buoyant hearts. Our happiness has deafened us, we'll say. It was only when we heard Willowjack, the master's fancy sorrel mare, protesting at the smoke with such alarm, that we awoke and went to help, as help we must, for no one wants to lose the manor house.

Now that we have reached our master's paddocks and his garths, we can smell and taste the straw. The smoke and flames are coming not from his home but from his hay lofts and his stable roofs. His pretty, painted dovecote has already gone. We expect to spot his home-birds' snowy wings against the smoke-grey sky. But there are none.

I know at once whom we should blame. When Christopher and Thomas Derby, our only twins, and Brooker Higgs came back from wooding last evening, they seemed a little too well satisfied, but they weren't bringing with them any fowl or rabbit for the pot, or even any fuel. Their only spoils, so far as I could tell, were a bulky, almost weightless sack and immodest fits of laughter. They'd been mushrooming. And by the looks of them they had already eaten raw some of the fairy caps they'd found. I did the same myself in my first summer of settlement here, a dozen or so years ago, when I was greener and less timid, though not young. I remember eating them. They are beyond forgetting. Just as yesterday, the last sheaf of that year's harvest had been cut and stood. And, just as today, we'd faced a break from labour, which meant that I could sleep my mischief off. So in the company of John Carr, my new neighbour then, my neighbour still, I went off that afternoon to Thank the Lord for His Munificence by hunting fairy caps in these same woods. I'll not forget the dancing lights, the rippling and the merriment, the halos and the melting trails that followed anything that moved, the enormous fearlessness I felt, the lasting fear (yes, even now), or how darkly blue the moon became that night, and then how red. I wish I'd had the courage since to try to find that moon again.

Last evening, when the twins and Brooker Higgs jaunted past our cottages and waved at us with gill stains on their fingertips, I asked these merry men, 'Had any luck?' They bared their sack of spoils at once, because they were too foxed and stupefied to conceal them, even though they understood my ancient closeness to the manor house. I pulled aside the dampening of leaves and inspected their few remaining fairy caps, saved for later revels, I suppose, plus a good number of golden shawls, which, stewed in milk and placed inside a dead man's mouth, are meant to taste so good they'll jolt him back to life. Accounting for the bulk of their sack was a giant moonball, its soft, kid-leather skin already smoking spores, and far too yellowy and dry to cook. Why had they picked it, then? Why hadn't they just given it a satisfying kick? What kind of wayward lads were these?

Here's what took place. This is my reckoning, calculated without recourse to any constable or magistrate — and just as well, because this place is too far off from towns to number such judicious creatures amongst our livestock; we are too small, and getting smaller. Our final day of harvesting was not as joyful as it ought to have been, and not only because the crop proved so frugal in the ear. A gentleman we did not recognise was watching us reduce our barley field to stub; a visitor, a rare event, exciting and unnerving. We mowed with scythes; he worked with brushes and with quills. He was recording us, he said, or more exactly marking down our land, at Master Kent's request. He tipped his drawing board for anyone that asked and let them see the scratchings on his chart, the geometrics that he said were fields and woods, the squares that stood for cottages, the ponds, the lanes, the foresting.

He was a pleasant man, I'd say. No more than thirty years of age and dressed much like the master, not for labour but for the open air, in sturdy boots, breeches, a jerkin, and a plain cap without feather, brooch or badge. His beard was shaped and honed to a point with wax. I have a narrow trowel that matches it. A townsman's beard. A wealthy beard. And he was lop-sided when he moved, with a stiff arm and shoulder on his left. His was a body not well suited to the balks and bumpy edges of a field. He was a

4

stumbler. And there was, I thought, a trace of past illness in his expression as well as in his step. But I've never seen a man more ready with a smile. We could not help but stare at him and wonder, without saying so, if those scratchings on his board might scratch us too, in some unwelcome way.

Still, there was essential work to finish yesterday, whatever our distractions. If we hoped for sufficient grain to last the year, we'd have to deserve it with some sweat. This summer's yield was not yet good enough. Plenty, here, has wed itself to Leanness. At the lower, shaded limits by the dell and on the more neglected stony slopes our plants have proven miserly. They grew as short, askew and weakly as our limping visitor and so were hardly worth the reaping. But the higher field, which we left standing till the last, has always looked more sprightly — and more promising. Since spring we've waited with our fingers crossed as our better barley steadily renounced its green and let itself go tawny. From the lane, looking down towards the tracery of willows on the brook, the top end of our barley meadow, bristling and shivering on the breeze, showed us at last its ochres and its cadmiums, its ambers and its chromes. And the smells, which for so long in this slow summer were faint and damp, became nutlike and sugary. They promised winter ales and porridges. The awns and whiskers of the barley's ears were brittle and dry enough to chit-chat-chit every time they were disturbed, nattering with ten thousand voices at every effort of the wind or every scarper of a rabbit, mouse or bird. They said, 'We've had enough. Our heads are baked and heavy now. We're dry. Bring out your blades and do your worst.'

Reap and gossip. That's the rule. On harvest days, anyone who's got a pair of legs and arms can expect to earn supper with unceasing labour. Our numbers have been too reduced of late to allow a single useful soul to stay away. There's not a hand that will escape the brittle straw unscratched. The children go ahead of us, looking for the grey of any thistle heads that have outstripped our rust-gold barley, then duck below the level ears of grain to weed out nettles, teasels, docks; 'dealing with the grievances', we say. The broadest shoulders swing their sickles and their scythes at the brimming cliffs of stalk; hares, partridges and sparrows flee before the blades; our wives and daughters bundle up and bind the sheaves, though not too carefully — they work on the principle of ten for the commons and one for the gleaning; our creaking fathers make the lines of stooks; the sun begins to dry what we have harvested. Our work is consecrated by the sun. Compared to winter days, let's say, or digging days, it's satisfying work, made all the more so by the company we keep, for on such days all the faces we know and love (as well as those I know but do not like entirely) are gathered in one space and bounded by common ditches and collective hopes. If, perhaps, we hear a barking deer nagging to be trapped and stewed, or a woodcock begging to make his hearse in a pie, we lift our heads as one and look towards the woods as one; we straighten up as one and stare at the sun, reprovingly, if it's been darkened by a cloud; our scythes and hand tools clack and chat in unison. And anything we say is heard by everyone. So there is openness and jollity.

The harvest teamwork allows us to be lewd. Our humour ripens as the barley falls. It's safe to spread the gossip noisily, it's safe to bait and goad, Who's sharing wives? Which bearded bachelor is far too friendly with his goat? Which widower (they look at me) has dipped his thumb in someone else's pot? Which blushing youngsters are the village *spares*, that's to say those children who've been conceived in one man's bed and then delivered in another's? Who's making love to apple tubs? Who's wedded to a sack of grain? Nothing is beyond our bounds, when we are cutting corn.

So it was hardly a surprise yesterday that once 'Mr Quill' in Master Kent's close company was attending with his survey sticks and measuring tapes to the shape and volume of our fallow field and so beyond hearing, we wondered, out loud, whether our visiting townsman had ever overcome his undisguised deficiencies to secure himself a willing wife. Was he a husband yet? And, if he was, what blushing pleasures might Mistress Quill take from such staggering and stiffness and from having such a likeness of her hairy private part upon her stumbling lover's chin? 'I'd like to take a scythe to him,' said my neighbour John. Another said, 'I'd rather take my wooden staff to her.' And then of course the

7

bawdiness increased with such play on the prospect of caressing Mr Quill's three-cornered beard and Mistress Quill's twin attributes that every time that evening and in our company he ruminated with his hand around his chin, as was his habit, the women there could barely plug their grins while their men looked on, biting their lips. 'And have you noticed his white hands?' one of our village daughters asked. 'I wonder if he's ever dirtied them . . . other than to . . . ' No, she would not finish. What she had in mind did not seem possible.

It was only when the gentleman returned in the fullness of the afternoon and stood at our backs on the bristle of the field to quantify and measure us that we began again to wonder what awaited these treasured neighbourhoods and to feel uneasy. What was he wanting from our soil, what were his charts securing? We saw his finger wagging on the count. We heard him numbering, until he reached the paltry fifty-eight that represented us. We know enough to understand that in the greater world flour, meat and cheese are not divided into shares and portions for the larder, as they are here, but only weighed and sized for selling. Was Mr Quill the confirmation of the rumour that had gone about our doors that Master Kent was in such narrows now he was a widower that he would need to measure and sell our land? No amount of openness and jollity could raise our spirits once that fear took hold. Our observer's ready smile was menacing.

We were slow to broadcast our alarm. But we tackled our last barley stands more silently, less

8

lewdly — and more scrupulously, as we were being watched. Now each barking deer or woodcock call was a warning. Each darkling cloud reminded us how nothing in our fields was guaranteed. We only muttered to ourselves, too anxious to raise our voices loud enough to reach our neighbours down the reaping line. Some of the younger men set faces which declared they'd defend our acres with their lives or with the lives of anyone that crossed them. The usual silent swagger. Rather than speak up, they turned their anger on the pigeons and the rooks, and on a handful of our master's near-white doves, which had descended on the stub and were already robbing fallen grain that, by ancient gleaning rights, should have been ours. These 'snowy devils', their out-of-season whiteness making them seem even more coldly pea-eyed and acquisitive than their grey and black compan-ions, were feasting on our bread and ale, they said, and sent the children to use their slings or shower them with handfuls of grit or yell the thieves away, anything to evidence our tenancy. The air was full of wings and cries. So our final harvesting gained ground.

By my account, once our complicated working day was done and all our flat-eared barley was gathered in and carted away, the Derby twins and Brooker Higgs, unmarried men in a village dismayingly short of unmarried women, set off for the woods, while most of us, the rest of us, restored ourselves at home, took stock. We shook our heads and searched our hearts, until we had persuaded ourselves that Master Kent was too good and just a man to sell our fields. He'd always taken care of us. We'd always taken care of him. Besides, what was the evidence of any sale? A bearded, skew-whiff gentleman? A chart? The counting of our heads? No, we should not be mistrustful. We should face the rest day with easy hearts, and then enjoy the gleaning that would follow it, with our own Gleaning Queen the first to bend and pick a grain. We should expect our seasons to unfold in all their usual sequences, and so on through the harvests and the years. Everything was bound to keep its shape. That's what we thought. We were calm and leisurely. But, unlike the three bachelors, we had not found and eaten fairy caps and then concocted ways of getting even with the thieving birds, especially the white ones from the master's cote. Nor had we stumbled on a moonball, fatter than a blacksmith's head, but too tindery to eat. Such a dry and hollow moonball is good, as any tree scamp knows, for taking flames from here to there. It's good, if you are so inclined, while everybody sleeps and only night's black agents are at work, for taking fire into the master's yards.

Of course, those fairy-headed men did not intend to kill so many of the master's doves. Or even mean to start a fire. Their plan was only to create a little smoke and drive the birds away. But when their moonball lantern was pushed before first light into the loft, amongst the bone-dry chaff and litter that the doves had gleaned and brought inside for nesting, it wasn't long before its smoulder took to flame and the flame, encouraged by the frenzy of flapping wings, spread along the underside of roof beams, fed by timber oils, and found the top bales of that summer's hay. A bird will stay away from smoke. So these doves could seek the corners of their loft, or beat themselves against the roofing laths, or try to peck an opening. But who truly knows what doves might do in fires? Perhaps, a dove will simply sit and coo, too foolish to do otherwise, until its feathers are singed black, until its flesh is roasted to the bone. Whatever happened, this is certain: the stable yard this morning smells of undeserving meat. And the twins and Brooker Higgs have woken to the worst dawn of their lives.

In any other place but here, such wilful arsonists would end up gibbeted. They'd be on hooks in common view and providing sustenance to the same thieving birds they'd hoped to keep from gleaning. But, as I've said, these fields are far from anywhere, two days by post-horse, three days by chariot, before you find a market square; we have no magistrate or constable; and Master Kent, our landowner, is just. And he is timid when it comes to laws and punishments. He'd rather tolerate a wrongdoer amongst his working hands than rob a family of their father, husband, son. Of course, the burning down of the master's stable and his cote, the loss of hay and doves, is not a felony that should pass unpunished entirely. If the perpetrators are identified, they can expect a beating, followed by a lengthy sojourn sleeping rough, beyond our boundaries. Some of their family stock — a pair of goats, perhaps, some weaner pigs — might well be claimed in recompense. But their lives will never be at stake, not here. So maybe it is better for the bachelors to hold their nerve, come out to fight their own fire, seem innocent, and hope that everyone will take the blaze to be an act of God. Bad luck, in other words, and not a soul to blame.

But Brooker and the twins are not practised at deceit. They'd not succeed as players on a stage as so many other renegades and cut-throats do, escaping justice in a guise. Their guilt is on display for everyone to see. They are too noisy and too keen, especially when Master Kent himself comes down, wrapped in the sleeveless mandilion his wife wove for him in the winter of her death, and stands in shock beside his rescued mare, well back, beyond the heat, to watch his stable disappear. His home and peace of mind are scorched. The guilty men do what they can to make him notice them, make him see how loyal and tireless they're prepared to be on his behalf. Unlike the rest of us, Master Kent included, they'll not admit to at least some errant, childlike fascination with the flames, the old and satisfying way they turn such solids into ash and air. Instead, they lead the rush to bring in water from the pond and cisterns. They make too great a show of beating back the flames with spades. The blaze has made their tongues as dry as hay. They show no fear. It is as if their lives depend upon the quenching of this fire.

Of course, they are the ones — and Brooker Higgs especially; he is the orator — who organise

12

the hunt for those responsible. It is clear at once — as soon as he suggests it — that nobody is ready to believe his claim that such a fire was caused by chance or by the natural overheating of a rick. A good rick's as solid as a cottage, bricked with sheaves. It can sweat, and bake itself. But what could have kindled it? There was no lightning overnight. No one burning farm waste close by sent a vagrant spark across the master's garths. No one slept in the stable block by candle-light. The master cannot be accused of having gone up amongst the doves with his tobacco pipe. No, this was done maliciously. Brooker is nodding his agreement. Whoever caused 'this Devil's work', he suggests, pointing at the black remains of the ricking ladder, which only this morning he and his own accomplices leant against the stable wall for access to the dovecote, probably intended to make off with the master's doves. To eat. Now who amongst them has so empty a stomach that they would need to steal a neighbour's food? Why only last evening the master himself said he would kill a calf to mark the end of harvest and their election of the Gleaning Queen. So who amongst them would steal and eat a dove and then find themselves too glutted to enjoy the veal? No, the finger of suspicion points not at a villager — the very thought! — but at a stranger.

There're newcomers, come out of nowhere to the edges of our wood, somebody says, precisely as Brooker hopes they will. This informer waves his hands towards the far side of the fields and that other damper, blacker plume of smoke that

13

all of us with eyes have seen this morning on our way to save the stable. From where we stand their smoke is still bending darkly on a breeze across the treetops.

'We'll call on them, I think,' says the master mildly. 'We'll call on them to test what answers they provide, but not before we've dampened everything and made my buildings safe.' He looks around and shakes his head. This has been a blow for him, another burden to survive. His eyes are watery. Perhaps it's only smoke that makes them watery. 'Well . . . ' he says, looking towards the smudgy sky above the newcomers, and lets his comment hang. He means that he is heavy-hearted at the thought — the logical suspicion, in fact — that the second plume of smoke will lead him to the dove-roasters. And then he knows his duty will demand a firm and heavy hand.

I understand that this is the moment when I should raise my own hand and say my piece, report the dry moonball. Or at least I should take Brooker Higgs aside to nudge him in the ribs. But I hold my tongue instead. A moonball isn't evidence. Nor is bad playing. Besides, I sense the mood is to let this drama run its course and die back with the flames. Today's a rest day and we want the air to clear — to clear of danger and to clear of smoke — so that we can enjoy ourselves as we deserve. This evening there's ale to drink, there's veal to eat, and we will choose the prettiest to be our Gleaning Queen. I'm sure I'm not the only one who elects to hold his tongue and does not, as he should, put up his hand. We do

14

not wish to spoil our holiday, nor will we value bales of straw and doves above our neighbours' sons.

In fact, my hand — the left — is too damaged to be raised. I was amongst the foolish volunteers who tried to roll some of the burning bales into the yard towards the line of water buckets so that we might save at least some of the master's winter feed, his great bulging loafs of hay. I soaked my neck-cloth in a water pail and tied it round my mouth against the smoke, and then, with neighbour Carr at my side, went into the stable block beneath the cracking timbers to see what we could save. We put our hands and chests against the closest bale, braced our legs against the paving flags, and pushed. The bale lurched forward, only half a turn. We braced to push again but this time my one hand plunged into the burning straw and smouldered for a moment. My fingertips are burnt. There's not a hair below my wrist. My palm is scorched and painful beyond measure. I have to say a roasted man does not smell as appetising as a roasted dove. The damage is severe. The skin is redder than a haw. I do my best to chew the pain, to not create a further spectacle. Still, I am not starved of sympathy. Even the master himself takes me by the shoulders in a hug to show his pity and concern. He knows a farmer with an injured hand is as useful as a one-pronged pitchfork. No use at all, especially at harvest time. No wonder I am more concerned at the moment with my own flesh than with any stranger's. Now I have to go back to my house and make a poultice for the wound from egg white and cold flour. Then a pinch of salt to pacify the blisters. I will have to be an invalid today. Today, at least, I will have to sit and watch the world. Whatever's bound to happen when my neighbours reach those newcomers who've set up home on the common outskirts of our fields will happen without me.

2

The village is aflame, but not with fire. This morning, once the master's stable blaze was deadened and so drenched it could hardly cough a puff of ash, my neighbours were in a bold and rowdy mood. The air was swarming with anxieties. With Master Kent, mindful of his horse's dung, riding politely at their rear on his recovered mare, they took the carting lane beside the manor house and strode with devilry in their steps — the kind that can flourish only on a day when there's no other work to do — towards the one remaining twist of smoke. Some of them were armed — or is it fairer to say *equipped*? — with sticks and staves, and 'meaner implements', John Carr reports. We're not a hurtful people, hereabouts. But we feel naked without tools. And it makes sense in such a distant place as this, where there is little wealth and all our labours are spent on putting a single meal in front of us each day, to be protective of our modest world and fearful for our skinny lives. Master Kent may own the fields. His titles, muniments and deeds are witness to the truth of that. The manor comes to him by right of marriage, through the old master, Edmund Jordan, and his only daughter, Lucy Kent, both deceased and buried not a hundred paces from my home in the church-yard with no church.

But what are documents and deeds when

there are harvests to be gathered in? Only toughened hands can do that job. And Master Kent, for all his parchmenting, would be the poorest man if all he had to work his property were his own two hands and no others. He'd be blistered by midday, and famished ever after. What landowner has ever made his palms rough on a scythe or plough? Ours are the deeds that make the difference. No, our ancient understanding is that, though we are only the oxen to his halter, it is allowed for us to be possessive of this ground and the common rights that are attached to it despite our lack of muniments. And it is reasonable, I think, to take offence at a ruling — made in a distant place — which gives the right of settlement and cedes a portion of our share to any vagrants who might succeed in putting up four vulgar walls and sending up some smoke before we catch them doing it — and to see these vagrants off, beyond our cherished boundaries. It's true, of course, that some of us arrived this way ourselves, and not so long ago. I count myself amongst those aliens. But times have changed. Our numbers have decreased in the years since I arrived as my master's manservant. Stomachs have fallen short of acres. We've lost good friends but not had much success with breeding their inheritors or raising sturdy offspring. We're growing old and faltering. Harvests have been niggardly, of late. There're days in winter when our cattle dine and we do not. Why should we share with strangers?

Anyway, what can you tell about a newcomer from smoke, except that he or she is wanting? Or demanding? We've heard from the occasional pedlar, tinker or walkthrough carpenter — who's hoped, and failed, to make a living in our midst — how there are cattle thieves beyond the woods, how travellers are stopped and robbed, how vagabonds and vagrant families descend upon a settlement to plunder it, like rooks and crows, and then move on. We have to ask ourselves, why have these people arrived just as the harvest is brought in. Is this another act of God? Bad luck, in other words, and not a soul to blame? A saint might think it so. A saint might want to welcome them and shake them by the hands. But we, more timorous than saints, might prefer to keep our handshakes to ourselves. Besides, to touch a stranger's flesh is dangerous. Do not embrace a soul until you know its family name, we say. We have been fortunate this year. No deaths from plague and only one appalling death from sweating fits so far. But contagion is known to be a crafty passenger, a stowaway. I can imagine hidden sores and rashes on the backs and buttocks of our visitors. And I can see why blaming them for what the twins and Brooker Higgs have done might be a blessing in disguise. No, I was glad to be at home this morning and not amongst my neighbours, even though it meant I missed first sighting of this creature who has so charred us with her fire.

I sat outside the cottage with my injured hand resting open on my knee, its palm turned up, and let the fresh air salve the wound. It was a rare event to have the row of dwellings to myself or, that's to say, to share them only with our poultry and our pigs. The quiet was curative, but it was also chilling in a way to survey, from the oaken bench I built myself from timber that I felled myself, the makeshift byres that once were family cottages. There was the creeper-throttled derelict next door to the Carrs' home, which when I first arrived was never free of voices; and then the unkept garden at widow Gosse's place, where her husband used to stand and boast his colworts and his radishes, his double-marigolds and thyme; and, after that, set away with its own path, the rubble of the tenement where Cecily, my wife, was raised. No, we have tenancy to spare, and could easily provide some newcomers a place to live, if the village was only minded to be less suspicious of anyone who was not born with local soil under their fingernails. Some extra working hands might be of value in the coming days, especially since my own left hand will be of little use and we are so hard-pressed for younger men and women. I rapped my good hand on the bench until my knuckles hurt. I did not deserve to feel relaxed.

These are the moments when I most miss greater places — the market towns, the liberties of youth, the choices that I had and left behind. My land-born neighbours now are ditched and fenced against the outside world. They are too rooted in their soil, too planched and thicketed, to be at ease with newcomers. They are not used to hospitality and do not want to be. There's not a village, sea to sea, that receives fewer strangers. In all the years since my and Master Kent's arrival not one other new soul has settled here for long, or hoped to. Who, after looking at this place and with no secret interest or association, would choose to make a home amongst these frowning residents? But I am now part of it and part of them. I have become a frowner, too, and I have learnt to make do with the Kindom of close relatives, where anyone who is not blood is married to someone else who is. One family's daughter is another's niece, another's aunt, and yet another's daughter-in-law. And if you're not a Saxton or a Derby or a Higgs yourself, you have a score of relatives who are. We live in a rookery. A cousinry, let's say. And just like rooks we have begun to sound and look the same. So many grumps, so many corn-haired blondes, so many wavy, oval beards, so many beryl eyes, so many thickset arms and legs, that no one needs to mention them, or even notice them, unless reminded by an out-of-pattern visitor like me. But even I have found myself with thickset arms and legs, though I arrived as thin and gawky as our Mr Quill.

The latest dwelling on our lands is by all reports a poor affair. Our hurried newcomers have only dragged some fallen timber from the wood and woven out of it, uncut, a square of fences better suited to restrict a pair of pigs than to house a family. These walls are fit for men who prefer to crawl rather than stand. They're pargeted with earth and leaves, and roofed with the kind of sacking that can stop neither the light nor the rain. Is this den enough to confer squatting rights? No one is sure. Though if it is, foxes, badgers, even moles could lay claim to their common rights and help themselves to fowl and fruit and firewood from our land. But then it is not expected that these newcomers, these funguses that seek to feed on us, these dove-slaughterers, will choose to stay amongst us for a second night once they've discovered how thin — and dangerous — our welcome is. They'll travel on. We'll walk them to our boundaries and set them on the way, glad to be of help.

The open hearth that sent up such a green-black plume at dawn was dead by the time my neighbours and Master Kent arrived at the shadowed clearing near The Bottom, where our land is cliffed by woods. Even Mr Quill had lurched along behind them, his parchment book in hand, as ever with such gentlemen, making notes and marking shapes and hoping not to be excluded from the dramas of the day. Though the smoke had run its course and some tidy housekeeper had already kicked away the remaining ashes and twigs, the confirmation that my neighbours were expecting — and Brooker and the twins were praying for — was on the ground for all to see. Bird bones, gnawed clean. Christopher Derby, the elder of the twins and usually the quieter, pointed at the remains with all the authority his index finger could muster and said, 'Our dear guests' meal. One of the master's birds.' Last night the newcomers had evidently gnawed on dove, as if they were 'great lords at banqueting', though by the looks of it, according to my neighbour, John Carr, who took the trouble to push his inspecting toe through the scraps and leftovers, this dove had dark feathers, short bones and a yellow beak. None of my other neighbours wished to be dissuaded, though. It was easier to believe that by a further cunning the arsonists had disguised their plunder as a blackbird.

There was no sign of any living bones about the den, and when its overnight inhabitants were summoned with a shout and beating implements to give an account of themselves, no one appeared. Brooker Higgs was the first to raise his stick and strike the dwelling on its roof, expecting, with a single blow, to bring it to the ground and earn himself some cheap applause. His stick produced an unexpected clonk as dull and firm as a bag of chaff, but the roof, after seeming to adjust itself, fell in. What thickset man cannot bring down a length of sacking? But the hurried timber walls were stouter than they looked.

Other men stepped forward with heavier tools and would have finished the task had not, before the second blow, a pair of strangers — a young mop-headed youth with a feathery, novice beard and a shorter, older man, the father, probably — stepped out of the trees with longbows raised and drawn to the ear. In common with every other man about these parts, they clearly knew how to loose an arrow if called upon. They seemed baffled rather than belligerent. They looked, in other words, more innocent than any of us would have liked. Their squinted eyes and furrowed foreheads said, 'What kind of villainy is this that takes a cudgel to a poor man's home?'

The twins and Brooker Higgs no longer

wished to be numbered amongst the front rank of their more aggressive neighbours, and not only because the strangers' arrows seemed to be pointing at Brooker's chest. He was the only one who'd done any damage yet and so was the most deserving of some punishment. He heeled his way into the crowd until his chest was not the first in line, and then — no fool — he let himself drop shorter. The women called their children to their sides and also backed away. The widow Gosse, I'm told, fainted and fell into some nettles. The other, more stalwart men made narrow with themselves, turning their shoulders to the arrow-heads and tucking their elbows into their waists, protecting their soft organs.

Master Kent dismounted from Willowjack and stood behind her. He was not being cowardly but sensible. The men spread out, widening the strangers' target and already calculating in their heads that the odds were on their side, that twenty sturdy men standing on their own God-given land with sticks and even one or two keen sickles were more than a match for two newcomers and a pair of arrows. As soon as those two arrows were released, no matter what damage they might do, the game was over and the beating could begin. As I've said, we're not a hurtful people. We are, though, fearful, proud and dutiful. We do what must be done. But at this moment, so I'm told, the mood was murderous. Two poacher-arsonists were facing us with bows. We'd never known such disrespect and brazen sacrilege. The day had darkened suddenly.

Mr Quill, for such a malformed man, showed the greatest bravery. Or was it simply courtesy? He clumsied forward wearing that ready, foolish smile which had kept us company in yesterday's field. For a moment it was thought he meant to strike the den himself and earn the recompense of being augered through the heart by a hardened poplar arrow-shaft. Indeed, one of the strangers turned his bow on Mr Quill, secured his hold on the fletchings and string, and said in an accent no one there had heard before, 'Step well away.' But the master's chart-maker did not step well away. He had other plans. What those plans were, my neighbours never discovered. Four or five of them took advantage of what they would later describe to me as Mr Quill's shrewd diversion. While he distracted them with his determined smile, holding out his palms to show they had nothing to be fearful of, our bolder men edged closer to the newcomers. Two more steps and it would be done. If Mr Quill was sacrificed in their attempt, then that might be a price they could afford. He was no cottager. They hadn't grown used to him. No matter that his scratchings would be incomplete. I will not say they may have thought his death convenient.

This was the moment that the woman showed her face. No witnesses are in any hurry to blot out the vision of her rising from the den. She had been hidden and confined below the sacking roof all along, I'm told excitedly by almost everyone who saw it. She is the burning topic for this evening. While her men — no one knows yet what kinship there might be between the three of them — were concealed amongst the trees, she was evidently sitting up inside her crude dwelling and peering out between the branches and the earthy daub at what I have to call a mob. She will have wondered at the anger they brought with them, their fearsome staves and sticks, the glinting silver of their sickle blades. She will have seen a stocky young man with the stone-green eyes of a cottage cat step forward and bring his clonking stick down on her roof — and on her skull. The face that showed itself was running wet with blood, and her black hair was further darkened with a wound.

The whole encounter was transformed by blood, I'm told. What was a routine stand-off between two sets of men, two sets of *armed* men, both ready to defend themselves incautiously, had in a trice become an occasion of shame. The woman's wound was too red and fresh not to take notice of. Indeed, the blood was marking her cheeks, like tears. At once the village women began to call out for restraint. Their men did not attempt those two more steps. They let their weapons fall away into the undergrowth or hang loosely from their hands. Again it was Mr Quill who didn't do what he was told. Despite the closeness of the bow, he moved forward awkwardly, pulled aside the topmost branches of their den, put out his hand and helped the bloody woman step into the light.

What were they to make of her? She was not beautiful, not on first encounter anyhow. She had what we might call (behind her back) a weasel face, wide-cheeked, thin-lipped, a short receding chin, a button nose, and eyes and hair as shiny, dark and dangerous as belladonna berries. What caught our women's eyes at once was the velvet shawl she wore round her shoulders, an expensive lordly weave in heavy Turkish mauve and silver thread. Their instinct was to call out, Mind your Cloth. Her blood was bulbing on her little chin and might soon drop to spoil the velvet. Their second thought declared, she's dressed beyond her station. A woman of her kind could not possess a shawl such as that without first stealing it. Even Lucy Kent, the master's wife, had never owned a shawl such as that. Indeed, a shawl such as that, so far as anybody could remember, had never crossed the village boundaries before. It's not surprising, then, that so many of our wives and daughters widened their eyes in envy, hoped to feel the weight of it between their fingers, and wondered what their chances were of wearing it themselves.

The village men were not so taken by the cloth. They noticed it, of course, and how it added a becoming colour to the scene. They could imagine making use of it, laid out in the hidden corner of some field, far from their wives. But, as men will, they were assessing her by standards other than her clothes. They surveyed her, hoof, horn and tail. And then they surveyed her two men. What they saw was someone who might happily infect their dreams, a wide-hipped woman who was enthralling to behold in ways they never could explain and all the more so for not being beautiful or statuesque but rather someone within reach, and someone who was

27

defiantly — and irresistibly — proud. She held up her head, flared her nostrils in disdain, pursed her lips, and did not even dip her gaze as she was helped by Mr Quill beyond the province of her broken home. She'd be, they thought, more than thirty years of age and so it was unlikely (and preferable, of course) that either of the men was her husband. The elder was already grey and balding, her father possibly, though any facial likeness was obscured by beard; the other was a man at least ten years younger than the woman, but equally as black-haired as her. A brother, then. This was a family. And it was safe to say the daughter of the house was still available, despite her age. She was a widow, possibly, with all that implies: she would be seasoned and experienced; she would have an unslaked thirst for company. In a village such as ours, where women die before the men, there are plenty of my neighbours who will have seen at once a tempting opportunity. While the women might have cast her as a subject of their kindom or a partner for their sons and might have nieced and cousined her, glad to have their breeding stock enlarged by some black hair, the men there will have chambered her and nested her the moment that she showed herself. Surely that could hardly count as sin. The local women were like land — fenced in, assigned and spoken for, the free-hold of their fathers, then their husbands, then their sons. You could not cross their boundaries, or step beyond your portion. But this one, this incomer, was no better than any other wild quarry on common ground. Like any pigeon, any hare, she was fair game.

Still, the written law should be obeyed. Our Master Kent, who had yet to show his presence and authority, mounted Willowjack again and brought her forward until he reached the clearing by the den, where the three newcomers and Mr Quill were standing like skittles, not uttering a word. I sympathise with Master Kent and what he chose to do. He understood that something out of reason had occurred and something out of reason had to put an end to it.

'Put those aside,' he said, indicating the two longbows. 'This is not a place for ruff . . . ' He would have called them ruffians had not the woman widened her eyes at him. 'This is not a place for rough manners,' he resumed.

She laughed. 'Those are the only manners we've seen since we arrived,' she said. 'What shame is it that you shake sticks at us?'

'I'm not shaking any sticks at you,' the master said. 'Nor shall I do so. But you two, sirs' — he pointed at the woman's men — 'must pay for dining out last night on fowl that don't belong to you . . . we've seen the picked-clean bones . . . by contemplating better manners in the pillory. Let's say one week. And let your offending bows be put underfoot and snapped in two. And each of you should have your head shaven, to mark you out as . . . well, suspicious travellers.'

One week, disarmed and bald? A modest punishment. And one which by happy chance would keep the woman on our land and separated from her men for long enough for every village hand to try his luck with her. She spat at this point, only at the ground between the horse's hoofs but still a shocking act and one that Master Kent could not ignore without losing face.

'Count yourself as fortunate we do not boast a broader pillory,' he said, not looking at her in case she widened her eyes at him again. 'And be thankful that we are too gentle here and careful of our water to duck you in our village pond. But you will lose your hair together with your men. And in the time it takes to lengthen you might consider your disdain for us.'

This time her phlegm reached Willowjack and left a rosary of pearls across her flank.

3

It is the evening of this unrestful day of rest and the far barn that has survived the fire is full of harvesters, lying back on bales of hay and building up an appetite on rich man's yellow manchet bread from Master Kent's elm platters. We're drinking ale from last year's barley crop. Again we benefit from seasons. Lanterns throw out such deep and busy shadows that my neighbours' faces are hard to place. They are grotesques, but only for a moment. I do not have to count the heads to see that everyone is here. There's not a soul who's stayed behind at home tonight. Even the twins' old mother, who cannot shuffle a single step unless supported at both elbows and lifted like a plaster saint, has somehow succeeded, with the help of a wooden winnowing screen — 'my lady's litter,' as she says — in being carried to the feast. There're parsley balls, salted offal pumps and stewed giblets. There's cured bacon too. And the little hand-reared calf, rejected by its mother in the spring and kept by Master Kent in this same barn, has been slaughtered for its pains, skinned in one and shafted on a roasting pole. For us. Its hide is hanging from a rafter beam above the fire, being dried and cured in the smoke and odour of its own flesh.

We ought to be content. The harvest's in. Our platters are piled high with meat. There's grease on everybody's chin. Our heads are softening with beer. Yet I can tell our village is unnerved. This morning's fires and skirmishes hang heavily, especially with the twins and Brooker Higgs but also with the men who far too quickly volunteered to hold the spitting woman on the ground and scissor her. To tell the truth there's none of us who feels entirely comfortable, who is not soiled with a smudge of shame. Chatter being what it is, I have no doubt that, apart from Master Kent and Mr Quill, anyone who wants to know who truly took a flame up to the dovecote will have worked it out by now. Secrets are like pregnancies hereabouts. You can hide them for a while but then they will start screaming. So we are all conspirators tonight. We can be absolved only if these three guilty friends pin their valour to their chests and whisper in the master's ear that the two so far nameless men who are now standing side by side, cuffed, collared and locked in the village pillory at the gateway to the church we never built, enduring the first chill of the evening and a little rain, should be set loose and brought into the feaster's barn by way of an apology. A cut of veal could be our recompense.

It's possible — no, likely, I will say — that Master Kent will not avenge himself on the twins and Brooker Higgs if they reveal the truth. Tonight they're family, to some degree. Tonight we all are family. And Master Kent, especially since his wife passed on and left her unattended looms but not a single child to him, cherishes the fellowship we provide. Besides, it does not take a great amount of ale to make him warm and soft.

Unlike a lot of us, the more he drinks the more he values harmony. So our merry men — so noticeably quiet, I see, and sitting in a huddle on the furthest bale, avoiding lantern light — could easily and without much fear design an almost-honest version of this morning's fire and make amends, both to the master and to the newcomers — and also to my smarting palm; I was the only villager they scorched. But they do not. They do not want to risk the truth.

And neither, come to that, do I. Despite what I have seen myself while walking to the barn, it is unjust but sensible, I think, to let the pillory alone. The cup of hospitality is broken already. So far as I can tell, it is not likely that our visitors, once their seven days are served, will want to set up home amongst us anyway. We've not endeared ourselves to them. They'll fold their sacking and go, the moment they're set free. So maybe it is wise for all of us to hold our tongues for the time being and let them soak up all the blame. Seven days are neither here nor there with men like that, men who have no land or greater family, men who have no roots but are like mistletoe. Further, there is an account on which I cannot yet confer my sympathy, being absent from this morning's scene, that says these newcomers are worthy of the pillory anyway, no matter who it was who took the fire to Master Kent's old beams. No one forgets the two drawn bows, the impudence of telling people they'd better step away, or else.

Nevertheless, we are certainly unnerved. Our pillory has not been used for many years. Its iron bolt key, which Master Kent keeps with a dozen others on a bronze chain somewhere in his parlour, is rusty and has broken wards. Its last frequenters were two cousins — both Saxtons, so related to my wife — who went to war amongst themselves about the title to a pig. That's no small matter. I'm not making light of it. Pigs are our backyard brethren, in a way, and worth fighting for. It took half a dozen of our lads to calm them down. To pin them down, in fact. It was an entertaining afternoon. The cousins spent only a night encased, as I remember it, and by the morning they had butchered their differences. They shared the pork out, snout to tail, two trotters each, weighing everything and even dividing the liver and the heart with the care of merchants cleaving an ounce of gold or cutting a length of cloth. Ever since they have enjoyed a reputation as our favourite rascals. They have only to grunt to have us clutching at our ribs. To this day they rarely miss an opportunity to claim, usually within each other's hearing, that standing in the pillory was not a cruel punishment, though being in their cousin's company was. And remains so. They'd paid too great a price for pork.

That was about ten harvests ago, during the second or third year of our master's marriage and his freehold over us. He's never thought it fit to put the pillory to use since then. It's been our village cross. We've little else. The plot of land that was set aside for a church has nothing on it other than our too many graves, a pile of well-intended but as yet unlaid stones and,

34

somewhere underneath the bracken, sore-hocks and willow herb, a flat foundation block. So far no one has made the time to dig a building trench, select a single flint for our church's walls or mix a pint of mortar. We do not dare to say we count ourselves beyond the Kingdom of God. But certainly we do not press too closely to His bosom; rather, we are at His fingertips. He touches us, but only just. We work cheek to jowl with breeds that cluck and snort and moo, but never with the Father who created us and them. I've yet to sense Him standing at our shoulders, sickle in His hand. I've yet to feel Him lightening the plough. No, we dare to think and even say amongst ourselves, there'd be no barley if we left it to the Lord, not a single blade of it. Well, actually, there'd be no field, except a field of by-blows and weeds; the nettles and tares, the thorns and brambles He preferred when He abandoned Eden. You never find Him planting crops for us. You never find us planting weeds. But still we have to battle with His darnel and His fumiter, we have to suffer from His fleas and gnats and pests. He makes us pay the penalty of Adam. Sometimes we're thankful that the nearest steeple is a lengthy day away (and so's the nearest ale-house, come to that!). We can't afford a living for a priest. We'd prove too small and mean a flock for him. Our umbrage would eclipse our awe. So we continue not irreligiously but independently, choosing not to remind ourselves too frequently that there's a Heaven and a Hell and that much of what we count as everyday is indeed a sin.

We do, though, have our wooden cross, our neglected pillory, standing at the unbuilt gateway of our unbuilt church. It's slightly taller than a normal man, oak built. The two hinged boards which form its wings and provide two stations for its prisoners are wider and a little longer than its upright. That makes our cross more muscular and far reaching than the usual, narrower crucifix. The orifices which in a crueller place would more regularly provide a fitting for the necks and wrists of miscreants have lately been a useful space for us to hang prayer rosaries or love chains made from flowers. It's here that Master Kent conducts our marriages and baptisms, where he delivers eulogies to those who have departed — my wife and his were celebrated on this spot — and comforts the bereaved. It's here we gather to consecrate our seed corn and give our harvest thanks and bless the plough.

So earlier this evening it was for me an unhappy and infernal sight to see the two men and their hanging heads and hands, secured to the village cross and left to sag for seven days. Up till that moment I'd witnessed only their smoke and heard about these newcomers, their defiance and their bows, through the vaunting, colourful reports of my brave neighbours, mostly John Carr and Emma Carr and the widow Gosse, with whom, in all honesty, I have of late established an occasional attachment. From her nettling description, I was expecting rougher men. All I could see from a cautious distance, passing by on my way towards the smell of veal and bacon, were the inoffensive tops of two hastily shaven and humiliated heads, as newly reaped as our great field, one ghostly grey, the other already darkening with tar-black stubble. The elder was the shorter man. He was on tiptoes and in evident discomfort. If he stood flat, he would be throttled by the wooden vice that bolted him in place. I decided then to find a flattish log for him to stand on when later I returned that way.

Master Kent is standing now, and drawing expectant smiles from us. These feasting times are when, fuelled by ale, he likes to recall for his soil-bound guests the life he led before his happy coming here. His are embroidered tales of a strange and dangerous world: imps and oceans; palaces and wars. They always leave my neighbours glad they'll not be part of it. But tonight his mood is clearly not a teasing one. Instead, he has invited Mr Quill to join him at the makeshift dining board and both of them have clapped us quiet. Is this a moment we should fear? 'Here is my good acquaintance, Philip Earle,' he says, taking hold of Mr Quill's elbow and pushing him forward for us to greet and inspect. 'You will have met him yesterday, and you will see him hereabouts for one more week. He has come to us in my employ to make a map of all our common ground and land. We will prepare some raw pauper's vellum for his task from that veal skin which is hanging now above my head. He will take note of everything and then draw up petitions for the courts. What follows is — with your willing, kind consents — an organisation to all of our advantages. Too many seasons have been hard for us . . . ' At this point Mr Earle (as we will never think of him) unrolls one of the working charts he has prepared and asks us to come up to see our world 'as it is viewed by kites and swifts, and stars'. We press forward, shuffling against each other to fit within the lantern light. 'These are more complete than yesterday,' says Mr Quill, but once again we only see his geometrics and his squares. His mapping has reduced us to a web of lines. There is no life in them. Now he shows a second chart with other spaces. 'This is your hereafter,' he says.

'Yes, our tomorrows will be shaped like this,' adds Master Kent. That Yes is more uncertain than it ought to be. He pauses, smiles. 'I will be exact . . . ' he promises. But not, it seems, for the moment.

Say it, say it now, say the word, I urge him silently. I don't have to be a swift or kite to know about the world and how it's changing — changing shape, as Master Kent suggests — and to hear the far-off bleating of incoming animals that are neither cows nor pigs nor goats, that are not brethren. I know at once; I've feared this 'Yes' ever since the mistress died. The *organisation to all of our advantages* that the master has in mind — against his usual character and sympathies, against his promises — involves the closing and engrossment of our fields with walls and hedges, ditches, gates. He means to throw a halter round our lives. He means the clearing of our common land. He means the cutting down of trees. He means this village, far from everywhere, which has always been a place for horn, corn and trotter and little else, is destined to become a provisioner of wool. The word that he and no one dares to whisper let alone cry out is Sheep. Instead Master Kent presents a little nervously a dream he's had. He hopes that if he can describe these changes as having been fetched to him by a dream, then we will understand him more and fear him less, for dreams are common currency even amongst commoners. Surely, we are dreamers too.

In this dream, all his 'friends and neighbours' — meaning us — no longer need to labour long and hard throughout the year and with no certainty that what we sow will ever come to grain. We have good years, we have bad, he reminds us. We share contentments, but we also share the suffering. The sun is not reliable. And nor is rain. A squalling wind can flatten all our crops. Mildew reduces it to mush. Our cattle might be ravaged by the murrain fever. Our harvest can be taken off by crows. ('And doves,' a small voice says. My own.) But wool is more predictable. A fleece of wool does not require the sun. Indeed, a fleece of wool will grow and thicken in the dark. A fleece is not affected by the wind or by the changing seasons, he says, warming to the task — for it is a task, a labour of persuasion. And, as far as he's aware, crows do not have a taste for wool, despite — he smiles, to alert us to his coming jest — their appetite for flocking.

No, Master Kent has had a dream which makes us rich and leisurely. Every day becomes a day of rest for us. We walk about our fenced-in fields with crooks. We sit on tussocks and we merely watch. We are not ploughing; we are shepherding. We are not reaping; we are shearing. We are not freezing to the bone on damp and heavy winter days picking stones out of the soil, wringing the necks of furrow weeds, or tugging out twine-roots and couch until our backs are stiffer than a yoke. No, we are sitting at our fires at home and weaving fortunes for ourselves from yarn. Our only industry is shooting shuttles to and fro as if it were a game, child's play. Our only toil is easy toil — a gentle firming at the heddles, attending to the warp and weft with just our fingertips, untying snags and loosening. Instead of oxen there'll be looms. Instead of praying for the stems of crops to stay straight and tall against the odds, against the efforts of the elements, and for their ears of corn to thicken and to ripen, we will be closing the sheds on broadcloth, fustian, worsted and twill. 'A stirring prospect, isn't it?' he says. Somewhere too far away to name, in places we can never see, a man is putting on a coat that we have shepherded and then made up with our own hands, a woman pulls a scarf across her head and smells our hearths and country odours in its weave. We start off with the oily wool on the back of our own livestock, our Golden Hoofs, and end up with garments on the backs of noble folk. It is a dream that, surely, none of us find vile. And still he has not said it: Sheep. Am I the only one to recognise what the dream is trying to disguise? The sheaf is giving way to sheep.

40

Master Kent has timed his revelation well. The veal is his. The ale is his too. We are no longer hungry. We're certainly not sober. We're in his debt this evening and know him well enough to want to trust his word, at least for now. His plans might be five years away. Or ten. Tonight's what matters, and tonight he's satisfied us with his feast. He only has to raise a hand to wave away anxieties and allow the drinking to continue. We have become like animals in our individual ways, precisely as the brewer's ballad says: goat drunk and lecherous; dog drunk and barking mad; bull drunk and looking for a brawl; pig drunk and obdurate. But mostly we are as drunk as post-horses — their thirsts are never satisfied — and so, for this evening at least, beyond anxiety.

We are, though, in the mood for music and for dancing. Young Thomas Rogers is our only piper, and our nightingale. He needs no persuading to pick up his instrument. At any chance, he fills his lungs, and empties them for us. He first drums up an uncourtly reaping rhythm with his foot and then commences with his holes and fingertips. We've heard his efforts many times before. When Thomas sits at night and practises, we can't escape his failings and his strains no matter how hard we try to sleep. But then we cherish him. Without him we would never dance. So we egg him on tonight. What we do not expect is this second voice that's joining him, that's joining in with greater mastery behind our backs. It's Mr Quill, Mr Earle. We'll have to call him Mr Fiddle now. He pushes forward with his

41

ungainly walk, leading with his shoulder, not his chest. He finds a place to sit at Thomas Rogers's side, lays the instrument across his knees and applies his bow to the strings. He first echoes, then ornaments, then commandeers what the piper tries to play.

Thomas Rogers does not look as pleased as Mr Quill at the warmth of our applause. The piper loses confidence and face. But the fiddle's voice — at least, when our visitor has settled himself on his backstool — asks both for our laughter and our tears at once. His tune is both glad to be unhappy and sad to be so gay. Quite soon the children come away from playing loggats, throw their last sticks at the staff, and take to the barn floor to slide around on the loose straw to the music. Now the few remaining wild-heads of the village — the Derby twins, of course, but other stewards of misrule as well — start the dancing, taking their younger sisters and their nieces by the hands and swirling them. It is the married couples next. And finally our handful of unmarried girls step up, with great solemnity at first, but soon their cheeks are red with effort and not blushes. One of them, the one whose piety and prettiness is judged most spirited, will be our Lady of the Harvest. She'll be our Gleaning Queen. We will choose her when the music has concluded, if that moment ever comes, if we allow it to. Tomorrow she will be the first to step into the vanquished barley field, to walk across the stub, to bend and find and save a grain against the colder times ahead.

Mr Quill the fiddler is shaping us again,

making us as congruous and geometrical with his melodies as he has done with his charts and ink. His dance is circular, then it is square; it's forth-and-twenty, swing and stump; it's reels and sets and thundering. The revellers are being asked to go beyond their normal selves, to be more liquid, actually. I am tempted to join in myself, though I'm a widower. But I dare not chance my smarting fingertips and palms amidst such taking hold and hand gripping. I stand and watch with Master Kent, that other recent widower, swaying at my side. The women skirmish with the men, stamping feet and swirling kerchiefs. The mopsies and the lads are far too close. They're holding wrists. They're touching waists. It's possible, in such a ducking light and with such happy havoc in command, that kisses are exchanged, and promises. We are a heathen company, more devoted to the customs and the Holy days than to the Holiness itself. We find more pleasure in the song and dance of God than in the piety. Thank heavens that we do not have a priest to witness it.

We should have guessed the spitting woman would arrive, just at the moment we were merriest. This is for me first sight of her. She's standing at the gate of the barn, beyond the reach of our lights and keeping so still that she also seems beyond the reach of pipe and fiddle. But there is no doubting who she is, unless we have a ghostly visitor, one of our wives or daughters resurrected from her grave, left thin by death. She's tinier than I expected, imposing in a smaller way than usual. But there's the heavy velvet shawl I've heard about, and there's the tufted, rudely shaven head. She looks as drenched as a pond-ducked witch or scold. 'It's Mistress Beldam,' Master Kent mutters to me, giving her a name I know will stick. Beldam, the sorceress. Belle Dame, the beautiful. The dancers have not seen her, though. It's only when our fiddler sets aside his bow, drops his tune and rises from his stool to look across my neighbours' heads towards our stubbled visitor that everybody stops and turns. She's hardly visible. She's little more than dark on dark, a body shape. We cannot see her eyes or face as yet, or make out the bloody scar across her naked head. She does not speak — perhaps we have imagined her; she is a spectre summoned up by ale and dance. The mood has changed. It's heavier. We were liquid; now we're stones. The night is closing on a broken note.

We know we ought to make amends for shearing her. That's why she's standing there, awaiting us. She's asking us to witness what we've done. I have a sense that some men in the throng might any moment offer her their hand, some women too, and lead her to our circles and our squares to swirl with us. For a moment, the temper of the barn is not that she has shamed our evening but that we've found our Gleaning Queen. We only need to bring her to the light and crown her there and then, and all is well. Another dream. In this, her hair is long and black again; her men are walking free, uncollared and uncuffed; our wooden cross is restored to holiness and draped in rosaries; and, no, we

44

weren't surprised by twists of smoke at dawn today; and there are doves. Yes, there are doves. They're circling, white consciences on wing. At first the sight of them is heart-lifting. But still they're circling. They cannot find a place to feed. This is their hereafter. They're searching for the gleaning fields, but there are none.

At the movement of the dancers, their lifting hands, the woman backs away, still facing us, not trusting us perhaps. She must know that if she hesitates the men will swarm round her like a cloud of gnats. It is only when she draws level with the gate that she turns towards it and the dark and goes forward, steps outside, and we are left to exchange, well, *sheepish* glances. We know the pipe and fiddle cannot play again. We cannot dance. We bid each other uncomfortable good nights, and hurry home to sleep the evening off, or lay awake, or worse.

I hope — like everyone — to find the woman when I leave. But I have better cause than them. Master Kent has asked me to. He says that I should bring her back, bring Mistress Beldam to the barn and let her pass the night with his straw bales as her mattress and a velvet shawl as coverlet. He does not count it proper that a woman, any woman, no matter what her felonies might be, should spend a night alone and unprotected from its dangers. I see him hesitate. He wants to specify what dangers there might be but does not think it seemly. There are no longer wolves to fear. We have not seen the traces of a wolf in living times. There are no bears or dragoncats. And Master Kent is not the superstitious sort that dreads the deeds of devils or spirits, of firedrakes or wood demons. There isn't frost or snow, of course. It won't be uncommonly cold tonight. What summer chill we can expect when the hours are small and the night is deep will not prove a danger to anybody sleeping wild and rough but only an inconvenience. Yet, having now seen the woman for myself and then observed the wisting in my master's eye, I understand what outcome he must fear for her; what he admits to in himself, indeed; what I have felt and still am feeling; what every man amongst us — even brave and bloodless Mr Quill — will be dreaming of tonight.

'Do what you can to make her safe,' he instructs me finally.

First I go to keep a promise at the pillory and cross. I will not be surprised to find Mistress Beldam there, attending to her men. Indeed, I pray that she is there. Amongst other things, I want her as a witness to my kindness. I leave the barn enlivened by my task, but my ardour is dampened straightaway. While we have been at the feast and dancing, deafened to the weather by the fiddle and the pipe, a greater Steward than Master Kent has noticed that our barley has been safely cut and stacked and told the heavens it is safe to rain. It's midnight rain, the sort that in the darkness has no form until it reaches you, until it strikes with the cold and keen insistence of a silver-worker's mallet.

It takes several steps before I realise how heavily it's raining. My neighbours have already scurried to their cottages, so far as I can tell. I do not see the outlines of another human soul. I ought to scurry home myself and save my tasks and promises until it is more dry. But the rain is pleasurable. It's washing out impurities. My fingers and my chin are soon rid of veal grease. My mouth is washed by water more pure and rewarding to the taste than anything our ponds and our obliging brook have to offer. Even my damaged hand becomes less painful in the salving of the rain. I run my tongue across my upper lip and savour the downpour. It's not quite sweet and not quite flavourless. It's sobering but, then, my drinking has been more moderate and tame than most.

Tonight, there is no moon in view, of course. The low clouds as I imagine them are a heavy blanket, woven out of black and grey. As yet, there's not the slightest trace of wind to take the rain away and irrigate our distant neighbours' lands instead of ours. We can expect this storm to settle in and persevere till dawn. Tomorrow will provide a motley of pools and puddles in our lanes and fields. Our ponds and cisterns will be full, and we'll be glad of that. Although it may not feel so now for anyone that's caught in it, we are the beneficiaries of Nature's dowry. Nevertheless, I doubt that Mistress Beldam will take much persuading that the barn is where she should seek safe haven from the weather.

I take the mud-caked lane away from my master's buildings, past his orchard gardens and his byres, towards the dreamt-of spire. I would benefit from light, though no lantern in the

47

world, no matter how enclosed, could survive the volume of this rain for long. I have to trust the scratchings and the marks that my dozen years of being here and working here and walking here have etched in me. The storm has robbed us of all colours — the usual blues and mauves that finesse the night. But I make out silhouettes; that crouching oak, its swishing sleeves of ivy, that little dusty elm that should be taken down and logged before it blocks the path. I recognise the billows and the swells of the hedges, either side, where there are gaps and gates, where there are peaks and branching pinnacles, where damsons can be scrumped. I pick up smells that I can name. The master's byres, of course. The sweating of his silage heaps. But other gentler odours too. The acrid smell — exaggerated by the rain — of elder trees. The bread-and-biscuit smell of rotting wood. The piss-and-honey tang of apple trees. I navigate my midnight village as a blind man would, by nose and ears and touch and by the vaguest, blackest forms.

I see the men before they hear or notice me, or that's to say I see the outline of their wide-winged cross and how bulked and heavy it's become, draped as it is with sodden prisoners. I stand and watch, not daring for a while to make my presence known but still enjoying what must be a further penalty for them, the unrelenting rain. They cannot harm me, that is certain. Their arms are pinioned and their necks are caught. My only risk can be a backward kicking. I'll have to treat them like a pair of tethered horses and not inspect their tails or rumps. I am holding my breath, not to be discovered. How silent it has become, beyond the pelting of the rain. I fear there's no one living anywhere. The night is ponderous. No owl or fox is keen to interrupt the darkness. It seems that even the trees have stopped their stretching and their creaking, their making wishes in the wind, to hold their breaths and stare like me towards the pillory.

If I could, if I had the powers of a wizard or a god, I'd build that church gate right away. I'd make it arch above the pillory. I'd build it with a canopy to keep these two men dry. Now that my eyes are more accustomed to the dark, I see them more clearly. This morning I persuaded myself that probably it's wise for all of us to hold our tongues for the time being and let these newcomers soak up the blame. But now, beneath these weighty clouds, I recognise my foolishness; no, let us name it as it is, my lack of courage and of honesty. *Soak up* is not a happy phrase, I think. This rain is pleasurable only for those not fixed in it, those who can look forward to a square of drying cloth, a roof, a bed, sweet dreams. Tonight's beneficiaries of Nature's dowry do not include Mistress Beldam's family.

So I approach them, and I speak. 'My name is Walter Thirsk . . . It's Walt.' There's no response. 'I was not there, this morning, when you drew your bows,' I say. They need to understand at once, I should not be numbered amongst their accusers. I did not shake my stick at them. I did not help to shave their heads. I did not march them to the pillory. They cannot know I failed to speak on their behalf. Indeed, I am the only one amongst the villagers against whom they shouldn't harbour any grudge. Still, they do not offer a response. They are like cattle feeding; their faces strain towards the ground. The rain drops unabated on their shoulders and their necks, channels down their spines. They each have a ropy tail of rain. The younger lifts his chin and looks at me, then drops his head again. He is exhausted by the weight of his own head, it seems. The shorter shuffles on his stretching toes.

Of course, I cannot find a log for the father to stand on, not in this darkness or this weather. The nearest fallen timber is a walk away, beyond our fields. I don't intend to go foraging so late at night. I should have planned this earlier. I could have sent a pair of boys out of the barn to fetch a log. I forgot. But I know there is a pile of large, roughly prepared stones intended for the church only a score of paces from the pillory. It isn't hard to pull one loose and lift it that short distance — at least, it isn't hard at first. Then my weeping hand which for the moment I have not remembered starts to hurt again. I've treated it too roughly, tested it too much tonight. Any crust that has been forming over it must now have torn again. I cannot see the damage, but I certainly can feel it. I drop the stone and try to roll it forward with my one good hand. The ground is far too rough and the stone is far too square for that. I tip and topple it once or twice but it has a mind of its own and none of the progress I induce in it is quite in the direction of the pillory.

50

I cannot think of anything at home that could serve as the older man's perch. I have a bench outside my cottage, but that is oak and heavy too. It takes two sets of hands to carry it. I have a chest and a smaller coffer, but not iron-bound and so too flimsy to support a man, even a short one. And both my kegs are full and too heavy to be moved about. Short of lying on the sodden ground myself and having him stand on my back, there's nothing I can do for him before tomorrow. I have to take care of my hand, if I ever hope to work again. Anyway, this problem at the pillory is not mine alone — and probably it's not as urgent as I thought. The older man has already endured the most part of the day on tiptoe. Surely he can tolerate the night. Then at first light I will call on John Carr and we can either share the burden of the stone or take, one-handed, an end each of the bench. Better, I can find those boys and send them log hunting. For now I have to guard my wound. I am suddenly embarrassed. I walk again into the downpour and the dark. Those men have not exchanged a word with me.

It is only now I can address myself to Mistress Beldam, and Master Kent's request, instruction actually, that I should hunt her down and bring her to his barn. I have seldom disappointed him before. I take great pride in that. My father was his father's clerk. My mother was his milk nurse. We are almost of an age and so must have been ear-to-ear when we were nuzzling infants, growing plump on the same breasts. I do not want to say he is my brother; our stations are too different. But we were playmates in his father's yards. He sometimes shared his books with me, and I was let to write and read and calculate. I managed these less clumsily than him, I dare to say. I have been his serving man since both of us were satin-chinned. I was the only one he brought with him when Lucy Jordan agreed to be his wife and he took charge of these estates and this old manor farm. And he was friend enough to me to let me go from his direct employ when I discovered my own wife, my own Sweet Cecily, and found such unexpected solace, for a man most used to market towns, in working with her and her neighbours in these isolated fields. I told him I was in love with Cecily, her hearty laugh, her freckled throat, her sturdiness, but also with the very crumble of this village earth. He said, 'Then you should go and plough the earth.' That is my history.

I will not forget those early playmate days or my family debt to Master Kent. I have always taken it as my particular duty to speak up on his behalf amongst my neighbours, if anyone's disgruntled. Or even to venture a casual word to him myself about any negligence or grievance that could damage his standing here. If Master Kent has ever taken me aside, to ask me to assess his stock, perhaps, or prune his fruiting trees, or patch some damage to his roof, I have done so at a snap and without a murmur or requiring an advantage in return. I do not mean to paint myself as some enamelled saint, haloed by obedience. I have been sensible — and loyal, in both our interests. *To all of our advantages*, let's say. Despite the shared and joshing friendship of our youths, I've never said, Your roof can wait. There're our own oxen need attending to. Or asked, What have you hanging at your sides, Charles Kent? They look like arms and hands to me. So prune your orchard trees yourself. No, I have warranted his respect by always helping him. So he relies on me and will be distressed — and disappointed, probably — if I go to him tomorrow to report I did not even try to bring the woman to his barn because my hand was painful. He'll think, Why does it take a pain-free hand to do what I have asked? He hasn't said that I should lift Mistress Beldam above my head and carry her.

Therefore, instead of squelching home, drying off, pulling on my quilted cap and sleeping out the storm, I only call in briefly to change my breeches and find my wide-brimmed hat and a leather jerkin. My one idea is to hurry down our lanes towards the clearing at The Bottom, where I saw this morning's darkest plume of smoke. No, *yesterday* morning's; the midnight has departed from us already. She will have sought the leaking shelter of her tumbled den. Where else? I will collect her there.

My thoughts are not entirely generous. Mistress Beldam has a hold on me, not like the enduring hold of my Cecily, but something new and different, something more uncomfortable. On first sight, my wife was at once a homely prospect, pretty, lively, comforting and warm. She left me calm and full of hope. To hold her on our marriage night — well, in truth, *before* our marriage night — was to arrive at a lasting destination from which I could not imagine departing for all and any of the years ahead. However, she was not the lightning strike that minstrels sing about. But that first sight of Mistress Beldam has put me out of character. Since seeing her in shaven silhouette I feel as if I have been feeding on Brooker Higgs's fairy caps. And now that I'm expecting to discover her, now that I am getting close to where she must have taken refuge, my head begins to dance with darker and more spectral lights; my heart is rippling; I feel a sudden fearlessness and then a sinking fear. I have been widowed for too long. If there's a moon behind these clouds, it is sensual and blue. There is wanting in the air, and sorcery.

Clearly, I am not the only one to think it so. There are men about. I hear the splash of other feet and catch a glimpse of walking figures, too tall and too broad-shouldered to be the woman we are hunting for. No doubt they're catching sight of me as well and saying to themselves, That wide-brimmed hat belongs to Walter Thirsk. What business can an old goat such as him have on a night like this, and so late? At least my errand is not clandestine. I'm doing what our master has desired. I do not have a wife or family to hide it from, like some of these other maddened figures in the night. I have not sinned against the woman yet, except the sin of thinking it, of thinking that she might not want to sleep alone in that great barn but would prefer a cottage bed. I will dry her with my damaged hand. My damaged hand will pay amends to her.

The den is hard to find but gradually my eyes have grown accustomed to the dark. The cloud to some extent has thinned. There is no moonlight but there is at least a muffled promise of the dawn to come, enough to make out shapes and outlines. There's the great black wall of trees, now heavily and noisily shedding water. And there's the pile of what was once her hurried, rough-and-ready walls. I'd call her name. It doesn't matter if my lurking neighbours hear. Let them understand that I have come with proper cause. But we have been too remiss in our hospitality. We do not have the woman's name. 'Mistress Beldam' will not do. Just 'Mistress', then. I call it out. But no reply. And no response when I step forward like a moonstruck youth with shaking hands to pull aside the sacking and the timber. The forest is a din of rain. Beyond the cascades and the waterfalls, I hear the fidgeting of feet that might belong to anyone or anything, a cough that could be human or a fox, the crack of snapping wood. I call out 'Mistress' twenty times, to no avail. She must have taken refuge in some other den. Or else she hears but will not answer me.

4

As luck would have it, I have been assigned to be Mr Quill's assistant for the week. My wounded hand excuses me from hard work in the threshing barns. Master Kent insists on it. Once more he proves himself my friend. I shouldn't try to grip tools or carry anything, he warns. Any pressure and I'll burst the cushioning of water-whelks and blisters that are already forming at the edges of the burn. I'm not fit for labouring, 'And never was,' he wants to say. (Perhaps he would employ me as his man again.) The grain can be separated from the chaff without my help for the next few days. My greater duty is to save my hand. There're men and women both of us could name who've lost a limb and then their lives because a wound has not healed properly. I have to keep it cold and dry but open to the air, so that the savaged skin at the centre can peel away or form a crust. At the moment it's too swampy to dry and harden. It's oozing liquids of the sort I'd normally expect to run out of my nose. And the pain, though not as searing as it was, is almost more than I can bear. It is unforgiving. I have not had a wink of sleep all night, well, that much of the night I spent shivering in bed and not out in the rain hunting for the sorceress. And now I walk with one hand raised and cupped in front of me. I am a beggar for the day, I'm told. My neighbours look into my palm, raise their eyebrows, wish me well, but I suspect they're jealous of my easy occupation. Already they have labelled me Quill-Carrier-in-Chief. They think we'll make a comic pair: the stumbler and the beggar, both damaged on the left and with only a couple of useful hands between them.

Still, I'm not so wounded that I want to avoid the gleaning field before my hands-free working day with Mr Quill begins. Our boys have been at the edges of the stub since first light, keeping off the birds with stones, clapping-boards and slings but not stepping on the field itself. That's not their privilege. Their dawn chorus prises us from bed and hurries us out of our cottages for an early meeting with our Queen.

Our village has been washed and muddied by the storm, but the clouds have cleared. It promises to be a steep and sunny day. Already it is bright and hot enough for us to shelter under rye-straw hats. We all feel harvest-worn to some degree, not thick-headed from last night's ale — well, not *only* that — and not only burnt back to the soul by yesterday's two fires and the smoke-stained turbulence that followed them, but fatigued by all the mutual labours of the year. Daily duties have deferred our weariness till now, then sapped us even more by giving us a day of rest. Our muscles are not used to it. An unused muscle stiffens like a drying rag. In this we are at one with everything we see and hear and smell. Despite the sweating soil and the enamelling of puddles from the midnight storm, the land itself is harvest-worn. So are the lanes.

We have been too occupied until today to see how beaten down by wheels and hoofs our cartways have become. They're shiny, worn away and sinking in from the season's slog and grind, and from our animals' exertions. Each step we've taken since the last frost at winter's end — an age ago — has left its imprint on our earth.

What wind there was yesterday after we dispatched the final sheaf gathered up and spread much of the lighter, finer chaff. The village has been freckled by the chaff. The service trees between our dwellings and the gleaning field are still embroidered with it and with straw, despite the rain. On the way between the harvest and the stackyard, unsecured bundles of cut barley have dropped on the verges from our wagons and our barrows, providing pickings for the ruddocks and the dunnocks to contest, and there are signs in the disrupted soil that someone's pigs are on the loose and have been snouting for fallen grain. There is a silent ripeness to the air, so mellow and sappy that we want to breathe it shallowly, to sip it richly like a cordial. No one who knows the busy, kindly, scented universe of crops and the unerring traces of its calendar could mistake this morning's aromatic peace and quiet for anything but Gleaning Day.

Now that we are gathered at the entry to the field, we stay and wait. With the sudden ending of our dance last night and the interruptions of the storm, we failed to nominate our Queen. Such negligence is bound to bring bad luck. We've never woken up before on Gleaning Day without a pretty sovereign to rule the stub. But Master Kent has said that we can settle it this morning. So all the girls and unwed lasses have put on their fineries, or more exactly borrowed firstly from their mothers' ribbon bags or dowry chests and then from their gardens and our hedgerows, making yellow drapes and garlands for themselves from tansy, ragwort and hawkweed blooms. Some of the more ambitious ones have smeared their cheeks and fore-arms with a golden petal paste. They look both pestilent and regal.

We can already see Master Kent bobbing high above the hedges of the manor lane as he rides towards us on his Willowjack. He too has made an effort for the day. His best high hat, usually reserved for marriages and funerals, is sashed with two woven cloths, one lemon-yellow, one apple-green, his wife's heirlooms. She was fond of brightness. Now we have some moments to inspect our girls and choose which one we'll raise our voices for. Here is a chance as well to look out across and down the sloping barley field and offer thanks, not to some higher being but to the soil itself. Can it really be almost a year since we last led out our oxen and took our ploughs to it, fixing our eyes on the leaf-bare treetops in the dell to keep our furrows straight and true, on what I recall to be a dull and chilling day? Then once the cold had nipped the cold, we came again for harrowing, flattening ridges to provide the fine tilth that best comforts barley, picking out the surface stones. Can it really be half a year since spring, when we fixed our eyes again on

59

those same tops to see them fattening with leaf and we spread out across the field in rows to broadcast seed, throwing our grain forward equally and to the swing of every step, spreading tiny vows with a plentiful hand? This year the first warm rains were late. The field was slow to blush with green, and what early shoots dared show themselves were shy and flimsy. We watched the barley with anxiety, first fearing drought and then, once our plants reached knee-height, praying that the sky would spare us gales.

That is our custom. We are daily nervous for the crop — though there are times, for me at least and especially at night in my cold cot, when I resent the tyranny of nervousness. I hear the stress and thrust of wind and unaccountably my spirits lift. My dreams are thrilled of late by flattened fields. I wake ashamed and cannot meet my neighbours' eyes. They might imagine I've fallen out of love with them, and fallen out of love with here.

When I first came to these vicinities I thought I'd discovered not quite paradise, but at least a fruitful opportunity — some honest freedom and some scope. Some fertile soil! I'd never known such giving land and sky. I do remember my first week, and — still my master's serving man — walking through the commons to the forest edge and not daring to go in, but touching everything. I'd found a treasury. I know I pushed my nose against a tree and was surprised by the ancient sweetness of the bark. I know I stood and studied ants, not guessing yet what ant-like labours were awaiting me. I know I picked a flower for my cap. And then I set my eyes on Cecily and saw a chance to build a future here. I wooed her by working at her elbow in her fields, attending to the hunger of her soil. My labour was an act of love. My unaccustomed muscles grew and ached for her. I put my shoulder to the plough for her. I became as tough as ash for her. I had no choice. The countryside is argumentative. It wants to pick a fight with you. It wants to dish out scars and bruises. It wants to give you roughened palms and gritty eyes. It likes to snag and tear your arms and legs on briars and on brambles every time you presume to leave the path. But this was precisely what I most liked about this village life, the way we had to press our cheeks and chests against a living, fickle world which in the place where I and Master Kent had lived before only displayed itself as casual weeds in cracks or on our market stalls where country goods were put on sale, already ripe, and magicked up from God knows where. It didn't matter if it rained or blew all day and night in town. We pulled on caps. We slammed our doors and windows tight. The weather wasn't any threat to us. Back then, the sun was neither enemy nor friend.

I cannot say I long for that again, but I am less content than I should be. I have my portion and my place. I'm fortunate. But twelve years here is not enough to make me feel utterly at home — not when I haven't truly got a home and haven't had since Cecily was pilfered by the fever, that overwhelming midnight pillager, as

61

brutal as a fox. Without my Cecily, my labour has no love in it. It's only dutiful. I'll never be a Rogers or a Derby or a Higgs, so woven to the fabric of the place that nothing else and nothing more seems possible. Their best riches are their ignorance of wealth. I'm not a product of these commons but just a visitor who's stayed. And now that these latest visitors have come — these three encroachers on our land; this lurching fellow and his charts — I am unnerved. I am reminded that there is another world clear of the forest tops, a world beyond the rule of seasons, a redrawn world, as Mr Quill has said, where there are 'hereafters'. I stand at the threshold of the gleaning field and wonder what the future has in mind for me.

Master Kent arrives in his cheerful hat and drives my troubled dreams away. In addition to the sashes around his brim, he has also knotted his ankles with golden ribbons and decorated Willowjack's mane with yellow strings. Mr Quill, who has accompanied them on foot, is trimmed at calf, cuff and throat in ribbons, a merry pillory of cloth. He is all smiles, of course. It's hard to read a face that always wears a masking smile. The master does not dismount — I think he feels that ceremony should keep him in the saddle; he also looks a little frail today and unusually anxious — but he manages to make a pleasant speech, addressing us from aloft like a huntsman talking fondly to his hounds or beaters. This is 'a noble day', he says, as usual. Anything we glean is ours to keep, of course. We are free to take any remaining barley we find to our kitchen pots, for stew or beer or stover. We do not need to add it to the common wealth, or store it in the stackyard for any general benefit. After us will come the livestock, he says, in order of their station: our cattle will be loosed into the field to reduce the stubble, then the geese, for fattening, and finally our hogs will be allowed to root and nose the soil. Surprisingly, he does not mention as he usually does each year that the hogs will precede the plough. This barley field is set aside for next year's winter-planted wheat (beer before bread, as ever) and so we need to go about its ploughing soon, before the summer parts from us. Perhaps I'm surprised with no good cause, but his silence on this matter, his preference for 'finally our hogs', instead of 'finally the oxen and the ploughs', is startling. The *organisation to all of our advantages* that he revealed last night might be more substantial than a dream, or an ambition that need not bother us just yet. It's possible that Master Kent does not expect our ploughs to be in use again. Our final harvest might have come and gone.

There is happier business to distract us, though. Master Kent suggests that it would be a pleasing courtesy for Philip Earle — our Mr Quill, our fiddler — to choose the Gleaning Queen: 'He surely can be counted on to be an even-handed judge.' The girls and lasses are brought forward to pout and curtsey in a line for him. He does his smiling best to be judicial but we cannot help but notice that he rests his eyes for longer on the older girls and that these older girls are more blushing than their sisters and more bodily. It's not that Mr Quill is a handsome or a well-built man, though his seeming wealth and kindness are bound to be attractive. Nor is there any sense that Mr Quill himself is bidding for a bride. It's just that this procedure has tows and currents which would not trouble us if every daughter in the line had yet to grow her breasts. The fathers there are both awkward and seduced themselves. They see their own daughters and their neighbours' daughters in a new, inconsistent light.

Mr Quill is thinking now, dramatically considering. He strokes his waxy, trowel-shaped beard to our amusement. Our laughter is lusty and excessive. We watch him looking out above our heads; perhaps he's expecting guidance from the trees, or hoping to catch sight of Mistress Beldam in her velvet shawl. Possibly our lop-sided fiddler, our even-handed judge, means to raise his hand for her and have her step inside our ring to be the Gleaning Queen. The men turn round and stare towards the woods and to where some of them at least, to my certain knowledge, hunted for her under last night's rain and where all of them, I'd guess, have wandered in their dreams. I half expect but dread to find a complicit smile on one of their faces, the smile of some quick-thinking lad who turned a profit from the rain by finding Mistress Beldam in distress and then providing somewhere snug for both of them to pass the night.

The judge opts sweetly for the one we least expect. He picks little Lizzie, John Carr's niece, and one of our suspected *spares*. She is not five years old, a gawky girl and hardly pretty yet. But she has clearly done her best to decorate herself. She is by far the yellowest. Her happiness at being chosen is innocent and unconcealed. So Mr Quill has made a gentle choice, avoiding older girls. She does not want to let him take her hand, however. She steps back when he draws close, a little frightened by his smile and his lop-sided gait. So Master Kent takes care of her. He removes the green sash from his hat and bends down from his saddle to drop it on Lizzie Carr's head. Her crown. She is to keep the cloth, he says. The older girls are hugely jealous now.

Lizzie Carr's father and her uncle, John, make a chair for the Queen by joining hands across each other's wrists and take her to the edges of the stub. She's not entirely sure what she's supposed to do. She only knows she is the centre of attention, not all of it well-meaning. Her own sister has already pinched and hurt her leg. She'd like either to run away and hide or to give vent to tears. But Master Kent has dismounted and come forward to help her from her chair. 'Take off your slippers, go barefoot, take the first step on the field,' he whispers to her. 'All you need to do is find a single grain, just one. Then we will cheer. And you will be our Queen for one whole year.' He pushes her shoulder gently, and she does what he has said, blessing the stub with her bare toes. The stalks are too tough on her feet at first, but she takes a few wincing steps, finding balder ground. And there she drops down to her knees and leans forward to search for her grain. The sash falls from her head. It is the field's only splash of green. But Lizzie Carr does not retrieve it yet. She has found more than a grain, she's found a complete ear, perfectly intact, as long and broad as a man's best finger, its awns as spiky as a teasel head. She's old enough to know how to separate out the barleycorn by running her fingers against the bristles. She blows into her palm to winnow off the flake. And now she's holding out her hand to show her barley pearls to us. The moment is always a rousing one. Our labours are condensed to this: a dozen tokens of our bread and drink, each tucked and swaddled in the oval of a grain, and sitting on a child's undamaged skin. What should we do but toss our hats and cheer?

Mr Quill is at my shoulder. He's grateful that I'm helping him, he says. He understands that I am handicapped today but all he has in mind for me is gentle work. He will be indebted if I can walk the village bounds with him, naming everything I see. He hopes as well that I can provide a shoulder for his bag of charting tools, and later use my single hand to help prepare his colour pots of paint and prepare the calfskin still drying in the dancing barn for vellum. He needs it urgently for Master Kent's land chart. Normally, I would not wish to miss my gleaning spoils. I could expect to come away with sufficient grain for some private ale and porridge flour, as well as winter feed for George and Gorge, the pair of long, flat-sided pigs I share with John Carr and his family. But Mr Quill proposes something more pleasing, and an opportunity when everybody else is double-bent and studying the stub to settle what has happened overnight to Mistress Beldam.

Master Kent stands back with us, enjoying the noisy rush of gleaners, their concentrated, thorough scampering. Already many of my neighbours have gathered up a worthy gleaner's sheaf; they hold it in their resting hands, a drooping horse's tail of flaxen stalks, while their working hands peck and pick across the stub like hens. The master has tucked a barley ear under his hat's remaining yellow sash, for good luck. He needs good luck. He knows my search for the woman failed. She did not seek shelter in his barn. He bashfully admits he waited for her there until 'the hour was insensible', meaning I suppose that when he finally retreated to his bed the casks of ale were empty. But he's more troubled than can be accounted for by ale or even by the seeming disappearance of a woman who two days ago was unknown to him and only yesterday he ordered to be shorn. He was embarrassed and at first a little shamed this morning, as he rode past the pillory at a polite distance, he reports, to be yowled at so stridently and manically and with such uncivil language by the younger of the two fastened men. No, he will not repeat the words on such (again) a 'noble day': 'It was as if I were the felon, in some way. The man's a ruffian, no doubt of it. I am a callous killer, it seems, and worse. He says he'll be revenged, and curses me. He shouted 'Murder, Murder!', as I passed.' The father did not even lift his head, and that in some way was an even heavier rebuke, he says.

It's just as well, I suppose, that I haven't yet succeeded in alleviating the short one's punishment by dragging up a log or stone for him to stand on. The men are proving insolent. But Master Kent can shrug off their insults. Any doubt he's had that they were rogues deserving of the pillory has been rudely shouted away. No, something weightier is troubling him this morning, something weightier even than the recent and costly loss of his stable and his doves. He has not looked so sunken and reduced since the day his wife Lucy and their infant girl both died in childbirth. I raise my eyebrows and tip my head to let him know he's set me wondering and that I am concerned for him.

'Come find me in my chambers, Walt, when Mr Earle dismisses you this evening,' he says, using the familiar form of my name, unusually. 'There are some matters to be shared.' He puts a single finger to his lips. He trusts me to stay silent.

Mr Quill is not a man who can move quickly. He's more the hedgehog than the fox. He's careful and he's leisurely. He doesn't mean to miss a thing. But his slow company is satisfying. I am required to take my time and look at everything anew. The ridge and furrow of our daily lives become less commonplace in the shadow of his scrutiny.

'Where will you take me first?' he asks, and the question itself confers on me some pleasing status and authority. I am grateful for his thoughtfulness.

'We inspect The Bottom, then ascend,' I

suggest, smiling to myself, for The Bottom is the dank depression which we know too as Turd and Turf. It's marshland, lower even than the brook, and so we count it safe to use not only as a charnel place for carcasses and skeletons and any animal too sick in death to be eaten but also as our open privy. It drains into itself, its own wet turf. The wooden closed latrines that we have built closer to the dwellings are more convenient, especially in the middle of the night and during winter, but many of us — though mainly men — prefer to empty bowels where Nature will take care of it, remove the stench as soon as it's produced. Our closed latrines hang on to smell, even when the gong farmer — we take our weekly turns at being him — pegs up his nose, wraps up his mouth, picks up his shovel and barrows it away. You cannot shovel up a smell. You'll never see a barrow-load of smell.

As we arrive at Turd and Turf, I make our progress as noisy as I can and raise my voice, letting it carry on the echo. Anyone who has preceded us will be glad of some warning, especially as I have a recent stranger at my elbow who might not welcome the entertainment of chancing on a working arse. But I do not expect to discover anybody here, even though it is a place where on normal days there are many tasks to carry out other than squatting with a furrowed brow and hoping for some solitude. There're rushes to collect for lights, ferns to pull for litter, clay to dig for bricks, peat and turves to cut for winter fuel and roofs. Today, though, I can account for all of us — well, all of us that I can name; not Mistress Beldam, though I live in hopes for her. They're gleaning barley until noon, and then will be gathered on the threshing floors and barn as late as dusk today and every day into the hungry months until the job is done. No, Mr Quill and I will have the margins and the commons to ourselves.

The path is overgrown here, and purposely neglected. It is portcullised by ivy vines, providing some seclusion for its visitors. I open up a gap for him until we're standing at the edges of The Bottom, our feet in mud from last night's rain but — I check — nothing less desirable. The marsh, where it's not shaded by curtains of beech and oak, is steaming, its vapours thickened and shaped by sunbeams. The air is unusually stewed and balmy today. If it wasn't for the flat blue sky, troubled only by the white pulses of a lifting mist, it could seem that thunderstorms are on their way. Otherwise, everything's familiar: the dome of cattle bones, the usual ruminating pigs feasting on unhealthy pannage, the swollen carcass of another of their kind that's died from cysts, the sinking, timbered path we use to barrow out our turves, the glint of oily water where the quagmire is deepest and the squelch is loudest, the coppiced hedge of goat-willows from which we take our sallow poles and behind which any man in need of privacy might clutch his knees and murmur to himself without an audience. There is no sign of Mistress Beldam here.

Mr Quill is too delighted by our tour to notice anything that does not bring him pleasure. The smell is worse than usual but, if he is aware of it, it does not bother him. He mistakes it for the unaffected countryside. He does not remark on the bones even, with their regiments of flies. He only says it is a peaceful and secluded place and 'humbling' in its beauty. He is blind to all the knot and thorn of living here. He takes hold of my arm in his excitement. He's pointing at the far side of the clearing and a swathe of longpurples, tall and at their strident best, as are the birds today, despite the nets that we have set for them. 'Listen to them juking,' he says. He holds a finger up and cocks his head. A finch commands him Pay Your Rent. A thrush complains of Tax Tax Tax.

I am a little shamed by Mr Quill, in truth. I don't wish to beat a drum, but there is something of myself in him, something that is being lost. I remember well my first encounter with The Bottom soon after my arrival here as Master Kent's man. It was, I have to say, a privy trip. And it was spring. The longpurples had hardly come to blade. But there were tall-necked cowslips nodding on the banks and king-cups, fenny celandines and irises in the mire. The trees were imping with infant leaves that seemed as attentive and pert as mice ears. So I was struck and 'humbled' by the beauty too, and only later by the carnal stench. I was an innocent. In that first season I tumbled into love with everything I saw. Each dawn was like a genesis; the light ascends and with the light comes life. I wanted to immerse myself in it, to implicate myself in land, to contribute to fields. What greater

71

purpose could there be? How could I better spend my days? Nothing I had seen before had made me happier. I felt more like an angel than a beast.

My new neighbours were amused by me, of course, my callow eagerness. For them an iris bulb was pig fodder; celandines were not a thing of beauty but a gargle for an irritated throat; and cowslips were better gathered, boiled and drunk against the palsy than stared at in the open privy.

'Where have we buried ourselves?' Master Kent once asked in that first year. 'Will nobody talk with me about anything but the fattening of grain and hogs?'

'Beer and bacon's all that matters here,' I said, sighing in agreement, because in those early days I feared that only those who had been cradled in this place could endure its agonies. But once I found my Cecily and put a hand to husbandry myself, I soon turned into one of them, a beer and bacon man who knew the proper value of an iris bulb. It did not take many working days before I understood that the land itself, from sod to meadow, is inflexible and stern. It is impatient, in fact. It cannot wait. There's not a season set aside for pondering and reveries. It will not let us hesitate or rest; it does not wish us to stand back and comment on its comeliness or devise a song for it. It has no time to listen to our song. It only asks us not to tire in our hard work. It wants to see us leathery, our necks and fore-arms burnt as black as chimney oak; it wants to leave us thinned and sinewy from work. It taxes us from dawn to dusk, and torments us at night; that is the taxing that the thrush complains about. Our great task each and every year is to defend ourselves against hunger and defeat with implements and tools. The clamour deafens us. But that is how we have to live our lives.

So it is an affecting experience this morning — and, I'm happy to discover, more valuable than gleaning — to be reminded of my younger self by Mr Quill's good humour. 'How should I name this place?' he asks, as we part the ivy vines again and climb to higher ground.

'No name,' I say. 'A marsh. A marsh. What should we call a marsh? We're dull. We have our names for animals but, no, not for the marsh.' I prefer not to have him spoil his charts with The Bottom, or Turd and Turf, or even the Charnel House.

'The Blossom Marsh, perhaps,' he says.

'Yes, scratch that down.'

We continue at our snail-like pace, beating the bounds of the village. I lead Mr Quill along the same route we follow every spring as a community, when we take annual stock of what we have in hand and what we hope to have in bud or shoot. That's when we bump our children's heads against the boundary stones, so that they'll not forget where they and all of us belong, and we challenge them to eat the grass they're kneeling on and taste the fodder with the mouths of cattle. Normally this would be our day for reconciling grievances but in company and in the open air, where grievances cannot be aired except with moderation and a placid voice.

I can predict already what will be grouched about next year, if next year ever comes. One of the Higgs women, let's say, will want her family stints increased. Now that they have another mouth to feed at home, she'll feel they should be granted rights to common graze a further pig or, failing that, some extra geese. Thomas Rogers's mother will complain that the laystalls where we throw our cooking waste for composting are too close to her cottage; she has to suffer all our kitchen smells and endure everybody's flies. 'We have to put up with your piping son,' we'll say. An older man as usual will repeat the enduring grumble — with not as easy a voice as he supposes — that the Derby twins for all their youth and energy are too often late to field and then too early to depart. But this coming spring there will not be the usual coo-coo-coo about the master's thieving doves: 'They take our grain; he takes their eggs; we see no benefit.'

Today this beating of the bounds is not a stock-taking and I will not be forcing Mr Quill on to the ground to bump his head against our boundary stones or require him to chew on grass. He does not see the parish with the dutiful eyes of a labourer or cottager. He does not want to hear our grievances or have me list the details of our working lives. He does not note that someone needs to drag the tangleweed off our pond if we hope to tempt some mallard to our traps, or what grand oak is now so frail and honeycombed that over winter it has lost its crown and bared its once proud head in preparation for our axes, or which land we ought to set aside next year for turbary and which we ought to save, so that the peat and turf can fatten and recuperate, or where the best reeds are for our thatching, or where the best supply of wood for firing can be found, or what walls and fences need attending to and which of us might do that job the best.

He does want, though, to stand in his yellow trim of ribbons and mark the detail and the beauty of each view. He's keen for me to name the plants. He makes a note of them and sometimes plucks a leaf or flower for pressing in his book, his personal 'Natural History'. It seems that listing them is his way of knowing them. I can easily put a name to all the herbs we discover on our way: the herbs for medicines, the herbs intended only for our beasts, the killing herbs, the devil's herbs, the herbs reserved for those already dead, the drunkard's herbs, the herbs with magic properties. I even name some of the weeds for him, though sometimes I invent the words. There ought to be a plant called purgatory. And another one called fletch. I point out prickly eringes, whose roots, he ought to know, can be prepared into a love potion. I show him burdock leaves, for wrapping butter in. And almond leaves for keeping moths away from clothes. He thinks I am the wisest man.

I suspect he is unimpressed by our local place names, however. He'd like me to put bright names to them, so that he can mark them down in ink, together with their measured angles and their shapes. But they're only workaday. 'East Field,' I tell him. 'West Field, South Field. John

Carr's flax garth. The Higgses' goose pen. Hazel Wood. The Turbary. The Warren.' We give directions in our titles, I explain, or we name a family, or we say what's growing there. We are plain and do not try to complicate our lives.

'I have a pair of pigs called George and Gorge,' I say finally. 'And Mr Kent calls his horse Willowjack, even though she's a mare, a Jill and not a Jack.' Those are the best names I can offer him. We do not even have a title for the village. It is just The Village. And it's surrounded by The Land, I add. Even Master Kent's freeholds and muniments do not provide a name. We're written down only as The Jordan Estate or The Property of Edmund Jordan, gentleman. 'He is deceased.'

'That is unusual,' Mr Quill agrees, but does not mark it down. Instead, for once and with evident effort, he frowns away the smile from his face and, first checking that we are not observed, takes me by the arm. 'I have a heavy confidence,' he says, 'which Master Kent is keen that I should share with you but with no other. There is another gentleman . . . we are awaiting him . . . another Jordan, actually, who has his claims upon' — Mr Quill makes a circle with his arm, beating our bounds with a single gesture — 'all this.'

And here at last I start to understand my master's evident distress. Old Edmund Jordan and his wife produced a daughter, Lucy, but not a son. So when her father died soon after Lucy married Master Kent, the manor and the property was her sole inheritance, which by legal document was to be divided equally on her death amongst her male heirs by blood, 'her envisaged sons', Mr Quill explains.

'There are no sons,' I say. 'She died in childbirth only this spring, but even that child was a girl . . . Master Kent is Mistress Lucy's single heir.'

'Not so. He is not blood. A husband is not blood. There is a cousin, though. Also Edmund Jordan. Those changes Master Kent proposes and which he has employed me to mark down are not his own. You cannot think he wishes them. Those sheep, these charts which I prepare, indeed, are demanded by the cousin. And he arrives today to make good what he counts as his entitlement.'

We have regained the higher ground before the impact of this news sinks in. The gleaning field is already empty. Today it is difficult for me not to see heavy meaning in its emptiness. There is no hint of green; not even Lizzie Carr's cloth crown remains. The acres seem to undulate and fall so endlessly and with such monotony of harvesting and tillage, such space and depth, that any bottom to them is lost not in the clouds or mist but in the duskiness of distance. What little pickings may be left are given over now to our cows and uninvited birds. Wild pigeons pause and jerk, full of fussy self-esteem and grain. I try to people it but I can hear only the weird and phantom bleats of sheep.

The Queen and all her subjects have taken to the threshing barn and are too busy when I arrive with Mr Quill to want to stop and hold a conversation with our inquiring visitor. The flail cannot cease its knocking on the floor just because of him. Every swing of it means food. There is today's allotment of sheaves to spread and barley ears to set aside; there's chaff to shake and separate from grain in wicker baskets; and then — unless we want weed bread or horse loaf — there's grain to sieve before it's sacked for storage in our lofts. What's left or dropped becomes the property of mice and rats and hogs. I plunge my good hand into a half-filled sack. It sinks up to my elbow as easily as if I've dipped it in a pond. Indeed, the grains run through my fingers in a liquid stream. I've known better harvests, years when the barleycorn was fat and milky. You couldn't pull a plumper bogey from your nose, we'd say. And I've known hungry years when yields were fibrous and parched, and we survived the winter on dry bones. Today the grains are good enough, but only good enough. We will not starve; we will not fatten either.

Mr Quill and I stand away from the great open doors and downwind from the winnowing, watching like gentlemen at a cockfight. He has his hands folded behind his back, perhaps aware of his soft and unworked palms, but certainly conscious of the price that everyone in front of him will pay for Mistress Lucy's failure to produce a son. I do my best to not betray his unhappy confidences on my face. I let my damaged hand hang loose on show so that nobody is in any doubt why I am not helping them today but still expect and still deserve my flour and my malt. I know my teasing neighbours. Their suspicion of anyone who was not born within these boundaries is unwavering. Next time they catch me sitting on my bench at home with a cup and slice, they are bound to wonder if it tastes all the sweeter for not being earned with labour. Do I need any help, perhaps — given my mangled hand — lifting the barley cake to my lips? Or any help with chewing it?

I hurry Mr Quill away. He's smiled enough, I think. But he is in such a considerate mood he will not leave the barn until he has said farewell to everyone. He is not rewarded with replies. The one or two who break their labour and lift their chins to look at him are only baffled. What is this stranger getting at? When no one plans on going anywhere today, what is the purpose of farewell?

We find ourselves at last back in the lane which will take us past the blackened timbers of the stable and the ashes of baled hay and towards the turret of the manor house. We've brushed the dust and chaff from off our shoulders, heads and beards, though Mr Quill's waxed wedge is still not clear of barley waste. We're deep in sombre conversation. It has been a restful and a pleasant walk, despite the weight of what I've learnt. Yet I feel as if I've made a conquest and also been beguiled. I like the man. And I've recognised an opportunity in him, a way to turn these changes to my benefit.

It is not until we near the church ground that I realise I've hardly given any thought today to Mistress Beldam or her men. I feel uneasy, suddenly. Disloyal. Indeed, I'm doing what I can to not catch sight of the wooden pillory. And I succeed. Or I succeed until we have very nearly reached the orchard where the lane-grass is bouldered with fallen fruit. I start to kick the largest apples down the path. I'm in a restive mood, of course. And with good cause. But Mr Quill has spotted Master Kent. From where we are, we can see only our mounted master's head and shoulders, his best high hat and lemon sash. He's circling the cross and talking loudly to himself. His voice is splintered and alarmed. He's rocking to and fro in the saddle, beating his thighs with his fists. And, as he has many times before on this piece of prospective holy ground, he is reciting obsequies and intercessions for the dead.

5

The younger Edmund Jordan has not travelled here before. He alerted us to his arrival with six blasts on a saddle horn as soon as he and a party of five — his steward, a groom, and three sidemen — gained first sight of our valley this afternoon. But they descended through our lanes and ways without encountering a working hand. I think Master Jordan must have counted on something busier and grander. Certainly he was dressed for that. At least he expected to be welcomed at the manor house and given time to rest before attending to matters of estate. But he was greeted not by offers of stabling and refreshments but first by the remains of a newly burnt-out barn and then by the sight of his host and cousin-in-law, Charles Kent, at the head end of a mutilated corpse. Mr Quill, his fixed smile now signifying his revulsion, was at the other end, while I, still excused from carrying because of my injury, followed on, leading Willowjack. They must have looked the strangest pair in their yellow gleaning cloths, their hands and breeches black with blood, their shoulders sagging from the weight as they finally reached the courtyard of the manor house and hoisted the body on to the long stone bench in the porch before an audience of these mounted visitors.

I don't know why we thought we could revive the man. Clearly he was dead and had been dead long enough for someone's loose pig to chance upon the corpse and tear out pieces of his foot and calf. One leg was so badly damaged that Mr Quill had to lift the body from the knees and tolerate what remained of the gnawed limb banging up against his own. But at moments such as this it would take a heartless man not to at least attempt some healing. Besides, once the three of us had gathered at the foot of the pillory and comprehended what had happened to the eldest of the newcomers, we were quickly in a hustle to escape the curses of the younger man. I have never seen such anger and such despair. His state was all the worse for his still being fastened in the pillory. His wrists and throat were purple with bruising. It looked as if he'd tried to pull himself free and didn't care whether or not he left his head and hands behind.

None of us had the expertise to make repairs, although we knew we had to be the first . . . to what? To make amends? So we did what little could be done — mostly wiping off the blood, closing the wounds enough to hide the grinning white of bone, changing the man's expression from one of wide-eyed agony to that of someone sleeping through a nightmare, and finally covering our newcomer in a shroud of baling cloth. Master Kent spoke a prayer, not quite out loud. It was as if he hoped to smuggle into the usual formulations an intercession for himself, asking for forgiveness possibly for being party to this death. I have to say I prayed myself, a rare event. But I could sense the thunder and the lightning closing in on us. A mighty storm of reckoning was on its way, if there was any justice in the world. The air was cracking with the retributions and damnations that, in my hearts of hearts, I knew that some of us deserved. I prayed that this was just a dream and that soon the couldn't-care-less clamour of the sunrise birds would rouse me to another day, a better day, a bloodless one, one in which, despite my hand, I'd do my common duty and drag up a log or stone to make that short man tall. I prayed that Time would turn back on its heels and surprise us with a sudden billowing of breath beneath the baling cloth. I might just as well have cried out for the Derby twins to bring their haul of golden shawls to jolt this man alive again.

This is my calculation, shaped once more without recourse to any constable or magistrate. Or any doctor, priest or undertaker, come to that. Yes, it's just as well — again — that we are so far from civil practice, because a constable or magistrate would have the will and power to lay bare the causes of this man's loose head and disfigured limbs. Here's what took place. Sometime between my sodden visit to the pillory last night and Master Kent's encounter with the two punished men this morning, when the younger was so manically uncivil, the elder man slipped or toppled from his stretched toes and snapped his neck. It might have been the rain that made him fall. Let's hope his accident was sudden and he was sleeping. Or, God forbid, it could have been his living efforts to fight off a hungry hog that made him flail his body to and fro until his bones were split. Of course, it might have been a stopping heart. I hope it was a stopping heart. Or something unexceptional. Whatever happened, it is clear that the father did not fail to lift his head for Master Kent this morning as an insolent rebuke but because he was already dead.

I'm not the only one who will blame himself, and will have good cause to blame himself. As soon as we established the body on the porch bench this afternoon and were standing back, shamed and bloodied by our efforts and not daring yet to turn and face the mounted visitors, I saw the looks on Master Kent's and Mr Quill's faces. A player in the theatre could not devise a greater exhibition of guilt. And once the word has spread, there will be many villagers who will regret their scythes and sticks of yesterday morning and others who will run out to their sties with fingers knotted for good luck to see if any of their pigs has broken free or already seems too satisfied by the taste of foot and calf to want its customary peels or brewing mash. And if the Derby twins and Brooker Higgs have any tenderness for strangers — a subject open to debate, I know — they will surely want to hurry naked to the woods to flay themselves with whips. This is a death that touches all of us, though we still do not even know the fellow's name.

But for the moment we are required — and thankful — to be hospitable. The four gentlemen by birth — that's Mr Quill, Master Kent, his cousin and the steward — are first ushered in to what passes nowadays as the parlour to the manor house. The three sidemen take care of luggage and panniers. I am assigned, as any common servant, to lead the way with Willowjack and show Master Jordan's groom where in the absence of a stable block their horses might be stalled. By the time I return, both chastened and annoyed by the groom's presumption and disdain — how does the solemn custody of saddles make a man superior? — the gentlemen have disappeared into the upper rooms. I can hear the hum and mutter of their voices, and once or twice I recognise enough to know that the master is giving an account of what has happened at the pillory and his cousin is expressing his dismay that what was evidently once a fine manor house has ended up 'as shabby and as threadbare as a beggar's sack'.

I hope to overhear the better. I remove my shoes so that I might move quietly through the rooms. I know that I am not expected to join the gentlemen. I should not offer any words of my own. Master Jordan will have recognised my station from the clothes I wear, especially my rye-straw hat, and from the ripened colour of my hands and cheeks. But I am determined to be the spy, though whether I am spying for myself or for my neighbours or for the master himself is not yet clear to me. Hearing them might make it so.

I see the inside of the house with a stranger's eyes, for once. Certainly, the manor is not a place to make us cottage-dwellers jealous. We have no need of windows, or an upper floor. All we require for our estate is earth for carpeting, rubble-walls, and a pair of hearty cross-beam timbers to keep the roof from falling in. But people of a finer pedigree want cosseting. We have heard reports of prodigy houses in other country villages, where gentlemen and ladies take their rest in timbered beds as sturdy as galleons and closed off from the great glass window light by curtains and softened with flock mattresses. They sleep in fine linen or silky camlet sheets with spaniels at their feet, while in the many chambers of the house the servants rise at dawn to put a shine on tile floors, buff up chairs with cushioned arms, shake out the moths and motes from the painted hangings, the tapestries and Turkey work, and put out breakfast trays of dainties — the suckets, comfits, carroways we'll never get the chance to taste. I've heard of yeoman palaces with lakes and deer parks in their grounds and so rich inside that a hungry mastiff is deployed all day to guard a cupboard where the mistress hides her costly silverware and brass and a casket full of jewellery. Indeed, when I was young and not yet come to this far place, I served Master Kent in a stone-built, courtyard residence with peacocks in a walled garden, a castellated tower, more than forty rooms and just as many helping hands whose only task was keeping house.

Master Kent's home has no such finery and so no need of any mastiffs, or even any spaniels. If there is any luxury or opulence, it has been well concealed, or it has been untended. The manor was busier and more cared for when Lucy Kent was alive. Its rooms were used and always

86

sweet with juniper smoke or strews of lavender. Some of our wives attended her each day, to help her dress and keep it clean and be her kitchen maids. But with her passing, her widower has preferred to simplify his life. The ancient gallery has been closed until this afternoon, as have all the sleeping rooms upstairs. Their fine wood panelling has begun to fade and scab for want of polishing. Mr Quill is quartered comfortably enough, downstairs, in what was, in the elder Edmund Jordan's day, the steward's room and where more lately Lucy Kent would sit and close the day with her needle; and Master Kent makes do in the parlour, his retreat, with its open fire. He has a wainscot bed, set against the wall but uncurtained and without evidence of any flock or linen. He sleeps on a mattress stuffed with chaff like everybody else and his summer coverlets are hap-harlots, the coarsest cloth. He has a coffer full of documents and manuscripts, an oaken trestle table where he sits to eat alone and rest his candle, a high-backed settle to protect him from the draughts and two reminders of his wife: her smallest loom, her hairbrush. He has more space, more possibilities, than us, but who can say he has more comfort? I would not swap accommodations with him, to tell the truth. Nor would I want to swap my life with his. Not now.

It is the first time for many years — since I had quarters in the attic and in the turret room, in fact — that I've had reason to pause and study the grander, second storey of the house. I have forgotten how melancholy these great rooms can be, especially when there are no dogs or children to misuse them. I am almost blinded by the dark as I draw close to the quartet of voices. It is still a bright afternoon outside. I have had to squint for much of the day. But even when my eyes grow used to it, the manor's lack of light is burdensome. The building is too old for the great wide-latticed windows and oriels of newer dwellings. It does not have a square of window glass but only recessed openings and loopholes. What light it has is blanketed by the red-black canopy of beeches planted closely to the house, as was the custom, to protect against lightning strikes. But at least the darkness affords me some disguise. I am able to ascend the stairs, skirting round what few narrow shafts of light there are, until I reach the landing at the upper gallery and what remains of the master's better furniture and brass-braced storage chests. And I can stay in shadow behind the curtain at the door to watch and hear the conversations at the far end of the room.

Only Master Jordan is standing. He is a tall, big-boned, round-shouldered man, dressed in a long doublet so hard-quilted that it stiffens him. He swings a casting bottle of rosewater in his hand, protection I suppose against the stench of this untended gallery. The once white-tempered mortar on the upper walls has dappled. The room is damp and smells of hair and mouldy laths. The other three are sitting neatly on a bench like courtiers, hands on knees, their heads lifted, listening. Edmund Jordan says, 'Of course, that's natural for you, I see,' to some remark that Mr Quill has made. It is clear he considers the

Chart-Maker a fool, a grinning and beribboned fool, with barley straw still in his beard. Even the word 'natural' is delivered with a sting. It is as if he's labelled Mr Quill The Village Natural — the local idiot who might be less annoying if he could stop airing his own opinions and only listen.

I am not a local idiot. I listen for a good part of the afternoon.

6

I sleep tonight in widow Gosse's bed. Once in a while of late I creep up like a midnight cat to brush my face against her door and call her name through the ajar as quietly as I can, so as not to be heard by anyone. Excepting her. Sometimes I'm not even heard by her and, in the silence of her no reply, there is a chance for me to come back to my senses and creep away again, unsatisfied and angry with myself. At other times — though less commonly, because her cottage sits back from the lane and so is less overheard and, thereby, better suited than mine to, well, our cries — she turns up at my door on a similar errand. I am touched and reassured by that. It is a sign that we are equal parties in our sin. This is not a case of fox and hare. Her pretence, her subterfuge, to use a stylish word I've heard this afternoon, is that she's come to borrow a length of candle or a little grease, but I'm not sure if she intends to make a pun.

Once or twice, I have affected not to hear her tapping on the door or, indeed, not to be in my bed at all, but on a night-time mission somewhere else. Down at Turd and Turf, quite possibly, and achieving a release of quite a different kind. At such moments I am reluctant to call out 'Kitty, Kitty, come inside', because this is the bed where Cecily, my little thrush of a wife, has slept with me. The marriage bed.

Though I'm not fool enough to think she's still watching over me, there's no denying that a woman leaves her mark, especially a woman who has shared your life for over eleven years and one for whom your feelings are not merely physical. Indeed, sometimes when I am in a melancholy mood, deep in the trenches of the night, perhaps, I slide my hand across the rough mattressing and find comfort in the hollows where my Cecily has slept (and died), where her shoulders and her hips have left their body ghosts.

My feelings for the widow Gosse are only physical, I have to say. I'm not even sure if she and I are friends. I think we hold each other in a low contempt. She finds me inexplicable — my self-absorption, my neglect of the small garden at the cottage back, my great abundance of uncommon words — and counts me as a town owl that's all hoot and no talons. She blames me for my cautiousness. I've been too schooled, she says dismissively. I find her limited and, except in matters of the field, dull-witted. But in bed when we are making love she's certainly no fool. Unlike my Cecily she has a lusty appetite. At night, her hand with her fingers spreading downwards is always on my abdomen, rather than lying more tenderly across my chest, as was my wife's. She has been a startling discovery. Possibly it is the intensity of our coupling that causes me so much shame to be her bedtime partner. We are, I think, like beasts, no better than a pair of forest beasts, unable to resist the physical and barbarous. It is not that she is beautiful or ever was. She must be very nearly fifty years of age. And since her husband died she has not taken much care of herself. Her clothes would benefit from mending — and from scrubbing, possibly. She has the usual warts and lumps of living hard and long. Her hair has greyed, despite the local patch of asphodels which other women use to keep their tresses stubbornly blonde. And it's difficult to tell, even when she's naked at my side, if Kitty Gosse is fat or thin. She's narrow-faced and narrow-hipped but large and softly comfortable about her waist and stomach. She calls it widow's spread and is not the least concerned — the opposite — when, lying on her back with me on top, her creamy stomach sways and frowns like a shaken posset.

But then I have to ask myself, What does the widow see in me? As I imagine it, I am still a scrawny fellow, thin-armed and pale but with a bouncy head of hair, unfashionably brown for hereabouts. I'm handsome even, I would say. Indeed, I have been told that I look pleasing, especially in a hat or cap. Certainly, that is how I last appeared in a looking glass. But I have not had ready access to a looking glass for some years now. Once in a while, when Mistress Kent was still alive and I had reason to be in the manor house alone, I risked the two steps to her dressing room and stood in front of her tall glass to take stock of myself. I stared upon the one face in the village that I seldom saw but was available to everybody else. Her mirror darkened me and frayed my edges where the reflecting magic crystals in the glass had made a dry black mould, a kind of glittered lichen which seemed

92

determined to encroach the clarity. But still, the body there was mine. I raised my hand and so did it. It replied to every smile. And when on more than one occasion I reached across to Mistress Kent's day couch where she threw her clothes, lifted free one of her heavy, decorated gowns and — wondering, just wondering; doing nothing worse than wondering — held it up against myself, that ashened, haunted woman in the looking glass was no one else but me.

For a year at least I have not even glimpsed my face. The duckweed in the ponds will not allow me to. The manor house has shuttered windows and no glass. The silver spoon the master gave us on our wedding day is tarnished and no longer repays any light. The worked copper on the brewing kettle picks up my shadow when I go close to it but the reflection is so tooled and beaten that my face is too pockmarked to be recognisable. In fact, I cannot think there is a looking glass in the parish, though no doubt there are some wives who have a secret sliver with which to horrify themselves and which they wisely do not seek to share. No, as far as I'm aware, our nearest likeness is two days' distant. The master, as is the husband's custom hereabouts amongst the gentlemen, sharded his wife's long looking glass and buried the pieces with her, for fear of being haunted by her trace. So, unlike the town from where I came, where everyone who stepped out in the street would first have turned themselves this way and that in front of mirrors and could not have stepped twenty paces more before reflecting on themselves in window glass, we in this village walk around in blinded ignorance. We close an eye and see no more than a side of the nose, or possibly some facial hair, the outer regions of a beard. We know our hands and knees but not our eyes and teeth. So truly I can only guess what widow Gosse can see in me. And I suppose it is the same for her. Perhaps, without a husband to be her informant, she doesn't even know how lined she is. That is the state of widowhood. We've no idea; we must hope for the best.

When I first started calling at her cottage, Kitty Gosse and I would hardly look each other in the eye. I was thinking of my Cecily — though Cecily was never this unbridled in my arms — and she, I must suppose, imagined herself unwidowed and back beneath the gouty, puffing Fowler Gosse, who died it's said between these very legs. Hugged to death, with hair in his teeth, some wag has claimed. But over time I've ventured to study every part of her and have found great pleasure in her enthusiastic limbs. Tonight, though, I leave neither of us satisfied. I am too anxious and too hurried. My purpose in coming here, in tapping on her cottage door, is not so much to spend myself in her and have her disburse herself with me, so that we might deserve a full night's sleep in company, but more to make myself forget or at least to banish from my mind for tonight the prospects I have overheard in Master Kent's dark gallery.

I cannot say that Master Jordan has proved himself — not yet — to be a rough or thoughtless man, though he shows a stony disregard for proper burial. He is efficient, that is

94

all. And unceremonial. He talks good sense, though sometimes sense is colder than an icicle. And sharper too. He listened patiently while Master Kent recounted the history of the newcomers: the doves, the fires, the bows, the pillory. And his replies displayed the mildest exasperation: 'It is my judgement, cousin Charles, that you make problems for yourself by being kind.' The two men in the pillory had only got their just deserts, in his view. If one had died, that was still within the bounds of what the law allows. 'A sturdy vagabond and fire setter' should expect to have his ears cut off and then be hoisted to the gibbet. That was not unusual. The younger man? Well, he should still serve out his week-long sentence: 'What is the case for being lenient? He has given the community offence and so should suffer justice in the full gaze of the community. Besides, cousin, you say he has already threatened you and holds you guilty of his kinsman's death. Would you have him walking free, in such a vengeful frame of mind? No, we will take him with us, far from harm, when we depart. We'll lash him to the saddle of a horse and set him free only when it is safe. Perhaps, we will equip him with a limp, as a reminder to be good, and wise. No doubt the woman you describe, the sister or the daughter or the wife, whoever she might be . . . well, no doubt she will follow her one surviving man away from here. In the meantime, let her be, let her peck about the forest like a goose. Do not concern yourself with her. A woman cannot do you any harm.'

What of the corpse? Again, Master Jordan could not see that this issue was problematic in the least. He snapped his fingers in dismissal. If Master Kent himself was too squeamish in such matters, he'd have his sidemen dispose of the corpse in the same place that any animal carcasses were abandoned. 'He has not earned a place on hallowed ground, I think. So let the pigs complete what they've begun.' He clapped his hands. 'You see, you see?' he asked, as delighted with himself as any boy. 'Nothing is as complicated as you fear. Now, gentlemen . . . ' His voice was lowered at this point. He did not want to waste more time on such frivolities. There were graver, grander things to talk about.

I listened to the squaring of the cousin's feet as he began to outline his plans for Progress and Prosperity. 'Do not blame me that I have an impulse to improve, a zeal for progress,' he told his audience this afternoon. 'It is not by design or any subterfuge of mine that this estate and the duties that relate to it have fallen in my hands . . . But any final testament should be observed whatever the consequences. I think we will agree on that.'

Well, let him make excuses for himself. I will skirt round the details of his methods and procedures, the sums and calculations that he's made, the reckoning. We've heard the drift of it before, from Master Kent's own lips, when he addressed us between the veal and the dancing. The cousin's version, though, was not so tender on the ear. There was no regret. He did not have a dream in which we 'friends and neighbours' were made rich and leisurely, where we were sitting at our fires at home and weaving fortunes for ourselves from yarn. I think he judges us rich and leisurely enough already. No, Master Jordan only had a scheme, a 'simple quest', for a tidier pattern of living hereabouts which would assure a profit for those — he means himself — who have 'the foresight'.

What matters most for now is that my master is allowed to stay. It is not the cousin's wish to be 'a country mouse', he said. He would prefer to remain in his great merchant house in his great market town and simply check the figures once in a while: what rough wool from these old fields has arrived in his warehouse, what cloth his hired women have woven on their looms, what varying profits have been made from selling their worsted, twill or fustian, their pickthread and their petersham, and what profits have been lost to greedy shearmen and staplers, cheating chapmen, and lazy fullers, tuckers and dyers. 'So many ravens to be fed and satisfied,' he said, letting his shoulders sag with the weight of his responsibilities. 'We should not deceive ourselves that in a modern world a common system such as ours which only benefits the commoners (and only in prolific years) could earn the admiration of more rational observers for whom 'agriculture without coin' is absurd.

'Everyone amongst us plays his part, for the good of the whole,' Master Jordan concluded. 'It is the duty of our part to make the others' part more comfortable. This is society.' He pointed at his smiling *village natural*. 'You, sir. Continue with your quills and charts, and let's complete your map-making before the week is out. This gentleman is Mr Baynham . . . ' Here I heard his steward civilly muttering his greetings. ' . . . and he, you will discover, is adept at preparing land for sheep. This is not the first community to benefit from Mr Baynham's stewardship. Of course, he needs to be acquainted with your land, my land. He will be guided by the charts. Before first snow he will have structured everywhere within these bounds with fences, dykes and walls, as he sees fit. He'll be reclaiming forestry. How can it profit us that there are trees, an oak, let's say, producing shade but not a single fruit to eat, except for beasts? We would be wise to hew it down and trade its timber rather than allow it to defeat the sun, for beauty's sake, at my expense. Likewise, the commons will be cleared and privately enclosed. You're pasture now. These lands are grass. We'll never need another plough. You, cousin — '

'We have a little short of sixty souls to feed hereabouts . . . ' Master Kent spoke up at last, his voice pinched and hesitant. And so it ought to be. But Master Jordan only spread his hands and shrugged, a shrug that counted our distresses as an inevitable proviso for his permanent advance. 'That's Mr Baynham's province now,' he said. 'I'm sure that there will be a place for shearers and for sheep-boys. Or for some, at least. He will employ what hands he needs. But we will sadly need to make economies — '

'I do not think that you will make economies,' said Mr Quill, who is, I have to say, the bravest soul for all his lumbering.

Master Jordan laced his fingers and looked down thoughtfully into the lattice they made. He offered Mr Quill a fleering, patient smile of his own. 'It is not my role to make economies but rather to provide expenditure,' he said finally. 'Do not imagine that I come here empty-handed. There will be charity. Gratuities, indeed. I will fund at last the building of a church and I will employ a priest. I bring you sheep, and I supply a Holy Shepherd too. There'll be a steeple, higher than the turret of this house, taller than any ancient oak that we might fell. This place will be visible from far. And I will have a bell cast for the very top of it to summon everyone to prayer. And hurry everyone to work. Those few that can remain, that is.' Again he stared into his hands, then added without looking up, as if talking only to himself, 'It's only Mr Earle, I think, who is not obliged to make economies, and has no duties other than with maps, and besides is so hellishly unstable on his feet he must have . . . ' He paused to find a witticism.

'Yes, I must have been kicked by a horse or struck by lightning. I've heard it all before. The heavens opened and a tongue of light gave me the body of an old gnarled tree. Oh, certainly, the devil himself concocted me in his cracked jar. And so I am deformed. Well, have it so, if that amuses you,' Mr Quill replied, with only the merest edge of temper to his voice; a practised speech, I think, which he has used to shield himself more than once before. And here my listening was hastened to an end by Master Jordan turning on his heels and striding down the gallery towards my lurking place. He was smiling — not unsweetly — to himself. I had to draw myself into the shadows until the man had passed.

Now I am sorely tempted to wrap myself round Kitty Gosse's back and whisper to her everything I've overheard this afternoon. It is a burden that might be lightened in its sharing. I have been privy to the pattern of our futures. I've seen the green and white of grass and sheep. I've heard the tolling of the steeple bell. I am the only one amongst them yet that knows our master is displaced, though still in place. We're all displaced, I must suppose. I have the sense to hold my tongue, of course — I must plan provision for myself, before my neighbours are informed — though feeling the warmth of the widow's back against my chest again while thinking as I must of Mistress Beldam pecking in the forest makes me effusive in another way. So she and I make love again. And I am sure we're not alone in that. The dark is stifling its cries in other cottages than hers. Their beds are creaking. There is whispering. Knees are pressing into straw. On nights like this, when there's anxiety about, there is a glut of love-making. Then the moon is our dance master. He has us move in unison. He has us trill and carol in each other's ears until the stars themselves have swollen and have ripened to our cries. As ever here, we find our consolations sowing seed.

7

We wake to learn that Willowjack is dead. The news is brought to Kitty Gosse's door at first light by Anne Rogers, our village piper's mother. She is amused but evidently not surprised to find me in my spacious underclothes naked from the waist up and pulling on my breeches at her friend's bed end. Someone 'with clever hands', she says, has taken a spike of metal, a tethering prong, from the winter tool chest in the standing barn and driven it with precision and with force into the horse's head above her ear. The large square stone that the slaughterer took from the church-yard and used as a mallet was found in the straw, syrupy with blood, when the carcass was dragged aside. It's sitting now on Master Kent's mantelshelf. Plans are afoot to hunt the hand that wielded it.

'It must have been a large hand,' says Anne Rogers. 'Someone big and strong. A man, of course. A man who might've done this sort of thing before. A man horses trust . . . ' She hesitates because she does not want to say what she hopes each of us is thinking, that Willowjack will have known her murderer. How could a stranger get close enough to hold a prong against her head and drive it home, even if it took only a single blow? It was never easy to get close to Willowjack; even unplugging a blood tick from her ear was rewarded with a nipping. Anne

Rogers means us to suspect our blacksmith, Abel Saxton, a second cousin of my wife and a man she once set her heart upon — until he married. Then he was despised.

'It might be anyone who's similar, of course,' she adds, seeing the look on my face and then nodding at my hands.

'I have my alibi,' I say, pointing at the bed and seeming for the women's benefit to make light of what is already upsetting me and will be insufferable for Master Kent. The knots that tie us to this tranquil place are loosening. 'Besides, this one hand's not entirely mended.' I show the healing wound. The scab has darkened and is flexible. If I'm not careful I'll be put to work again. 'It's painful still,' I promise, not quite certain why both are laughing. 'I couldn't squash a fly with this.'

'Or even strip a bit of barleycorn,' she says.

So now there are two bodies to be taken down to Turd and Turf, the master's cherished mare and the abandoned man from the pillory. I do not know whom we should hold responsible for the horse's death. My first suspicion lays its eggs beneath the skin of Master Jordan's groom. I was not impressed by him when, yesterday, I showed him where his horses could be tied. He looked at Willowjack with a narrow lip, I thought. 'She'd benefit from brushing down,' he said, though by any rule she was twice as fine a horse as any of his mounts. Envy can be maddening. Perhaps she's nipped him, and he's taken his revenge.

I could as well make out a case that lays the blame again at the feet, well, at the hands, of

Brooker Higgs and the Derby twins, all three of whom are known for their great fists. Perhaps word has already leaked out — from outraged Mr Quill, or possibly the cousin's sidemen — that the village as we know it and our employments are to be surrendered to the yellow teeth of three thousand sheep. We'll be outnumbered fifty to one — and soon. Our trio of bachelors would once more have cause for anger and indignation, though no more cooing doves to vent their outrage on. And no bleaters yet. They might have listened to the love-making last night and grown restless, naturally, wanting trills and carols of their own. They might have eaten the remaining fairy caps from the visit to the woods on what seems a thousand evenings ago. And only then they would have found the wicked pluck to hammer Willowjack, a horse that everybody loved and so the creature most deserving of their blows. But I have seen how Brooker and the twins have slunk around like chastened dogs these past few days, fearful that their dove-baiting will catch them out. The roasting of the birds was bad enough, though it was warranted to some degree. But the newcomers were punished unjustly because of our men's deceit and silence, and now the smaller one is dead, strangled at the pillory. No, there's not a mushroom strong enough to make these young men kill the master's horse. They're frightened of the shadows now. In any other place but here, they would be frightened for their lives.

Another possibility: I blush even to name my

neighbour, dear John Carr. He is a placid man, greatly loved by his fellows and close to animals. John Carr can stop a drove of running cattle in their tracks, even ones made frisky by the company of bulls or young. I've seem him root a maddened dog to the ground with just a fingertip: one firm touch on the nose to stop the barking, and another to set the tail wagging. It's a gift, and one that he is called upon to use whenever we've an animal to butcher. It was John who dispatched the little calf we feasted on the other night at Master Kent's expense. Its skin is still soaking in brine under the rafters of the barn, though today it is amongst my challenges to lift it out before it's entirely fit and attempt to fashion some serviceable vellum for Mr Quill's shape-shifting chart. Yes, John Carr is the village slaughterman and more than anyone I know possesses all the skills and speed it took to execute Willowjack with the calm efficiency Mistress Rogers describes. But neighbour Carr has small and stubby hands, a pair of how-to hands, worn short with work. And he is kind.

Anne Rogers will not be the only one to count our blacksmith, Abel Saxton, as a suspect, that's for sure. One of his hands is big and strong enough to hold a hoof completely still while he's shodding it with the other. But I discount that idea straight away, as Abel Saxton has been too intimately involved with Willowjack — her welfare and her tack, her clobber and her shoes — to wish her dead under any circumstance. The master rewards him well for his leatherwork and smithery. The man's a fool, but not the kind of fool to spit in his own hat.

I'm mystified, to tell the truth. It does not take me long, once Mistress Rogers has run off to spread the gossip of where 'old Walter Thirsk' has laboured overnight 'again', to mutter a rosary of names between my lips — the twenty or so men in the neighbourhood tall enough to level with a horse's ear — but still not find a likely candidate.

'It will've been the short one did it,' offers Kitty Gosse as she prepares our porridge for the day. I have forgotten how hare-brained and vexing she can be.

'You mean the little man that died? Yes, that does seem likely, doesn't it?'

'Who else? If you've been throttled in the pillory for burning doves, and half devoured by pigs, murdering a horse is just the sort of mischief you'd enjoy,' she says with certainty. 'There's motive, isn't there?'

'The man is dead.'

'The dead men are the ones to fear. A soul can't rest until it's satisfied, until the fellow is revenged.'

'He's far too short to reach the horse's head.' I'm trying to be reasonable.

She stares as if I am the world's buffoon. 'Everybody's short, when they're kneeling down,' she says, and looks at me cock-eyed. Of course, she's right. I've been half-witted. The horse wasn't standing; it was down and sleeping when it died. It was in the hollows of the night. What does a horse do, then, other than to fold itself into the straw and sleep? The killer didn't have to be familiar. The killer didn't have to reach. The killer didn't even have to lift that finger-stretching rock far from the ground. The killer might have used two hands. Far from being the work of a hefty, muscle-fisted man, the killer could have been a woman or a child. Not counting widow Gosse's ghost and his pilloried companion but including Mr Quill and Master Kent's six manor house guests, there are more than sixty sons and daughters of Cain who might have crept back to their cot last night with horse blood on their hands and clothes.

Indeed, that is the stain that Master Jordan wants to chase, once everyone is gathered in the threshing house ready for another day of barley work. Horses have enormous pumping hearts. A loop of blood fountained out of Willowjack's head the moment that the prong went in. The straw is black and sticky with its splash. Whoever was responsible for this death will not have escaped entirely dry and unspoilt. All the masters need to do is find the pile of red and sodden clothes. The cottagers are told, therefore, that none of them must stray a step beyond the barn today. Their dwellings and their gardens will be searched. And we must prepare ourselves, in the absence of a lawful gibbet, to see a neighbour hanging from an oak before the end of day.

'And who are you?' That is a question no one dares to ask as Master Jordan stands before them. The cousin does not even give his name or offer the briefest account of his status and intentions. All my neighbours see is a man of

106

blunt authority attended by three menservants who are affecting to be dangerously bored. They all four look extremely clean and pale. Spotless is the word. No worthy flea would want to spend a night with them. The menservants are dressed in matching breeches, jerkins with flaxen collars and brimless caps, like foot soldiers. From behind, where I am standing at Master Kent's shoulder, they are indistinguishable from each other. Their lord — for it must seem that he's at least a lord — has thrown aside the leather riding-coat and padded doublet he was wearing yesterday and, as befits the summer warmth, is attired more loosely in trunk-hose — or onion pants as they might as well be called — and an embroidered linen smock. There's not a tuft of wool on him, I see. His beard is barbered and his hair, so far as we can tell, is pinned. But what holds our attention and most persuades he is a man we should not trifle with is his high-crowned hat, his copotain, which he's adorned not only with the Jordan family badge but with both a feather and a gemstone clip. That hat alone says power, wealth and provenance. That hat alone could purchase each of us.

In truth, this lord, this gentleman, is having trouble keeping his hat in place. He has to raise his hand and hold its brim as he describes — in gestures and in words — what he expects from us today. In brief, he wants an end to all the nonsense that has disturbed our country peace so thoroughly of late. We are too far from 'ordinance and regulation', he says. We have forgotten Benefits of Law, Just Punishment, the

Dues and Customs of all citizens 'and countrymen', he adds. So far 'the reckoning', for which we all could well be held to account, comprises only property of the manor house — some buildings and some creatures of great consequence.

'Someone amongst you here, beneath this roof, will be found and held responsible for the theft of a mare of great value,' he says. 'That person cannot expect to walk these lanes tomorrow, nor should he hope to claim a holy burial . . . He will meet the rotting carcass of the horse he killed, in your charnel field. He will meet his brother miscreant too — the one who foolishly thought he could set fire to barns and doves and only pay the meagre price of one week, at leisure in the pillory, but has instead today been dragged by his bloody heels to join the skeletons.'

I cannot help but look for the twins and Brooker Higgs amongst the silent gathering. When they're not gaping, they're swallowing. They're picturing the pair of carcasses already at Turd and Turf and wondering which of them now standing in the barn will sleep for ever with Willowjack and with the pig-chewed, throttled newcomer. But that's the same for everybody here. It's as clear as any thunder cloud that troubles are approaching fast, that lightning is bound to strike a villager. This high-hatted man, whoever he might be, whatever his conjunction with the Jordan family badge, will not be satisfied until the reckoning is paid.

Master Kent himself says nothing to explain.

Everyone can tell by how he hangs his hands behind his back and bows his head, nodding too self-consciously — he's nothing but a listener today — that, whoever this new gentleman might be, their own master of the manor is balancing on a lower rung than him, and knows it. This is a new experience, and baffling. No one has seen the master standing with such anxious deference before. We're used to knowing he's in charge even though he's never been too keen to remind us of that fact. He has always tried to be an even-handed, subtle Caesar in our midst, more ready to achieve his purposes by throwing an arm around our shoulders than shouting in our ears. Our Caesar now seems powerless. Of course, he has been saddened by the loss of Willowjack and might have such a heavy heart that it has dragged his tongue into his throat. We can expect him soon to lift his head and take our reins again. But, no, this evident submission to the younger man is touching on the servile now. It's almost fearful. And made all the more so by the other man's officious bearing, his icy forthright manners which expect and get compliance from everybody. 'God Bless you all,' he says at last. 'And God help one of you.'

Master Kent is glad to have me at his side once we have left the barn. He needs 'a calming hand'. Not only has he lost his mare, he's had to fight to save her body from the profiteers. 'My cousin tells me I am wasteful, not to have the 'useless' carcass baked for its grease,' he says. 'I told him that the horse was far too loyal and loved for such rewards.' And Master Jordan's reply was that he himself had valued his mastiff, Blunt, just as much. He evidently was a dog as fierce and unimpeachable as any constable. But he still yielded thirteen pounds of grease when he was too old for the job and had to be dispatched.

'I am improvident for not putting Willowjack to the same good use,' adds my master, leaning closer so that he is not overheard. 'But I have insisted on my way, and won the argument . . . for once. If only I could always win the argument with cousin Edmund . . . ' He puts a finger to his lips, nervous suddenly. 'The two of us should hold our tongues. You understand?'

My master assumes that Mr Quill has, by now, explained to me the cause and reason of his cousin's country trip. He is asking that I keep secret from my neighbours not only what surely now seems obvious — his cousin's lawful usurpment of the manor and the land — but also the details of our coming woolly plight. He hopes to win some further arguments, before any cloven hoofs make their first imprint on our land. He means first to negotiate some blunting of his cousin's blades before he talks to us, his friends. It will have been his plan, I'm sure, as soon as he was warned, before the barley was cleared, that Master Jordan was descending by road to harvest his inheritance, to make a fight of it, to protect us with his arguments, to find some means of, say, saving at least some common ground where we — the shearers and the shepherds of next year — can let loose our beasts, to do his best, as well, to preserve some forestry. 'So long as all my neighbours here are safe,' he'd say, 'and they have work and food and dwellings that are assured until the thresholds of their graves, then I am equally assured your flock of sheep will meet with hospitality . . . '

But it has not been so. Somehow the village was already burdened by misfortune before its future rode in on a horse, before the Dream of Golden Hoofs came near. There were the fires. There were the doves. There were those raised, unfriendly bows. There was the woman and her disquieting face, breaking short the dance. There was the body at the pillory, or that much of the body left behind by pigs. It feels as if some impish force has come out of the forest in the past few days to see what pleasure it can take in causing turmoil in a tranquil place. And now, the worst — if it is right to count the death of a horse as worse than the death of a man — his Willowjack is dead. That is heartbreaking. She was Mistress Kent's own horse. And it is frightening too, because whoever killed the mare was stabbing Master Kent as well. Of course, he cannot talk to me or open up his heart just yet. We are surrounded by the cousin's men. And Master Jordan himself is never out of hearing. My master only offers me a shrug, a pulse of hands and chin and mouth but sadly eloquent. It says, These are the blackest days for us, old friend. I raise my eyebrows in reply. Indeed, we've never known a more alarming day.

We have gone beyond the hearing of the threshing barn. The flailing and winnowing continue steadily behind. Only Mr Quill, the steward Baynham and the groom are unaccounted for, though I imagine the first two are working as an awkward pair on manuscripts and charts. I hope to be at Mr Quill's side this afternoon preparing paints and parchments as originally intended, but for the moment I am regarded as 'cousin Charles's fellow' and required to lead our party to the family homes, the heart of everything, identify the absent occupants by name and then stand by with Master Kent while Lucy Kent's cousin-by-blood and his sidemen step indoors to pull away the coverings, lift the matting and the reeds, upturn all the storage chests, shift the barrels and the benches in search of bloody rags. It's rare for me to peer into so many private rooms, to glimpse how cramped some places are, how full the beds, how modest their possessions, how buckled is the furniture. I am surprised by neatness and by dirt, by evidence of last night's food and evidence of none. It's certain that you cannot tell from how a person works or how a person strolls behind her hens what kind of life they live in secrecy.

I am embarrassed when we reach the Carrs' dwelling. John and I do not put up our feet at each other's hearths. We are good friends but meet and talk only in the open air. We sit outside and understand that neighbours should not pry. Neighbours should be deaf and blind. 'Take care,' I ask the men as they go in. But they are too impatient and detached to take much care. I sense my request has only made them more suspicious of the Carrs. I have to step away. I cannot bear to listen to the evident disruption. John will never understand why I did not go in to try to stop the breakages.

It is embarrassing as well to wait outside the widow's house and hear the thudding of the overturning bed, still warm, as I suppose, from me and her. Still rocking, possibly. But thus far there has not been any sign of butchery, not even in Abel Saxton's cottage. The only blood they find is on a kerchief in my place. I have to match my hand to it and have the master vouch for me, report my 'courage' in the burning stable block. I evidently saved the best part of his hay. Only then can Master Jordan be persuaded I am not a suspect.

So we reach the last of the village's twenty or so inhabited dwellings and we are allowed to rest while the sidemen go to check the sties and byres, the whitehouse and latrines, the brewing shed, the outbuildings and any nooks and crannies where a bloody shirt might readily be hid. It is Master Jordan himself who walks up the tangled path towards the tenement where Cecily was raised. And it is Master Jordan himself who almost at once re-emerges into the light with a cry of satisfaction and holding a heavy, bloodstained wrap of cloth. At first the master and I think it is too dark to be the woman's velvet shawl. But all too soon the truth is unignorable. First, the sunshine catches on its silver threads, and then the shawl is opened up and the colour is confirmed, the rich and heavy Turkish mauve. Shake it one more time, I want to call out to the man, and see who topples out into that thistle bed.

Actually I hold my tongue, and so does Master Kent, even when his cousin throws the shawl across a fence and invites us to identify its owner.

'Give me her name,' the cousin says, addressing me, the villager, but one he seems to trust, though possibly only because I'm not as stolid or corn-haired as the rest.

'I truly do not have a name for her,' I say, and indeed it's not entirely a lie. I can put a face to her. I can describe her roughly sheared scalp which must by now be softening and blackening with hair. I'd not mistake her dark and shiny bella-donna eyes for any other woman's in the village. But other than the byname Mistress Beldam conferred on her by Master Kent, she has no title of identity. 'I've never seen one of my neighbours wearing that. By all my heart,' I say.

I leave it to my master to recognise the garment and the culprit, and do his heavy duty. He will have judged by now that the woman who spat at Willowjack also slaughtered her. She crept into the barn where so recently she brought the dancing to an end, searched the tool chest for a spike and somehow lifted up that heavy, church-yard stone to bring it down with spiteful and indignant force. From any other man but Master Kent I would expect a response of matching spite and indignation. He loved his Willowjack. But he does not even seem surprised to link the woman and the horse. He does not think her actions justified. Why visit anger on a horse? But clearly she was righteous in a way. Her kin — and still we do not know what kin he was, her father probably — was taken to the pillory on Master Kent's command and was abandoned there to be consumed by pigs. What man with any heart could say the woman had no grounds? And so I am not surprised when Master Kent does not identify the owner of the shawl for cousin Edmund Jordan. He is prepared to blame himself for Willowjack. But neither does he hide behind a tricky truth, as I have done. Instead he says, 'That shawl was my wife's, your cousin Lucy Kent's.' There's not a cottager round here who'd have the means to gain a shawl like that, and nor the opportunity. That much is clearly true.

Master Jordan nods. 'Then who . . . then who lives in that derelict? It seems to me that someone's sleeping there.'

'A vagrant, possibly. Some passing midnight pillager.' The master shakes his head, biding time by making show of his bewilderment. The tale that he eventually suggests is this: someone has come through overnight, a ruffian. He's crept into the manor house and, finding it too occupied by lightly sleeping men, has taken leave with only Lucy's velvet shawl as his bounty.

'It was hanging at the back of her old loom until last evening,' he explains. 'Our mothy visitor means to sell it when he reaches any town, most probably — or he only meant to sleep in it, up there in that old tenement. But first he took the opportunity to steal the finest mount for his future travels.' Master Jordan is nodding yet again. 'He will have chosen Willowjack, of course, rather than one of your serviceable horses, cousin Edmund,' Master Kent continues, warming to his narrative. 'But Willowjack is loyal and skittish. I think we can presume the fellow took a kick from her. Or else she nipped him hard. A vulgar, violent person would have sought revenge for that.'

Master Jordan has pursed his lips. He is considering. It is not that he is such a stony-hearted moralist that he is looking forward to the gibbeting of a local man. But it will serve his purposes if through the death of this old mare he is able without cost to make his sudden mark on this inheritance. There's nothing like a show of heavy justice — and a swinging corpse — to persuade a populace not used to formal discipline that their compliance in all matters — including those regarding wool and fences — is beyond debate. He's made his threats and promises. He has already disturbed and violated everybody's home. He will lose face and thereby some control if what Master Kent describes is true. The miscreant was not a local man; the miscreant has come and gone, it seems.

'So be it, then,' he says reluctantly and does not seem to mind that my master has taken up the velvet shawl, heavy with his horse's blood, and says that he will have it washed and put back in its place, where it belongs, on Lucy's loom.

But Master Jordan is still looking for ways to save his face and demonstrate his loyalty to justice. 'That man who spends an idle week at your pillory, he was the one responsible for burning down your farm buildings and slaughtering your doves? Is that correct?' he asks eventually, smiling almost. My master only dips his chin. Not quite a Yes. 'And he, I think, has promised to revenge himself on you?'

'That's true — but only in the heat of his dismay. Besides, he is securely fixed and cannot have visited any injury on Willowjack, except by sorcery,' the master says.

The cousin is not listening. 'I do not mean to blame the horse on him, unless of course your proposal of sorcery can be proven. But we must question him,' he says. 'At least I think I owe it to your dignity, dear cousin, to lay the charges of sedition and incitement at his feet. You are my witness. He has said that he has plans to murder you. Now I am unwittingly the master of this place and so discover myself to be its de facto magistrate. I think it's time we took his case to court. I say so with a heavy heart.'

Here he turns full circle, sweeping the horizon, taking in the width and span of us. It's clear the conversation's at an end. He is maddened by our way of life. He is exasperated by the disarray he has discovered in our village. He sighs dramatically, to leave us in no doubt. We've brought these troubles on ourselves. And he will bring them to a sudden and impatient end if needs be. I catch his eye. 'So, Walter Thirsk,' he says, just listing me. He's wondering, I think, how useful I might be. I nod, admitting to my name, no more. But possibly he takes it as compliance on my part. He sees me as a man who not so long ago — twelve years — must have seen this village as he sees it now, a slow-paced commonwealth of habit, custom and routine, of wasting time and sauntering, of indolence.

Again he circles, but this time he is smiling. He lifts his arms and, palms up like a preacher, spreads his fingers, at all the land in sight. 'Nothing but sheep,' he says, and laughs out loud. His joke, I think, is this: we are the sheep, already here, and munching at the grass. There's none more pitiful than us, he thinks. There's none more meek. There's none to match our peevish fearfulness, our thoughtless lives, our vacant, puny faces, our dependency, our fretful scurrying, our plaints. I can tell he wishes he could see the back of all of us. He'll put an end to all the sauntering. He will replace us with a nobler stock.

8

I am in Mr Quill's good company this afternoon and cannot help but dream about the sort of life I might spend with him should I escape the fleecy prospects of our fields by leaving here in his employ. At least, that is my maturing scheme. I could be gone within the week, if he takes to me and if my current master gives me leave. It is a fearful prospect, parting from Charles Kent, after what has been a lifetime of his company, his fellowship, but not as fearful as one in which his unremitting cousin is my master. So I do my best to be visibly meticulous for Mr Quill, though — truth be told — I have embellished my expertise in readying the quality of vellum he requires for the final presentation copy of his enclosure charts. The best vellum, he says, rubbing his own inner arm by way of an example, takes weeks in preparation; even so, my brisker efforts might still be expected to produce a surface that is uniformly smooth 'but textured still'. And it should be thin enough for the light of a candle to shine through it. I'll do my best to reproduce his skin. It cannot be dissimilar to tanning leather for an apron or a shoe.

I have removed the calfskin from the sink of salted water, dung and lime where it has been soaking and bating for the past two days, since its removal from the rafter in the barn, and brought it, dripping brine and grease, past the site of Willowjack's demise, along the farm lane and into the manor house, where the scullery corner has been set aside for chart-making. My hand is much restored, I am relieved to say. The wound has not defeated me, though it is still too tender at its centre to be much use amongst the threshers and the winnowers and their heavy tools. But it is a relief to be working usefully after what have been almost three days of anxious idleness.

Mr Quill requires me to prepare the skin while he makes a paper audit of our fields and commons, finally transferring to the square in front of him what he has witnessed in the round. We keep our voices low so that neither Master Jordan nor his serving men catch any word of my account of this morning's evasions and intrigues. The threats.

'I fear for us,' he says. His use of us is accidental — he has only been with us for, what? not quite four days — but it is revealing. I can tell he has surprised himself with us. Evidently Mr Quill is putting down a root just as I am pulling up my own.

'It is the woman who must fear the most,' I say.

We are agreed that Mistress Beldam — for whom we clearly both have put down roots, despite her misdeeds and offences, though possibly because of them — should be found and warned. It can't be long before our novice magistrate or one of his lieutenants connects the velvet shawl to its most recent owner — there's not one of us who hasn't seen her wearing it,

120

either at the morning visit to the newcomers' den on our rest day or at the feasting barn that night. Someone is bound to talk. All that Master Kent has done by claiming the cloth as his wife's is to gain Mistress Beldam a little time, a stay of execution, possibly, and to earn himself the final contempt of his cousin.

We could and ought to put our tools aside at once and walk off to the tenement where the bloody cloth was found. Both of us fear that Mistress Beldam will have already returned to where she evidently made her refuge overnight. And that is perilous. No doubt that trio of sidemen who currently have nothing else to do except inflate themselves as constables will be poking noses into every nook and cranny as we speak, hoping to provide some extra bodies for the Jordan court. Neither of us wants those three gentlemen to catch even a glimpse of Mistress Beldam. We understand too well the impact of her face and hair. Especially her hair, which, now it's shaved as short and shy as rabbit fur, only intensifies her native insolence and vulnerability. She's too inviting to the eye. Such gentlemen with time to spare will not be kind to Mistress Beldam if they find her on her own and in a tumbledown beyond the hearing of the threshing barn. We only hope she has the sense, since her revenge on Willowjack, to scurry back into the forest from where she came and make herself another nest of logs and turf — but across the parish bounds, where none of us are free to stray.

'We'll look for her,' says Mr Quill. His voice has thickened, just from saying it. 'But not until

121

we are' — he points a finger at his ear — 'not overheard.' Steward Baynham is close by, it seems. We hear him moving in an upper room and then we hear him on the stairs. He's flitting like a bee about a plum, and bees — as I at least have learnt in these past years — adore sweet mischief more than anything. Something ugly and unusual has happened to us all. In just a few days we have become even more suspicious of the world.

'She might be anywhere,' I say. 'But there is one place she's bound to visit.' Her surviving kinsman must be fed and given drink. She will not let him wither on the branch of our village cross. She's bound to come at night when it is safer and she can be unseen except by owls and foxes, and the moon, to comfort him and take good care of him. That's a duty none of my neighbours are expected to assume, but one which Mistress Beldam can be certain to fulfil. So it is agreed that once the Jordan party have retired for sleep tonight, Mr Quill and I will become like owls ourselves, round-eyed and patient, waiting on the scuttle of some little feet. We'll be dark-feathered in our drabbest coats, and in a hideaway of leaves. And when she comes? Well, we can think of nothing else. We're happy to seem busy with our work. And we can think of nothing else but her.

I clear away the carpeting of straw to find bare tiles and stretch the calfskin on the scullery floor. Now I can see the puckering where that little hand-reared animal, which was so moist and succulent for us at our gleaning feast, was cut along the spine, peeled off the ribs and then spread out for butchering. Her twin flanks are still joined at the girth, along an uneven ridge of skin. They provide for Mr Quill an amply proportioned square, almost a good reach in length along each side. I arm myself with a blunt-edged knife and kneel down, holding the saturated skin firmly under both knees while I scrape away from me with my good hand. The knife dislodges any waste, any nuds of lime or tags of veal, but I have to snap out hairs at their bulbs with my fingers. The skin is not yet leathery. I should say vellumy. It's far too coarse still, and resistant. I should have soaked it for a week or more. I have to limber it. I will not say it's easy work. I will not say I enjoy being this intimate with an animal I've known and liked (and eaten, actually). But I see the task as a test. It can stand as proof to Mr Quill that should he ever need a manservant then none can do a better job than me. So I try my best not to complain. I concentrate on smooth and thin and uniform. I am determined I will pass the lighted candle test.

At such close quarters, the smell is nauseous. What flesh has not been loosened and washed away in the soaking has begun to putrefy. I have to sit back every little while to breathe less heavy air. Stand up too quickly and I'll faint. But slowly I can feel the calfskin surrendering to my hand. It's thinning and it's softening. I do not think the vellum I produce will be the finest quality. It's not sufficiently prepared. I'm rushing it. I have no practice or proficiency. I've made mistakes. I doubt that it was wise to dry the skin in the smoke of its own roasting flesh. I'm not even certain if I should have steeped the skin with lime and dung. Till now, there's not been any call for vellum hereabouts. Mr Quill, though, does not seem dissatisfied when he steps across the room to view my progress and test it with his thumb. Evidently my surface is very nearly fibrous enough to hold yet not absorb his inks and paints.

Mr Quill is working on his preliminary sketches. He is experimenting, hoping to discover what coloured patterns he can devise to make the story of our farmscape — and our sheepscape — easy to decipher. It sounds to me, from my position on the floor, as if he's doing women's work. His tools are cutlery and grinding blocks, and pestle dishes hardly larger than a shell. I half expect to smell the spice of cake. Nutmeg, at least. But all I get above the rot of veal are the cloying odours of his binding gum and lye. He is clearly content in my company, speaking freely now, not whispering. It doesn't matter if he's overheard by any of the Jordan men. He's only talking processes, informing me, but also reminding himself, of each step in his recipes for colour. He uses words I've rarely heard before — like *lapis lazuli* and *smalt*. They are somehow related to the emerging blues that are already in evidence on his fingertips — and across his cheeks and in his tapered beard. I am supposed to see the difference — although the light is low in here — between the florey and the litmus and the indigo, which he displays for

124

me on little parchment tags. He is as snug and personal with his kitchen colours as I have learnt to be with clouds, let's say, or even with the sky's own wash. I have my blues: this blue betokens harvest days (it will not rain), and that one promises a cracking frost; another — higher, darker and more ponderous — reveals itself only silently and briefly when the sun has already withdrawn into his bedchamber but the windows of his heavens are not yet quite closed; this is the blue that says we're free to stretch and finish work and rest.

So our afternoon progresses cosily, drawn on by the prospect of our owlish rendezvous tonight. There is a touch of winter in the room, not in its chill but in its busyness — and that is comforting. What I will miss the most, now that Cecily is gone, now that I myself am tempted to depart, are those still and icy, cloud-weighted times in the dead season when, if I were fool enough to step outside my cottage into the cold and moonless dark, all I could expect to see would be the ducking of my neighbours' candle flames and all that I could expect to hear, other than the cracking of the frost beneath my feet, would be the industry of far-from-summer tools. This is for us the mending time and the fixing season: boys carve their spoons from yew or plug the leaks in mugs and jugs; their dads replace the handles on their scythes and sickles, or fashion willow tines to renew the teeth in forks and rakes; their wives and daughters make new clothes or darn the old. Every home is embering before its fires in concentrated silence, and getting ready for the coming year.

And in our house, my wife and I set to work on the reeds and withies I gathered in the autumn, making trays and baskets for anyone that asked and could provide us with a ham, let's say, or a honey pot by way of exchange. Such evenings were our most tender and consoling, no matter that the spring was far away and all we had to eat was barley bannock bread and broth, every day a Friday with no meat. So here, in Mr Quill's attentive company, I hear those busy sounds again. So long as I do not look up across the scullery, I am lost in lost and happy times.

For a while, the encounters and discoveries of this morning are almost forgotten in the engrossments of our work. Our talk is soft and intimate. Mr Quill has the grace to show an interest in my story. Here is my chance to say how, now that Cecily is dead, I am eager for a change. A change and an adventure. 'And not one that involves a single day of shepherding,' I add. 'Though making vellum is a pleasing craft.' He nods while I am speaking. He takes my meaning, I believe. His nodding gives me reason to suppose he will discuss the matter with his host. 'And you, sir?' I ask Mr Quill. 'Are there adventures calling you?'

His story is a shorter one. He has never been in love. He has no wife to widow him, and both his parents are deceased. His eldest brother has their property: the family home, a warehouse and a riverboat for trade and carriage of anything from fish to cloth. But Mr Quill is not a wealthy man, he says, 'not in possessions, not in my body

. . . as you see. This left side is wooden from the shoulder to the ribs. A sudden palsy. Something in the bones. When I was a child.'

'So not an accident?' I mean to ask him if he was struck by lightning or injured by a bucking horse, as I overheard him say to Master Jordan last afternoon.

'That was my schoolroom jest, my regular defence against . . . ' he starts to say, but shakes his head. He evidently does not want to mention lightning again. 'No matter, though. I have been raised to understand I am unfit to work out of doors and too great an encumbrance to be employed within. I cannot help my brother in his warehouse or his boat. What use am I? In such a clumsy state, I cannot even find myself a wife. I take my happiness from this . . . ' He indicates the paints and sketches on his desk. 'Step forward, Walter. See how my colours have ennobled all my marks.'

While I've been working vellum from the skin, Mr Quill has turned his scratchy charts and drawings into something odd and beautiful. There is no lettering as yet. Just shapes and lines and colouring. I recognise their intrigue and their sorcery. I've seen equally compound patterns, no less ineffable than these, when I've peeled back bark on dying trees, or torn away the papering on birches. I've seen them sketched by lichens on a standing stone, or designed by mosses in a quag, or lurking on the under-wing of butterflies. I've found these ordinary abstracts in the least expected places hereabouts: I have only to lift a stone, or turn some fallen timber in the wood, or reverse a leaf. The structures and the ornaments revealed are made purposeful simply by being found. But none of these compare for patterned vividness with Mr Quill's designs. His endeavours are tidier and more wildly colourful — they're certainly more blue — than anything that nature can provide. They're rewarding in themselves. They are more pleasing than a barleycorn. 'This one,' he says, 'is here and now, my true account. It's what you have before Edmund Jordan the Younger brings in his improvements — '

'King Edmund the Second!' I suggest.

'Yes, let the man be crowned as that.'

Can I identify the barley field, Mr Quill wants to know. I look again, hoping for some clues, from the charcoal-dark lines, perhaps, or from where the paint has crusted heaviest, or where it's thinned and tonsured on the bubbles of the paper. It is not until he turns his painting through two quarters that I think I recognise the twists and fall of the field, the low redundant parts where barley grows on hostile soil, the sweeping upper wings where cropping is the best, the darker shading of the baulks, the snaking signature of what must be our snaking stream.

'Exactly so,' says Mr Quill, when I indicate my answer with a finger, lifting a smudge of paint as I do so. 'And here I've plaited in your boundary line.'

Now I can see the boggy path and Turd and Turf, not yet identified as the Blossom Marsh. There's our top end. And there's our deep and tall and goodly wood. Our fortress walls of thorn and scrub. Our unbuilt church. Our commons and our cottages. Our one-time safe and kindly realm.

I look again but squintingly, and not at the particulars. I've never before had a true sense of how our estate is shaped, how stars might shine on us, or what those hawks and kestrels see. It has been too many years for memory since I last observed our land from any greater distance than our clover hill — that first day, in fact, twelve years ago, when I arrived with Master Kent and saw, far off, from the pale green of the higher downs, the true green bowl — no, *valley*'s not the word — of this isolated place nesting, hidden, in those blank spaces between far rivers, nameless and beyond. But otherwise I've put no shape to it. Now I know the village is a profile of a brawny-headed man — a bust, in fact. His neck and shoulders are our pasturelands. Our cattle and our goats are feeding there. The four great fields make up his face. His ear — our pond — is small enough to be a child's. He almost has a nose, where I suppose that little clovered hillock is. The forests are his hair.

It is an odd experience, unnerving in its way, to look down on our woods, our commons and our fields at once, to see them side by side, or separated only by the thickness of my thumb, when I have never seen them on the ground with such adjacency. Here the sap-green-painted fallow is seemingly attached by the madly dark blue stitching of a ridge-top copse to the grey-cum-yellow stubble of our barley field. They look like neighbours, exchanging glances through the trees. I've walked that thickness-of-my-thumb a thousand times. It's easy going till you reach the ridge. The fallow field has a subtle slope, so it drains well but keeps its soil. There's seldom any mud. But there are pebblestones to set your feet against. You have to take the cow track at the ridge and go downhill a little with the copse thickening on your right until you find another rise, and there's an open gap which lets you pass along a lane of thorns into the field where now, this afternoon, you'll find our cattle gleaning grain. This is the point, at the brimming of the trees, where neither field can be seen. You're too closed in. Indeed, there's nowhere on the walk — which takes a little while and some exertion — where both the fallow and the barley field can be looked upon at once. You'd have to climb a tree for that. Or be a bird.

So Mr Quill's true account of here and now is not as honest as he hopes. He's coloured and he's flattened us. No shadows and no shade. We are too mauve and blue; he's planted long-purples everywhere. There are no climbs or slopes. The land is effortless: a lie. He hasn't captured time: how long a walk might take; how long a piece of work might take; how long the seasons or the nights must last. No man has ever seen this view. But it is beautiful, nevertheless. And so, come to that, although it's hard to acknowledge it, is Mr Quill's map of the sheep fields that are looming over us. This chart is even busier with colour, and more patterned to the eye. Its patchwork is much tidier. The fields are smaller, broken up and edged. The dark of the wood, with its clustered symbols showing trees, has almost disappeared. I cannot find an eye or ear. The brawny-headed man has lost his face.

'What do you make of these?' asks Mr Quill. I take his question as a test. I do not want to say his paintings aren't as honest as he thinks. But it isn't hard for me to praise them fulsomely for what they are as pretty things, a kind of vision of the world — our little world, in fact — that I have never seen before and which has left me moved and oddly breathless. With his help these coloured papers, unmarked as yet with any names or guides, make sense to me at last. They complicate to simplify. I have translated them. I can tell you where we are on them. I could stub my finger on the spot where I am standing now. But still I'm left to wonder where we'll be on them in days and years to come. And so my breathlessness. There's something in these shapes and lines, in these casual, undirected blues and greens, that, for all their liveliness, seems desolate.

9

Little Lizzie Carr and her green sash are in Master Jordan's custody tonight, as is (or so the rumour has it for the moment — Mr Quill and I have yet to see the living evidence) the widow Gosse, *my* Kitty Gosse, together with Anne Rogers, her best friend. We need to organise ourselves, of course. This is the moment when our wildest hotheads should raise their sickles and their sticks. But John Carr thinks the hottest heads have already packed their bags and gone. Certainly, Brooker Higgs has not been seen since dusk. And the Derby twins were spotted heading off towards our top end and the setting sun, bundles roped across their backs and walking faster than they've ever walked before; their mother looks as grey and blank as pewter, and only shakes her head when questioned. Three of our sons are vagabonds, untethered strays, who clearly feel it's safer to be anywhere but here. That has never happened to our sons before.

Whose version of events should I believe? The loudest voices that I overhear are decided — as am I, reluctantly — that the shaven, black-haired woman is behind it all. A dozen different stories hold Mistress Beldam responsible for all the disarrangement of their cottages — and then for every odour that's not pleasing, for every jug of curdled milk, for every darkening of cloud. And she will take the blame, I know, for driving sheep

132

into our fields. Everything's uncertain and unhinged because of her. She's brought a curse on to our land, she's blighted us. My neighbours say she'll not be satisfied until we're all dragged off to rot away with Willowjack. When the threshing barn was inspected at midday, they told the 'new gentleman's' serving men as much, and that the bloody velvet shawl claimed by Master Kent to be his wife's was not his wife's at all but the property of this fierce, alluring woman. But no one listens to them any more, they now complain. No one's been hunting for 'the sorceress' despite their warnings. Those men are picking only on the innocent, on local women and a girl.

What's certain, according to these flapping tongues, is that while I was on my knees this afternoon making pauper's vellum from the calf, Lizzie Carr, still very much the Gleaning Queen in her green cloth and bored with sorting barley, slipped out of the threshing barn, hoping to renew the yellow blossoms she'd been wearing since her crowning. She was bound to be noticed by Edmund Jordan's men. And they were bound to challenge her. This girl, bedecked beyond her station in a valuable cloth and mustardy with flowers, like a fairy child, was far too young and tame to fit the description of the savage woman they'd only recently been informed about by the less wary of my neighbours and whom the sidemen were now very keen to meet. But she was baffling. And her clothing was suspicious. The men supposed that all expensive cloth — Lizzie Carr's green sash, that woman's bloody

133

velvet shawl — must provide some necessary clue in their pursuit of Willowjack's killer. The meaning of those shawls and sashes, not to mention Master Jordan's too easy-going cousin's lies, would reveal itself in time no doubt, and after thorough questioning, beginning with this mystifying child.

As I imagine it, the men will have held Lizzie Carr by her irresistible plaits — like her uncles will have done a thousand times before, like I have done myself. They would have been more playful than spiteful, at first, and meant only to prevent her skipping off. Why was she in the lane at all, they'd want to know. Hadn't she been instructed quite clearly by Master Jordan that nobody must stray today beyond the barn? And, more to the point, how was it that a common little girl like her was sporting such a fine and pretty dressing on her head? When she told the truth, that Master Kent had given it to her, and that she was the Queen for one whole year, they were bound to doubt her word, tighten their great hands round her willow arm, and march her off to answer more practised and judicial questions in Master Jordan's presence.

What is not yet clear — at least not clear to me because it seems that, for the moment, I am not included in the village circles — is how the two women became involved. Anne Rogers is the fiery sort, I know. It's never wise to disagree with her, even if you're family. And Kitty Gosse is mulish when she wants to be. If they were working at the entry of the barn, in plain sight of the lane, and witnessed Lizzie being taken off by those three coarse and stony men, who only this morning were party to the prophecy that we should expect to see a neighbour hanging from an oak by sundown — 'God Bless you all, and God help one of you,' he'd said — I can't imagine them standing aside. I can imagine, though, a tug of war between the women and the men, with this year's Gleaning Queen the scrap of flesh they were fighting for. The women wouldn't have stood a chance. They'd have been outnumbered, for a start; outmuscled too. But it might have taken some kicking and some bruising before they admitted defeat and allowed themselves to be dragged away like sows to face the consequences of their meddling.

No doubt the sound of Anne Rogers's battling voice reached the barn. Everybody would have hurried out, glad of the excuse to put down tools and see the last tugs of the struggle in the lane. Those clod-heads in their matching uniforms who were so churlish and so dangerously bored earlier in the day were now setting upon two village women and a child and dragging them off to who-knows-where and with who-knows-what in mind. Of course, the threshing and the winnowing came to an early end at once. This would have been the moment, I am sure, when Brooker and the twins, our arsonists, judged it best to pack and go before their secrets were uncovered. They wouldn't want to decorate that sundown oak.

I know my neighbours well enough to share their anger and alarm — though it seems they're still not so keen to have me in their company and sharing anything this evening. They reply to any simple question I might put with, Why are you asking that? and, Who needs to know? They're closing ranks already and I am not included, despite my dozen years of standing at their shoulders. Old friends avoid my eyes. They duck away from me. Even John Carr is reluctant to talk. He hardly offers me a phrase. My once darker hair is clashing with their blond again. It is their reminder that I am the master's man before I am a villager, that I have spent my afternoon with Mr Quill, preparing for the coming of the sheep, and not with them, helping with the wintering of grain. I did not join them when they faced drawn arrows at the newcomers' den. I did not join the dancing in the barn. I did not even join the gleaning of the barley field, and that was inexplicable. They know that when their cottages were so roughly pulled apart this morning, I was there to witness it but not to stop it. The knowledge that I spent last evening naked in the widow's bed will not have come as a surprise, but then it will not have done me any favours either. The half of the village most related to Kitty and Fowler Gosse will see me as a poacher; and the other half are Saxtons or Saxton kin and will count me as a traitor to my — and their — sweet Cecily. The envious men will be the most outraged. Many of my neighbours nurtured a seedling for Kitty Gosse and will resent my success. Maybe even one or two of their wives might once have nurtured shoots for me. I must have represented all the world for them when I arrived, and then when I became a widower . . . well, I had sweet-natured offers, let me say, but stepped away from all but one of them. So I cannot condemn my neighbours for closing ranks. These are nervous, jealous times for all of them.

And I know their expressions well enough, even in this evening gloom, to understand that these are also dangerous times for me. If there are offerings to be made, if there's a name that should be whispered loud enough for this new master to overhear, a name that might conveniently connect a suspect with a crime or might divert suspicion from a native-born, better it is mine than any of their men's, better I'm dragged off to sleep with Willowjack than anybody else. Unlike the twins and Brooker Higgs, already lost to us, it seems, I never was a local tree, grown in this soil from seed, to die where I was planted. I can be done without, and with no lasting harm. I'm no great sacrifice.

I do not blame them, honestly. I'm not a person they should trust, not at the moment anyway. I've not been loyal of late, or even tried to cling on to their love. I have kept too many secrets and too many confidences to myself. I have not told them what I overheard in the manor house gallery or what Mr Quill has divulged to me about the older Edmund Jordan's will and its entitlements. I plead guilty to the charge of being too tight-lipped, though I might say my silence was judicious rather than dishonest: I cannot serve each master and each friend with equal shares. I do not even know myself who it is I want to please, besides myself, or where I most want finally to rest my head. In Mr Quill's employ, I think, although there's something in his coloured charts, his hawk-high version of the world, that makes me wonder if he is too skittish and too vulnerable for me with his never-fading smile, his wooden lurch. He said as much himself this afternoon: 'I am the roughest piece of furniture.' You won't be comfortable with me, in other words. I am reminded of that country saw, Only a fool would strap a saddle to a wooden bench and hope to ride it home.

Perhaps, now that I am fallowed by the cottagers, I ought to speak my piece to Master Kent, persuade him to re-employ me as his man. He might let me move back to the manor house. I'll take the attic rooms again. He'll need an ally when his cousin claims command, however distantly, and when the sheep invade his fields. He is my only brother in a way, though I cannot think he is my family. But whatever future I can devise for myself, I cannot be light-hearted about the present. I am furrowed sad tonight to see the village back away from me. My neighbours leave me standing on my own. Now I wonder if I've been a fool about this place; my restlessness is just a curse, a moling demon in my heart whose mischief is to have me leave the only acres that can provide me happiness. But then I understand too well, from what I've heard and seen, that any happiness — or at least the lands that nurture it — will not survive the autumn frosts.

So I stay a little to the side, forgotten or at least ignored in the shadows, and do not add my voice to theirs as they discuss what should be done about their disappearing sons, the pair of women who are held, and little Lizzie Carr. We're the majority, they protest. We must be listened to. I hear the word *petition*. I could tell them, had they not decided to be deaf to me, that numbers amount to nothing in such matters. Dissent is never counted; it is weighed. The master always weighs the most. Besides, they can't draw up a petition and fix it to the doorway of the church as other places do. It only takes a piece of paper and a nail, that's true. But, even if they had a doorway to a church, none of them has a signature.

Of course, the loudest voices are the ones that want to arm themselves with sticks and blades and march up to the manor house like maddened geese to save their goslings from the law. But they are only honking, making warning sounds. Nobody wants to storm the manor house, not with Master Kent inside, not with the echoes and impressions it has hoarded in its corridors. Besides, those three sidemen look menacing. They will be used to seeing off a crowd, the angrier the better, for then the greater their excuse for banging heads, and breaking bones, and leaving scars and bodies.

Some other neighbours say it's best to let the evening run its course: the master's bound to intercede on their behalf. There'll be some displeased questioning of the women, no doubt. There's been a scuffle after all. And who can say that Kitty Gosse and Anne Rogers weren't too fierce and fiery in the lane? That's no surprise. It might be wise to let the matter boil and steam tonight. It makes no sense to lift a scalding pan. It's best to let the water settle first, and cool. So, wait, is their advice. The three arrested villagers will be home by midnight, or by tomorrow midnight at least, and none the worse for wear.

It is the Saxton cousins, those two comic grunters who were once so famously divided by the partition of a pig, who suggest the favoured strategy. They will not arm themselves. They will not wait like children while the water cools. Instead, they will present themselves at the manor house tonight — at once — as meekly as they can. They will wear smiles, remove their caps, and let the masters understand that any troubles that have occurred in these past days have been the work of newcomers and that they propose tomorrow, at first light, to search the alcoves of their land until the culprit — here they mean Mistress Beldam — is caught or driven far away or the victim of an accident.

I am not there to witness their entreaties at the manor, nor to make my own appeal for Kitty Gosse, as I should, because when we reach the unbuilt gateway to our unbuilt church, I discover Mr Quill — as was arranged this afternoon, though in the mêlée I've forgotten it — in conversation with the one surviving tenant of our pillory. It is his third night fastened here. My neighbours do not even pause or lift their caps for either of the men; their business at the manor house is more urgent. But there is a stifled, communal cry and a shaking of heads. The night is swarming with a hundred tuts. Clearly they're unsettled and displeased to discover this new

140

conjunction, these two contrary outsiders unified in whispering. They see that Mr Quill has spread his arm across the young man's shoulder. They see the gap between the mouth and ear. And it is disturbing. Yet every one of them will admit in their heart of hearts that we have not been just to this ragged, shaven visitor and certainly not to the older man who died; his fate is far too cruel to contemplate. That is why no one has come in these few days to throw windfalls at the remaining captive or to cuss at him, for fun, as would have happened if he were genuinely culpable of anything more serious than not belonging here. And that is equally the reason why none of us has been more kind, offering to share his burden of bereavement, a crust and rind, at least, a gift of ale. A greeting, anyway. A wave. We've been ashamed, I think. And bewildered, truth be told. Bewildered by ourselves. These are not the customary village ways. Our church ground has been desecrated by our surliness. Our usual scriptures are abused. This body on the cross is not the one that's promised us. Yet, once again, it's Mr Quill who teaches us our shortcomings. It's Mr Quill who's intimate and kind. It's Mr Quill who's valiant. It will not make him popular.

The woman and the man are husband and wife, Mr Quill explains as we settle down with church-yard stones as our bench for our long wait for Mistress Beldam to appear. They are fugitives from sheep, exiles from their own commons, six or seven days away on foot. They've come to us because their ancient livelihoods have been hedged and fenced against their needs. And the man who died was Beldam senior, her father. This, I suspect, is information neither of us has hoped to hear. Our imaginations have been fed by having her as a sister and a widow, a woman, that's to say, free of ties and so within our grasps. We are, the pair of us, one bachelor, one widower, unspoken for — but now we are required to feel less ravenous. A married woman's out of bounds, in principle at least. But, though I cannot speak for Mr Quill, my attraction for the woman, based on that glimpse of her in the lamp-lit dancing barn and on the recent sight of her blood-soaked shawl, has not abated but only quickened at the knowledge of her kinship to this man. The marriage of an older woman to a thin-bearded youth is something that appeals to me. I can imagine being younger, being him . . . well, I will stop. These are the stories that we tell ourselves and only ourselves, and they are better left unshared.

Except I cannot stop. I find myself too keen to catch the woman stepping through the night. I can see her stretching on her toes to kiss the cheek and ear where just a while ago Mr Quill almost pressed his lips. I can see her kneading all her husband's muscles and his joints, to drive away the stiffness and the pain of three nights hanging on the cross. I can see her taking from a wrap a supper she has foraged from the woods — there're apples there aplenty now, and blackberries, and game. And I can hear them whispering: she's saying that his sentence is almost half served and that he must endure; she's saying how our village will be punished for its sins; she's promising the fire they lit to stake their claim on common ground will be remade and lit again; she's drawing bows and firing arrows at the night; she's making love to him.

Mr Quill is silent too. His hands are gripping tightly on to his knees. The moonlight catches us infrequently tonight but when it does I see the paint stains on his fingers and knuckles — some blues and greens, some lustre work — and I can tell that apart from his plain cap he has dressed himself in finer and more gentlemanly clothes than those he wore for me this afternoon. He's like a decorated stripling at a fair, come to spy himself a girl. We sit like this in brewing silence for a while, busy with conjectures of our own and only lifting our heads slightly whenever we're disturbed by snapping twigs, a shifting animal, a bat, the hint of footsteps coming close, raised voices from the manor house, and all the usual, rowdy ardours of a fading summer night.

It is, I think, the husband who hears her coming first. The top beam of the pillory rattles, bone on wood, as he tries to turn his shoulder and his head. I do not know if he's aware that Mr Quill and I are sitting only twenty paces from his back. I do not know what Mr Quill has said to him or what arrangements they have made, if any. I wouldn't be surprised if Young Beldam (he has a name of sorts, at last) calls out to her. A warning. There are other men about, he'll say. Best run. But he says nothing, only whistles lightly, no more than the whistle of a breeze. I think he wants to let her know, as she comes close, that he still has breath in his lungs. She will not find another corpse.

Mr Quill touches the back of my hand with a single finger and lifts his chin to point towards our left, where beyond our tumble of stones the church ground falls away a little into a ditch backed by thorn scrub and sore-hocks and, then, the groping night-time silhouette of trees. He cocks his head. I do the same, until I hear the rustling. It could be another roaming pig, come to feast on someone else's shins, but it's too delicate and purposeful.

I have forgotten how small she is, and how silent is her brightness. My memory has plumpened her and toughened her. But without the heavy wrapping of her shawl she's even more birdlike than she appeared on that night in the barn. Now her shoulders seem especially narrow, particularly given the fullness of her hips. Could such shoulders really find the strength to drive a prong of metal through a horse's skull? She has not seen us, evidently, because she walks between us and her husband's back, not carelessly but not on tiptoe either. She's confident. Perhaps she knows that everyone has gone to shake their fists — politely — at the manor house. Her hair, so far as I can tell from her grey silhouette, is no longer grinning with the exposed white of her scalp. It's slightly darker now — a few days of defiant growth — and velvety. At least, I think it's velvety. At least, I think of touching it and finding out. I think I'd like her to turn round. I want to see her face a second time. That first time she was hardly visible. She was little more than dark on dark, a body shape, as I remember it. If only she would spin round on her heels and the moonlight would oblige, I could persuade myself she's real and not a spectre summoned up by loneliness.

She's carrying a piece of sacking, heavy with food, in one hand, and a dark, stoppered bottle of cordial in the other. I recognise that stoppered bottle: William Kip has got a shelf of them — pippin juice or burdock or rosewater, mostly — his summer bottled for winter. I think he'll find that one is missing now, unless she plans on taking back an empty. It seems that Mistress Beldam has been foraging but not, as I expected, in the woods. Again Mr Quill puts a finger on my hand. He means we should stay patient and not be tempted to show ourselves to her with our warnings for her safety until her husband has been greeted, comforted and fed. Then we will reveal ourselves. We will reveal ourselves to be her friends.

It's hard for me to watch her kissing him but it's not an ache that lasts long. She's hardly lifted the bottle to his mouth when the hubbub of my neighbours now returning from the manor house along the apple-strewn lane reaches us. We look in that direction, all four at once, like cattle in one herd, and when we turn our heads again, she's gone. Mr Quill darts forward, throws the stolen bottle which she's abandoned at her husband's feet into the sore-hocks, and hurries off with his strange gait, right shoulder first, in Mistress Beldam's midnight steps.

10

I have persuaded neighbour Carr to talk today. He'd rather not. But I have him cornered at his door. He's too embarrassed and too profoundly kind to rebuff me entirely. Still, he is not comfortable in my company and will not join me on the outside bench where it is cool and shaded. For once, against our custom, he prefers to duck into my stuffy, cluttered home and find a place out of the door light where he can't be spotted from the lane. I touch his elbow as he squeezes by, but there is no response. I think he even pulls away. When he feels secure enough to speak, I can hardly hear his voice. He won't be overheard by other cottagers. I suspect he also would prefer not to be heard by me. His story is 'a spiky one', he says. No one has yet laid eyes on either of the captive women or on Lizzie Carr, his niece. Indeed, the treatment of the crowd of supplicants at the manor house last night was 'not considerate'. He's being cautious with his words. He's testing my allegiances. We know each other well enough to judge such things from how we sit and fidget, how we breathe.

'John Carr,' I say to him. 'Let's put an end to this.' I reach out for his knee and rather than grasping it as I might have done a day ago, I drop my closed fist on it, two gentle almost weightless beats, the softest of rebukes.

'I know,' he says. And that's enough. He

straightens up, takes steady breaths, leans forward with his elbows on his knees, so that his face is looking into mine. 'Lord help you, Walt, if you're deceiving us.'

'Lord help you, John, if you believe I would.' I'm glad he cannot see my flushing face in this half-light.

He settles back, deciding what to do. He's caught between a nettle and a thorn. 'And so . . . ?' he says. He's waiting for a prompt.

'And so, how was it 'not considerate'?'

'Here's how. Those serving fellows kept us waiting at the porch like dogs and horses,' he says, a mite less guarded than before. Master Kent was 'not available', it seems: 'He's always been available. I've never known him not available.' John Carr shakes his straw-grey head, warming — heating — to his tale. 'And as for this new gentleman? He is a Jordan, so we're told. And some devilry has given him our land.'

I cannot tell if I'm included in the *our*.

This latest Master Jordan was also 'not available' last night, John tells me. The villagers could smile their smiles and doff their caps until the end of time, but still he would not meet them at the door. At last, his steward, Baynham, showed his face. 'Matters are in hand,' he told the villagers, so gravely it was worrying. His only answer to their questions was a shrug. It was as if their worries were of no account. 'I hear that there is witchery about,' the steward offered finally.

'What witchery? No one has ever thought there's witchery,' I say to John. I overheard the

147

mention of a 'sorceress' just yesterday, but that's less burdensome a word. We can be tempted by a sorceress, beguiled by her even — but witches? No, their crafts are uglier and heavier. I am concerned and genuinely surprised by John's report. A formal accusation such as that brings turmoil every time. The very mention of it is bad luck. It is a charge we tell our children not to make, not even as a tease. Say 'witch', we warn them, and Master Havoc will come with Lady Pandemonium to keep their crone bad company. 'There's never any witchery,' I repeat.

'That's what we told the man,' says John Carr. 'But he replied that he knew better. They already had three of our she-devils in custody. He said we'd better go away and start collecting faggots for their fire. That's when our tempers flew apart . . . ' He stops. I hear his humiliated sigh. Now he's the one that's flushing and ashamed. Again, he's forward, elbows on his knees. 'Or should I say that's when our tongues got loose. We did ourselves no favours, Walt. We didn't do you any favours either. Sad to have to tell you that, but it is best you know. We had to take care of our own.'

It's no surprise. I'm not included in 'our own'.

As far as I can tell from John Carr's brief, discomfited account of what then took place last evening at the manor house's porch, Mr Quill and I are said to be part of some conspiracy. For reasons of our own that are too dark for telling, we have teamed up with the three dove-burners who arrived so recently and so coincidentally at the same time as the Chart-Maker. My

148

neighbours will not call him Mr Quill again, it seems. That name does not sound devious enough or tie in with the excessive colours of their newly woven tale. If that fine shawl belonged to his departed wife, as Master Kent has claimed and they are now no longer determined to doubt, who was better placed to steal it from the manor house and wrap it round that woman's shoulders than the master's guest, the Chart-Maker? It was the Chart-Maker who offered his hand to the woman on the morning of the fire when her den was being levelled to the ground; it was the Chart-Maker who made her welcome at the dance; it was the Chart-Maker who was discovered only yesterday evening at the pillory with his arm round the younger vagabond's shoulder. They evidently were old friends. Perhaps they were related in some way. Blood-brothers, probably.

As for Walter Thirsk? Well, according to the blurtings of last night, I am not the same man they have known and trusted for so long. I now spend my hours only with the Chart-Maker. I no longer see the need to work at the shoulders of my neighbours, or to stand with them outside the manor, even when my own 'sweeting' is inside. Master Kent, to whom I should be grateful till I die, is neglected by me, his one-time loyal man. I am, it seems, to be suspected. That is the benefit of accusing me. In the spreading shadow of my guilt, Anne Rogers, the widow Gosse and little Lizzie Carr must be considered innocent of . . . well, innocent of anything this younger Jordan could accuse them

149

of, but which should be laid more properly at other doors, including mine.

'I'll repeat you to the master, word for word,' Mr Baynham promised them, according to John Carr, whose word, I must believe, is trustworthy. Equally innocent, by the way, my neighbours added for good measure — and to the increasing amusement of the steward, who by then was nodding with a knowing smile but with the door half closed — are the three good young men who thought it wise to keep away from these conspiracies and have already packed their few possessions in a cloth and gone but who knows where.

'I think you would be wise to do the same, Walt,' says neighbour Carr, already standing up to flee my cottage. 'Follow Brooker and the Derby boys, and save yourself. Go back . . . ' He stops. He will not say, Go back where you belong.

I am alarmed, to tell the truth. Our snug and tiresome village has burst apart these last few days. Master Havoc and Lady Pandemonium have already set to work. We are a moonball that's been kicked, just for the devilry, by some vexatious foot. Our spores are scattering. And it seems I ought to scatter too. Perhaps at once. It's always better to turn your back on the gale than press your face against it. Indeed, I am already looking at my possessions and wondering which few of them I ought to bag across my shoulders and by which path I might best secure my liberty.

* * *

Actually, I am the only one who may safely stay. For the first time since the day I found my mottle-throated Cecily cold and lifeless on the bed, Master Kent has come into my cottage room. He is sitting in the place so recently warmed and dented by John Carr. He seems in shock. At least his hand is trembling, and his breath is evidently being ladled from a shallow pool. But he has news that is reassuring for me, though not for anybody else.

The captured women have endured a night of punishments, Master Kent reports in a sunken whisper. I have to turn my head to catch his words, although his words are almost beyond bearing. Last evening, before my neighbours even thought of marching mildly on the manor house, Kitty Gosse had already confessed to what Master Jordan has decided will best serve his purposes.

'I have the sense my cousin is taking pleasure from sowing these anxieties, in the same way we take pleasure in the sowing of our seed,' says Master Kent. 'I fear his harvesting. I think he means to shear us all, then turn us into mutton.'

My master cannot claim to be a witness to the shearing, though. He was required to go back to his room and rest himself, until called. 'They had that smaller fellow' — Master Jordan's groom, I suppose — 'lean against my door, in case I counted it my duty to step out, and try to be a hindrance,' he says. 'What could I do, except stay toothless in my room?' But floorboards leak and timber carries sound; he heard the crashes and the cries from the gallery above all too clearly.

151

The one word *witchery* has licensed the Jordan sidemen to do precisely what they want. Evidently, Kitty Gosse took less persuading than Anne Rogers, but then, once the inquisitors had discovered on her naked body her warts and lumps and judged them perfect teats on which the Devil readily might suck, she was exposed to fiercer questioning. Besides, she is in her own way, as I well know, the more attractive of the two and, therefore, will have suffered more in their efficient custody. Their master must have promised a free hand in their tormenting if they produced the witchery he wanted, and the name. They will have asked, Was Anne Rogers also an enchantress? And was the little girl some kind of flowered sacrifice, some sort of offering, perhaps, or was she also being nurtured as a country hag?

My master is reluctant to say much more about what his ears have heard. He is ashamed, I think, to have proved so powerless — and under his own roof too. But I already understand enough about these sidemen to suppose how their evening might have advanced. They were not quick-witted, that's for sure, but they would have been fired up by each other and by the stirring circumstance of being entirely in charge for once. They were far from their own wives and mothers. And they were far from a restraining word. And there were no witnesses that counted. No matter what they did last evening, they could claim they did it only at their master's bidding. They were provoked by him. So Kitty Gosse will have done her best but very soon would have understood that there would be no respite until she told them what they said she must — although, of course, these men might very well prefer her not to offer a confession too soon because then they'd have to finish with their torments, they'd have to put an end to taking turns before they were entirely satisfied.

From what Master Kent is saying, I can presume that Kitty Gosse will have identified herself, as they required, to save herself. She might have done no more than nod almost imperceptibly when they mentioned Anne's and Lizzie's names again. Certainly, she had the spirit, the master says, to give her word that neither she, nor her friend, nor the child were ringleaders in any way, but only — 'Only what?' a sideman said. Well, only foolish followers. 'Who, then?' Kitty, joined by Anne Rogers by now, and too bruised and exhausted to do anything but cooperate, screamed out half a dozen names. My master, his head tipped towards the ceiling planks, heard every one of them. 'I think she picked on women who were not her cousins and were not Rogerses either, or who had never been especial friends to her,' he says. And then a moment later, she began to list the men.

I am surprised to hear that neighbour Carr is included in the lengthy cast, though I am not. I surely would have been an easy pick — the outsider without the faintest trace of blond. Perhaps I fool myself, but it is tempting to imagine she's protected me. If she's ever free again, she will not want to go without an old friend in her bed. But Master Jordan's sidemen

153

were not satisfied by this. These village names were not of any interest. They hadn't even called on Mr Baynham to bring his ink and write them down. 'So were these also 'only foolish followers'?' they asked. Both women answered Yes, at once, seeing there a chance to redeem a little reputation for their men and friends. Then who did they consider most responsible? By now they had run out of names. Who was there left to take the blame? 'The gentleman,' said Anne Rogers.

'Which gentleman?'

'The gentleman . . . ' Master Kent heard her pause. One of the sidemen laughed, he says; she must have mimicked Mr Quill's uneasy walk, crunching up her shoulders, possibly. 'This gentleman.' She didn't need to volunteer his name.

Now it was a pleasure for the men to tidy up and step downstairs where Master Jordan and his steward were smoking their long pipes. After fierce and tiring questioning, they reported in bragging voices loud enough for Master Kent to overhear, they had laid bare a covenly intrigue. Once Lizzie Carr was brought wet-cheeked into the room after having been tied all afternoon, and promised that she might keep her green sash if she could prove herself a wise and honest little girl, it was easy to find corroboration of what the women had alleged. Not that Master Jordan needed much corroboration. However, he was a lawful, tidy man who by nature wanted to seem thorough. It was just as he had expected. This grinning Mr Earle — was that the fellow's genuine name? Was he the erl-king of some kind?

154

— had always clearly been a busy devotee of the arts, to which the black arts were akin. Lizzie Carr confessed she had been frightened by the man. He was the one who had 'made me Queen, and tried to put his hand on me'. Dark practices, indeed. Besides, hadn't the man admitted only yesterday that he'd been struck by lightning or some such wizardry?

'He said the heavens opened up for him, I think,' agreed Mr Baynham, 'and a tongue of light gave him the body of an old gnarled tree. He is deformed thereby. By alchemy. Something about the devil and an old cracked jar.'

'Collect him, then, and bring him here.'

Mr Quill was not found in his room, of course. By that time he had already slipped away to throw his arm around the shoulder on the pillory, and then given chase to Mistress Beldam through the night. But there were objects in his room which only deepened his complicity: pestles, grinding blocks and bowls too small for kitchen work, together with powders, paints and grounds which, if separated from his parchments and his brushes, could not seem anything but menacing. There was a fiddle, Satan's instrument. There was a Natural History of plants, handwritten with his recipes for making potions and procuring spells, and with suspicious vegetation pressed between its leaves. And there were wordless charts too colourful and incautious to be the kind of maps a landowner might need. No, Mr Baynham had never seen such reckless maps before, although he had experience in such matters. He would expect some helpful keys and labels. These were

155

more like incantations shaped by paint.

So it was that my neighbours arrived too late last night with their doffed caps to ask for the release of their two women and their girl: the captives had already spilt the cats out of their bags and were tied by their wrists and ankles to the heavy newels on the upper landing of the stairs. The three sidemen, looking both excited and shamefaced, were waiting with their cudgels in the lower hall for the sorcerer's return. The steward was sent out to brush aside the villagers. 'I know I should have answered them myself,' says Master Kent, 'but I was still confined behind my door. I could have shouted, I suppose . . . ' For Mr Baynham, though, it didn't matter who my neighbours named. His master already had the name he wanted most. He'd use the others if he needed to. Besides, much of what they said supported what the sidemen had discovered. The Chart-Maker — a sinister title, wasn't it? — was the Trouble Maker too. And, in addition, it seemed he was, according to the local word, the one behind the theft of the velvet shawl belonging to Master Kent's dead wife. And he was, as well, connected in some way — related, possibly — to the vagabond woman, who was evidently loose about the place, and her kinsman on the pillory, who was evidently not. The bloody killing of the mare began to make a little sense to them now. It was part of some dark ritual. No, matters were indeed, 'in hand'. And this was where the steward told my neighbours, 'I'll repeat you to the master, word for word.'

'And was my name put forward there as part

of some conspiracy? I'm told it was,' I ask.

'Indeed, it was,' my master says. 'I thought my heart might stop from hearing it.' He sounds a little nettled. 'But, Walter Thirsk, it seems you are a man my cousin has determined he can . . . rely upon.' He spreads his hands and ducks his chin. He means it is a mystery, and one that bothers him.

'And what occurred when Mr Qu . . . when Mr Earle returned last night?'

'He has not come back to the house, not yet,' my master says, covering his eyes with a hand as he speaks. He is embarrassed by the answer he must give. 'He will have slept' — he spreads his hands in front of him again — 'elsewhere. My cousin's men are hunting for him now.'

11

I have forgotten Master Jordan's groom. I suppose I should have guessed how jealous he would be of the sidemen and the time they spent with female captives in the gallery. I am sure he will have overheard the quizzing and the probings and would have liked to creep upstairs to make his contribution. But he was not allowed. You're just the horses man, they will have said. And so his comrades had the pleasure. He had none. He had to be the guard outside Master Kent's bed-parlour. He was ungratified, and therefore he'll be dangerous. Already, he has been left with too much leisure on his hands these past few days. Of all the Jordan party, he has had the least to do. Once he has fed and groomed his mounts and let them loose on the master's edges to crop on wayside grass, the body of the day is his to waste. He wanders idly through our village lanes and makes a nuisance of himself with any pretty face he meets. He bothers livestock and scrumps our fruit. He pokes his nose through gates and doors that should be barred to him. He is the only one, as yet, who has the inclination and the time to test out rotten apples and putrid curses on Mistress Beldam's husband at the pillory. He is the only one who's been constant in his hunt for the woman herself. Today his efforts have been redoubled because, as he now understands from the events of last night at the manor house, in which he sadly has not played a satisfying part, there is a free-roaming sorceress to lay his hands upon and one not set aside only for those pampered sidemen to enjoy.

It is his misfortune, though, to be spotted standing and facing me, while I sit on my bench hoping for a greeting from a neighbour. He wants to know where I suppose a woman of her kind might find some secret refuge from where she can emerge at night to carry out her killings. I do not think he knows what enemies he's made for simply being in the Jordan crew. How can he guess, in all his innocence, that I'm not popular today and that being in my company will not seem widely sociable? Certainly, he should have calculated for himself how rash it is, the morning after such occurrences, to walk into our village midst with nothing for protection except a length of rein. I must suppose he hopes to lead a chastened Mistress Beldam to his master on the knotted end of it.

On any other day but this he would be safe. We'd all be threshing, winnowing and sacking, and would shrug him off as nothing but a nuisance, as nothing worthier than chaff. But our women and our Gleaning Queen are still unaccounted for, beyond that talk of witchery. I know better than to enlighten them with Master Kent's distressing news; they will not trust a word I say. What's more, our three sons whose beds were cold and empty last night are still missed and missing from their homes. The master and myself are not the only ones to have despairing hearts. So we — yes, *we*; I still say *we*

— are as tense and volatile as wasps. No one, not a single soul of us, has taken to their tools today. Even I, with my scarred hand, have not gone early to the manor house to labour on the thinning of the vellum square, its pumicing and chalking. I have no duty there, not even if the Chart-Maker returns. I can be of no use to him, except perhaps to find him and warn him about the welcome he'll receive. I will hunt for him. I have a duty to the man. But since I last saw him scuttling in Mistress Beldam's steps, I do not like to contemplate where he might be. I fear his injury. I fear that he is intimate with her. So, for the moment, I am sauntering about the lanes or loafing on my outside bench, approachable, but listless with unease.

Our village would seem leisurely to any passers-by. At least, our hands are idle. But this is not a feast day with pleasures to anticipate. We won't be dancing to Thomas Rogers's pipe tonight, or Mr Quill's fiddle, come to that. Our sluggishness is no more purposeful than our scurrying. Already our village fabric is unravelling. The harvested barley is uncared for. A sack has toppled, and spilt. No one is even seeing off the rats. There are sour cattle droppings waiting to be spread, molehills to be kicked over, cow ticks to be removed, unless we want our animals enfeebled by the theft of blood. Whoever was the gong-farmer this morning has not done his duty. The barrow is still clean and free from flies, and the latrines are not worth visiting. Our pigs have not yet received their morning scraps. That diseased bough from the Kips' old cherry tree has fallen finally, and blocks a path, but none of the Kips has dragged it away or offered it an axe; there's two night's winter fuel there at least. Anyone that chances on it barely gives it a glance, but steps around the trunk with a vacant face. The cattle are protesting on the common land, heavy with milk. A gate hangs loose — the rarest sight — and cocks and hens are walking free as if they know these lanes will soon be theirs. But there are greater matters to resolve than hens. A congregation has been called, I hear, for noon. I will not go, of course. Until that time, my neighbours are as bored and puzzled as a pack of parlour cats with nothing close to scratch. With nothing close to scratch, that is, until they see me talking to the groom, not telling him where Mistress Beldam might have found her hideaway.

He is a smaller man than any of the Jordan constables, and lighter even than the steward, who, though quite short, is built of oak. That's not to say the groom isn't dangerous — but he'd be more dangerous to women or to the horses in his charge than to Lizzie's father, Gervase Carr, a quietly violent man when it most counts. Where is his daughter, he wants to know, asking roughly but from a distance, at first. The groom just shrugs, but doesn't turn. He knows enough about the weighing of the world to judge that a gentleman's groom will tip the scales more heavily than a clodhopper. Gervase takes a step forward towards the bench where I am sitting and towards the groom's back. Another half a dozen steps and he will be able to reach out and seize this fellow by his scruff. 'It's Lizzie Carr I'm talking of. You've seen her, haven't you? She's just a little twig of a girl. Your master has her at the house — '

'She's owned up to all her wickedness,' the groom replies. He really ought to step away. Instead, he turns around finally. He miscalculates the situation he is in, although he can't but be surprised to see the swelling crowd at Gervase Carr's shoulder. He attempts a quip. 'If she's a twig, then she'll burn very nicely with those other sorcerers,' he says, pushing out his hands as if to warm them at a fire. 'We'll have a bit of charcoal from her yet.'

It's Lizzie's mother who reaches him first. Gervase is slow to take the groom's full meaning and is looking more puzzled than alarmed. But his wife is cut from quicker stock. She takes the fellow by the ear. She has two sons, and so she's practised at that art. She twists, and then she has him by the hair. Gervase is next. His wife has marked the way. Then all I know is, there's a sudden rush. The others jostle in. A body hits the far end of my bench and I have tumbled backwards, falling awkwardly and with no dignity into the pebbled rain ditch at the foundings of my cottage. A second blow topples me before I can get back on my feet. A booted foot has kicked me in the face. An accident, I hope. But I am wise enough to keep myself rolled up, like a hedgehog, with my back turned to the oddly quiet scrum. No one is calling or saying anything. All I hear is thud on thud, a farming sound, a livestock sound. A thousand stinging grievances are settling on the groom; a hundred angry, waspy fists are hurting him. He might still walk away with bruises and not wounds but then one of the Saxton lads decides to outdo his brothers by stepping forward with his pruning blade and widening his victim's quipping mouth, from lip to cheek, with one efficient strike.

Without the sudden show of blood, which leaves its mark not only on a dozen of my neighbours but also across my bench and breeches, nothing would have stopped the punching, I'm sure of it. But blood unsettles us. We step away from it. Unless it's ours, we have to wipe it off at once. And so the beating of the groom loses its nerve as quickly as it was found. Gervase Carr retreats to swab his bloody knuckles in the grass. The Saxton lad runs off to wash his blade. Two sisters spit on each other's aprons to help scrub out the appalling splashes. Everybody checks their clothes.

Quite soon we are alone once more, the Jordan groom and I. I'm stunned and angry and alarmed, slow to stand and find my footing. He's hardly moving, but he's certainly alive. A dead man never made such noise. But I'm the only one to hear his pain, and I'm the only one, I have to say, who hasn't hit the man. I'm glad he has survived to stand as witness to that truth — if that mouth can ever speak again.

The lane has emptied suddenly. They're running now. There's not a person in the village who won't have realised at once, with the spurting of the groom's blood and the gory gaping of his face, that everything has changed for the worse. It's almost safe to roast our master's doves; it's possible to kill our master's mare and not be caught for it. But beating up and cutting through a Jordan man will throw us all at the mercy of a less forgiving outside world, one that will not rest or let us rest until its duty has been done, until its justice has been satisfied. God bless us all, and God help all of us. There isn't one of us — no, *them* — who's safe.

★   ★   ★

I'm not surprised this afternoon to see it is the Carrs and Saxtons who leave the village first. They know they have the most to fear. It was their fists and their pruning knife that did the greatest damage. There's no escaping punishment. Even neighbour John and his wife, Emma, have been persuaded that it's best to pack their burdens and their sorrows in a shoulder bag and join his brother's family in their flight. No one with that name is safe, not once the groom has dripped his blood-blinded way back to the manor house and shown the stabbing and the beating he's endured for being nothing else but Master Jordan's loyal man.

John is hollowed out, a husk. His shoulders slope not only from the weight of his bundles and packs but also, seemingly, from having to leave behind the bones and body of his customary life. This will be a bitter day for him, for all of them. He does not look at me when he steps away from his front door for what could be

164

the final time — we made our lasting peace this morning, in the darkness of my room — but should he have chosen to I would not have tested him on the fate of his young niece. What else are they supposed to do? I know it's not their intention to abandon Lizzie coldly to her fate. But there are other Carrs to think of now, other Carrs to be protected first. They need to make them safe beyond our bounds, and then I'm sure there must be other plans to make the family whole again. A farmer knows to gate the herd before he hunts the stray. Fleeing now can make no difference. And staying in the village would not secure the girl. She'd still be orphaned; her parents are the instigators of the beating and so cannot expect to live, once enforcers have arrived. Already they have heard the whinnying of a horse, protesting at its saddle and its reins. And they have harkened to the hoof-beats of a rider — Mr Baynham, I would guess; the sidemen will be needed now, to bruise and bully us — setting off up the same lane along which he descended when the Jordan party first arrived. It is not long before the village hears the four blasts on the steward's saddle horn to let us know that he has ridden into safer ground.

Our village is not purposeless this afternoon. It's like another working day. Except it's busy with the tying up of bundles and the stitching up of skins. It's busy with farewells, from which I find myself excluded. I only watch, and hug my neighbours in my dreams. The next to confess their departure are the Higgs and Derby families. For them it is an easier choice. Their sons have gone ahead of them. They're following. They'll be reunited on the road. Each of the four remaining family men takes a corner of the winnowing screen which serves as old mother Derby's litter. She shares it with their luggage and their clothes, but does her best to keep it light by lying still, with her knees drawn up against her chest. There are no tears as they set off, so far as I can tell. They're being calm and competent. They are not fools. It's best to get away before the trouble really starts. They've guessed what Mr Baynham's mission is. He'll come back either with a pack of twenty sidemen, meaner than the three already here, or a troop of soldiers, armed for a battle and disappointed if they can't start one. That saddle horn has sounded their defeat.

At first, some of the more reluctant families, the ones who've hardly punched the groom and so imagine they'll be spared the very worst of punishments, say they'll take the risk and stay. They have not quantified the risk; they've only quantified the loss. The tally they draw up contains the anxious and the menial — 'We haven't finished sacking up our barley yet. What happens to the hens?' — but also the weighty legacies of family and land, too weighty to be carried on their backs. 'We've ploughed these fields since Adam's time,' they say, counting back the granddads on their fingertips. They're ancient families. They'll not easily be driven out before the torrents of the law, to disappear in towns or villages where their names and faces cannot ring a bell, robbed of their spirits and their futures, as well as of their fields. But people who have bounced between feast and famine all their lives are nothing if not tough-minded and hard-nosed. A sack of barley is not worth a life, they realise, as they watch the afternoon sun dip into the latticework of trees. They're short of time. And so they start to gather up their things. There'll be no ploughing if you're dead, or anchored to the wall of some dark cell. Besides, departures do not need to be final, they tell themselves. The prodigal comes home. The swallows and the swifts return in spring. It's prudent, though, to fear the worst and run for cover if the clouds are black enough. And the clouds are clearly black enough today. No matter how these ancients play it through their minds, the stabbing of a master's man, on top of everything, must mean the end of their tranquillity. They'll have to find tranquillity elsewhere. Surely life beyond these fields cannot be as sinister and dangerous, as fearsome, loathsome and bizarre, as Master Kent has claimed when he is drunk and telling them of imps and oceans, tree fish, mermaids, cannibals, men with hoofs and women who lay eggs. He is only teasing them. Surely, he is only teasing them.

So the numbers swell throughout the afternoon, until finally everybody I have known in this placid line of cottages accepts that it's best to put some distance between themselves and Master Jordan's men, especially that groom, especially his freshly carved gargoyle face. They shudder at the thought of him. Once the decision has been made, I can see — and I'm surprised and touched by it — a kind of determined, turbulent happiness taking hold. If there is grief and anger in the air, there is also jollity. Some of the younger ones are almost smiling with relief as they set off to cross our village limits for the first time in their lives, relieved to get away before they're caught, of course, but also glad that what's ahead of them is not predictable. They've found a reason to stride bravely off. Their hearts are leaping and their heads are clear. They're free at last, and filling up with hope with every step. Perhaps they will encounter marvels on the way.

Most of them take the widest lane, the one that Mr Baynham followed on his horse, because it means they at least can lead a cow or goat with them, or carry their hens and geese in baskets on their barrows and their carts. The Kips even succeed in putting an ox between the shafts of a hay wagon and setting off with almost everything they own, including all their stoppered bottles of cordial and their gleaning sacks. Of course, their names are going with them too. All of the village names that count are moving out. Soon they will have gone beyond the hoof-trod paths and drift-ways on The Property of Edmund Jordan, gentleman, and will have reached the wonder of a gravelled surface, the wagon ways of post-horn carriages, packhorse trains and carting loads. They will have joined the restless, paler people of the towns.

Only the Carrs and Saxtons take the slower, deeper, forest route, despite their lifelong dread of going for too long without the certainty of either daylight or the moon. The trees at the forest's heart might not have seen a human face before. There might not even be a path. That means these neighbours cannot draw their carts or take with them any of their more valuable animals. They'll leave them to find forage of their own. 'Let them eat wool,' I mutter at my neighbours' backs, making light as best I can of all their troubles, present and forthcoming, their lamentable *hereafters*, as Mr Quill has titled them. But going by the forest route does mean they're safe at least from mounted pursuit. With any luck they'll not be caught, they'll not be hunted down like deer. Who knows, within a day or two they might have reached another line of bounds and someone else's common ground, where they can put up their hut — four rough and ready walls, a bit of roof — and light a fire. They'll build a place; they'll lay a hearth; they know the custom and the law. Their smoke will give them liberty to stay.

* * *

I am in Kitty Gosse's bed again. She isn't stretched out at my side, of course. Tonight the only fingers fanned across my abdomen are my own. I've not laid eyes, or hands, on her since early yesterday. Her absence is an agony. I am surprised to feel so sick of heart because, of late, my wider carings have been narrowed by my wife's too recent death. Kitty and I have not been honeyed lovers, after all, but falling short of that — something simpler, I suppose, something less affecting. But, still, the knowledge of her torments at the manor lies leaden in my stomach, a heavy, undigested stew which increases in its girth the more I ponder it. I'm brimming now with fret and bile, because of her.

I hope to find escape in sleep. But before I even try to sleep, before I dare to fall asleep, I have to tidy up the mess left by the three sidemen during their ransacking, the same three men who pained my Kitty Gosse. I had my choice of many beds, of all the village beds, in fact. There's not a neighbour's home that's closed to me. But the habits of half a lifetime will not be shed so suddenly. I don't feel free to trespass in their forsaken rooms, let alone rest my head and body in someone else's dents, without their first inviting me. I think I'm hoping to recover some of their trust even though they are too far away and too long gone to witness my timid, loyal observance of our country practices or even care what I might do. But Mistress Gosse's home has on occasion let me in quite willingly, and so I am pressed into dents that do, to some extent, belong to me.

I could not have slept comfortably in my own bed — at least, I did not want to take the risk. What I must regard as John Carr's final, kind advice — that I was named as part of a conspiracy and should, therefore, pack up, move out and save myself — is unsettling still. My head is bustling with bitter, bruising possibilities. If Master Jordan's men are looking now for Mr Quill, no doubt they would be pleased to capture his assistant too, his vellum-maker, his companion on the bounds. It's all too easy to imagine what might occur if I were sleeping in my bed at home, wrapped up in my own rough cloth inside my own rough room. I'd be woken by the breaking open of the door. They'd drag me by my ankles to the manor house. My cheekbone's already cracked today, and hurting; it's fractured, possibly. My jaw is stiff. Chewing on the apple and the stub of bread I had for supper was hard work. So I will be punished all the more if I am bounced amongst the windfalls in the lane. I see myself laid out on the long bench in the porch on stone already moist and cold from Mistress Beldam's father's corpse. I am the one who sleeps with Willowjack. My everlasting paradise is Turd and Turf. I take the blame for everything.

I must remind myself that Master Kent has told me otherwise. He says I am not counted as a suspect. I'm ashamed to say, the opposite is true. I'm taken by his cousin for a man he can 'rely upon', that was the way he phrased it. Unlike neighbour Carr, Master Kent was privy to last night's excesses, even though a floorboard blocked his view, and so his word has some authority. He promises I've not been named by widow Gosse. He could be wrong entirely or the circumstances might change, of course: each day the story of our lives is forced on to a different track. Nothing seems impossible. But my instinct almost persuades me he is right. There has been something in the way Master Jordan looks at me — he's weighing me; I'm livestock in his eyes — to make me wonder if he hopes one day to find me useful, a beast of burden he can put

171

to work. He must realise I'm truly not a villager. He knows I used to be the manor man. He sees I stand apart. I'm separate. Indeed, I haven't felt as separate in years. Perhaps it's just as well, this recent, saddening detachment from the drove. I almost welcome it. These loose roots might save me yet.

So I find some calm in Kitty Gosse's bed, though fleetingly. My naps are fly-by-night and fugitive. I cannot stay asleep. Because the demons come again. They're taunting me with: You're Master Jordan's donkey now; You don't deserve kind neighbours and good friends; You did deserve that hearty kicking when you toppled from your bench into the rain ditch this afternoon; There's more and worse to come for you; Watch out. I imagine for a second time that breaking open of my door, that dragging of my body by its ankles through the night. It is not the sidemen beating me but Saxtons, Rogerses, Gosses, Derbys, Kips and Carrs. Yes, someone that I must have thought of as a neighbour or a friend has struck me in the face today. The bruises have flowered on my cheek and the pain is ripening, I find myself so saddened and incensed that I can hardly hope for the salve of lasting sleep.

Counting sheep is not the remedy. The night itself is also keeping me awake. Its wind is pelleting its buckshot stars across the sky. The trees cry out already for their departed friends. Abandoned animals are demanding care, despite the dark. It is as if they know I'm here and are impatient for my services. I ought to drag my aching face out of the widow's bed and attend to

172

them, attend to everything and anyone that needs me in the night. For there is no forgetting there are other human hearts out there, more damp and cold than mine. I'm haunted now by the thought of Mr Quill, not only by the fear that he's been caught, but also by Master Kent's report that the missing man slept *elsewhere*. The last time I saw him was at the pillory. One moment he was putting his finger on my hand, the next he was almost out of sight, crashing through the sore-hocks in Mistress Beldam's traces, and her scent.

I am not being generous or sensible. What does it matter if he captured her? What loss is it to me? Indeed, it might be best if that were so, if he caught up with her elsewhere and hushed her cries to tell her of the danger she was in. But then surely he would have gone back to the manor house at once, his duty done, his conscience clear, and not slept elsewhere. And I am bothered by the thought, the tormenting drama, actually, of that cropped head on Mr Quill's bent chest. I almost put his lips on hers. I almost see his graceless body — bared, as white as moonlight — in her arms. I am so bothered that I placate the tension with my hands, alone in widow Gosse's bed, where so many times of late the tensions have been stroked away by her. Of course, I'm left more bleak than I began. My loneliness is evidenced in wasted seed and empty cottages.

Who are my neighbours now? I'm counting them on gluey fingers. My tally is the strangest one. There's not a willing soul remains within our bounds who entirely belongs to these commons and these fields. Apart from Kitty Gosse, Anne Rogers and Lizzie Carr, if they're alive, no one who's stayed was born close by. No one who's stayed has family. My reckoning provides me with just seven bodies freely sleeping under a roof: four Jordan men — the steward has already ridden off for help — the two masters of the manor and dissenting cousins, and myself (though not quite sleeping yet). There is the husband at the pillory, of course. I must remember him. He has no roof. And then the missing couple, unaccountable, the sorceress, the Chart-Maker. I have to say it: beauty and the beast.

I force myself to concentrate. If I can only ponder on a single task — forget the woman, Mr Quill, my bruises and the neighbours who provided them, all talk of sorcery, the horrors of the coming dawn . . . no, stop. If I can only find a single task to think about, to practise in my weariness, I will sleep. I know that I will sleep. Labour is the gateway to a night of rest. I take myself off to the barn. I close my eyes and fly there like a bat. And there I find discarded tools. And I commence — at least restart — the threshing of our barley crop. Quite soon I've made a rhythm with my flail. My neighbours should be proud of me. I work the thump, until it's beating with my heart. I dream of ploughs and oxen, furrows, grain.

12

Master Jordan seems a calm and happy man today. He says I'm just the hand he's looking for. Indeed, when I walk across to the manor house as soon as it is light with nothing clear in mind except to show my damaged face and take the consequences, he meets me at the door himself and leads me from the porch into the room where he is eating breakfast. He has me sit. He offers me his bread and ale, though not the cold meats and the cheeses. He's being civilised but thrifty. I cannot tell what's happened overnight but clearly it is to his satisfaction. Even Master Kent, when he comes in and sits with me on my side of the table, seems less ashen and less shaky than he has for several days. This morning he's breathing from a deeper pool. It is as if a truce has been brokered and both men claim the victory.

But first — to earn my bread and ale, it seems — they ask for my account of what happened in the village yesterday. Has anyone remained, they want to know. Did anybody speak of their return? And when my answer to both questions is a No, Master Jordan claps his hands, his signature for being pleased, and laughs out loud. 'What frightened mice your neighbours are,' he says. 'And so the meek shall inherit the world!' He means his sheep, of course.

Edmund Jordan might seem a very pleasant

man when he is relaxed and smiling. I do not find him dangerous. And so I risk a question of my own, though I select it carefully. I will not ask about the girl and women in his keeping, even though they cannot be detained more than fifty paces from his table. I cannot seem to be concerned for them, if they are witches in his view. I dare not even mention Mr Quill. I'm too associated with the Chart-Maker already. Instead, with a nod of apology to both men for my temerity, I say, 'I worry that my dear master is deposed entirely.' I reach an arm out, stretch along the bench, until I can lay my hand on Charles Kent's elbow. This is my show of loyalty. This is my reminder that we once drank at the same breast. I'm stepping back into his yard. That seems my only option now.

'You should not squander any fluster on your master, Walter Thirsk,' he replies, then pauses, smiles, tips his head, says 'Water! Thirst!', laughs merrily and claps his hands. I've never seen a man so happy with himself so early in the day. He leans across the table to lay a hand on each of our fore-arms. 'Your master is my cousin through marriage, as you know. He's family. He's country kin. I cherish him, of course. No, my benefit is that he benefits. We have a plan. We leave today. We leave with cousin Charles in our good company.'

Now I am required to listen to a lecture on the principles of stewardship. The province of a hundred people out of every one hundred and one is to take and not provide direction, he says. He mentions Profit, Progress, Enterprise, as if they are his personal Muses. Ours has been a village of Enough, but he proposes it will be a settlement of More, when finally he's fenced and quick-thorned all the land and turned everything — our fields, the commons and 'the wasted woods' — into 'gallant sheep country'. 'And, as misfortune has it,' he concludes, marking that Misfortune with a happy show of teeth, 'the villagers who most would benefit from these advances have preferred instead — as one, it seems — to impose their villainy on my good groom and then seek another place where their idle subsistencies can flourish. So the land has come back to the Lord, I mean myself, who owns this property of soil. I have the chance to start from scratch. Or, as our Mr Earle might say, I have the chance to start on a spotless sheet of parchment.'

'Has Mr Earle finished with his charts?' I ask. I cannot see the risk in that.

'Ha, Mr Earle will never finish it, I think.'

'You mean because he is accused?'

'Accused of what?'

'Of unclean magic, can I say?'

Master Jordan leans across the table again and presses his thumb into my forearm. 'Your face is very cruelly bruised,' he says. His smile has thinned. 'I hope the injury has no cause to spread. I would not want to see your other cheek as scarred. No. Again, you must not squander any fluster there. You will not. That is what I say. Magic, clean or otherwise, and sorcery . . . such things? We should not mention them again.' And on those words, as if ordained, the first sunlight

177

of the day finds passage through the red-black canopy of sentry beeches and lays a glossy stripe across the table top. At last I understand the hope in Master Kent's face, and his composure in these torrential times. His resignation too. There'll be no trials. There'll be no burning at the stake. There'll just be progress of a sort.

What the cousin proposes and my Master Kent supports, with many nods and nudges of his knee on mine but without speaking a word, is that when the Jordan party leaves, as leave it must by noon today, with the three prisoners in tow, I am to stay behind to be the new master's ears and eyes. His steward has already ridden off to organise the purchase of the sheep — so not to summon soldiers, then — and in the coming months I can expect the arrival of hired hands who will lodge in our empty cottages while trees are cut, and hedges struck, and drystone walls and winter folds built. I can expect, as autumn comes, a pair of shepherds to arrive, or even three perhaps, and they will carry with them coins for my wage. But for the coming weeks I can count only upon myself for company. 'Yourself and Mr Pillory,' he says. 'It is my reckoning the man has three more days to serve. Today, tomorrow and the last. As you are honest, do not show him leniency, but set him free only when the hour veritably lets him free. I have your word?'

Master Kent nods encouragement. He will explain when we're alone, he seems to mean.

'You have my word.' I hate myself for saying so.

'Then start your day in my employ by preparing our five horses for the journey. My groom has not the heart or face for it. He's keeping to his bed. I thank him for that. He is a fiercely ugly man today.' Master Jordan stands at the table, offers me his hand. I cannot help but reach across and shake it briefly. My finger joints clack against his rings. His palms are cool and vellum-soft and smooth.

Master Kent comes with me to the orchard, where, carelessly, since the groom's disablement, the horses have been left untethered overnight. We could be mistaken for ranking equals as we walk at each other's shoulders down the lane, two greying men of more than middle years, no trace of finery, bulked up and burnished by our living on the land.

'I thank you, Walt,' he says, taking my hand. We are old friends again. 'I cannot say how glad I was to see your face today. Despite your bruises. I feared you would have fled like everybody else. I'd not have blamed you if you had. I've been tempted to take flight myself. I've even thought to take a light to it, my home, and finish off what was begun in my dovecote and my lofts. Rather than be witness to . . . ' He does not want to list the changes that will come. 'These are sad and hasty times. In what . . . five days, six days? . . . the village has been . . . lost to me. It has been lost to all of us.'

Nevertheless Master Kent has managed, he reports, to salvage at least some advantage from the exodus. As soon as his cousin learnt the village was cleared out, dispersed and chivvied

179

by alarm, as Master Jordan always must have intended, his interest in the captives and in any talk of sorcery waned quite suddenly. A triumphant stillness flooded through the manor house. Any mention of Mr Earle, my Mr Quill, was rewarded only with a yawn. Mistress Beldam didn't matter any more. Alchemy and sorcery were trifling affairs compared to the Land of Progress he proposed.

'And so I risked an intercession on behalf of little Lizzie and the women,' says Master Kent. 'If my cousin counted their undoubted sins — their foolishness, let's say — a minor matter, surely he could end their punishments. It would be kind and wise of him, and honourable, of course — the man loves honour almost as much as he worships wool — to end their punishments.'

'You do not mean that I should end their suffering at once?' the cousin teased. 'Is it your plea that I must let them meet their Maker straight away? Can I use faggots from your log pile for their fire?'

'I propose you let them meet their Maker in their own good time, and for the moment let them walk afar, untethered.'

'Walk afar as sorcerers and sinners?' Master Jordan was amused by his older cousin's unproductive tenderness.

'No, only walk afar as country folk who have been sundered from their families, and will do nothing worse than follow them, and never trouble you again. Nor trouble me . . . my conscience, that's to say.'

'We would not want your conscience to be bruised or even tested, cousin Charles.'

And that is what Edmund Jordan has consented to — although he clearly wants to number me amongst the many forfeits Master Kent has to pay. If I agree to stay behind and watch over his land until the sheep have taken charge and tainted our earth with their yellow splashes, then he'll agree to 'untether the witches'. 'But they'll not step free on the estate of Edmund Jordan the Younger,' he says. His lands are closed for ever to Rogerses, Gosses and Carrs. 'Their greatest sorcery has been to make the clock stand still. Their mischief is to shade my path. I'll not pardon them for that.' So the girl and the two women will be escorted off in custody and released only the moment they reach the marketplace, three days away. Master Kent will keep them company to make sure his cousin honours his word. 'It is my wish to witness it,' he says. 'To see that widow, daughter, wife walk freely in the free streets of a town. But, for myself, I cannot think that I will ever come back to this place.'

Now he has me in his arms, and we are almost toppling on to the apple-strewn ground beneath the horses hoofs. Any hawk looking down on the orchard's cloistered square, hoping for the titbit of a beetle or a mouse, would see a patterned canopy of trees, line on line, the orchard's melancholy solitude, the jewellery of leaves. It would see the backs of horses, the russet, apple-dotted grass, the saltire of two crossing paths worn smooth by centuries of feet, and two grey heads, swirling in a lover's dance, like blown seed husks caught up in an impish and exacting wind and with no telling when or where they'll come to ground again.

13

It is midday already and I am waiting with the horses in the courtyard's remaining rectangle of shade. The manor's outline is straight-edged and motionless. Its sharpness has unsettled them. They resisted their saddles this morning, and are still peevish and resentful. Being in the sun under open skies and busy trees was preferable to this. Up till now, the last few days have been amongst the most unruffled of their lives. What space and liberty. They've not been fed before on hay as fresh as I've provided for them or, until yesterday, on such an uninterrupted abundance of apples. Had the groom been working and not nursing his cut face, he would have tethered them away from apples — especially the bitter codlings — and the fermenting colic they will cause, the fatal torsions and the windy flux. But I don't care about the welfare of these strangers' horses. I've watched them munch. I'll let them suffer from our fruits. I will not wish Godspeed on them. By this time tomorrow they could well be too sick for travelling and my masters might be required to exercise their own legs for once. But for the moment the cobbles are clacking with hoofs and the air is murky with horses' breath. They will not settle, no matter what I whisper in their ears. They know that soon they will be laden down with panniers and men.

I am relieved when the sidemen bring out the

luggage and start to prepare for the journey. I am allowed to stand aside and be ignored. The sidemen do not want to meet my eye. I like to think they are ashamed, or even a little fearful of me. Perhaps they've heard I am their master's latest chosen man, his eyes and ears, his watchman and custodian. They'll be as glad to ride away from me as I will be to see their errant backs retreating from the manor house.

The final piece of luggage that they bring is the groom himself. He's carried in a matting litter with not much care. I cannot see his face or any of his wounds until he's helped to stand and lifted bodily on to the smallest and the least skittish of his mounts, a gelding with a mottled rump and flanks. The damage has been dressed, but his head and hair are caked in blood, and I can tell by how he holds himself, as shivered as a moth, that every movement inflicts pain on him. Three days of riding on rough ground, I think, and he will be either a mad man or a dead man. His little horse, if he survives my apples, will have requital then for every whip and switch the groom has ever laid on him. I would step forward for a closer view. I want to look the groom in the eye. I suppose I want him to see the bruises on my own face, of which he is to some extent the cause. But I have hardly taken one step forward when the door in the manor porch opens and the prisoners come out, in a line, and tied at wrist and waist. I think I'm seen at once by Kitty Gosse, although the sun is in her eyes and I am hidden in the wedge of shade. Her face contorts, although that might be pain and not the sight of me. Then Anne Rogers and the Gleaning Queen appear, their hands crossed on their aprons, their shoulders down like penitents.

I hesitate. I ought to hurry across the yard and comfort them. I might even give them hope. I would not want them to travel out before first understanding that soon, thanks to Master Kent's interventions, for which I am to some extent the ransom price, they will be freed, to walk afar, untethered, in another place. But I'm afraid, and I'm too shocked by them to move. It's not that they are wounded like the groom, not visibly, at least. It's just that they are not the women I have known. And Lizzie Carr is not the girl. She still wears her green sash, surprisingly. She has it tied round her throat. It's dirty now, I see, and torn. It might be bloody, in fact. But I am reminded briefly of how she once appeared, that little nervous scrap, exhorted by my master to step out of the chair of hands provided by her father and her uncle John and find a single grain, 'just one. Then we will cheer. And you will be our Queen for one whole year.' She'd been the sweetest and the yellowest that ancient day. I'll not forget her blowing on the grains to winnow off the flake and how the barley pearls were weighty on her palm. But now she is like chaff herself. A sneeze could lift her up and take her off. She's hollowed out and terrified. What can it mean to her that she is being fastened to the saddle of a horse? What can it mean to Kitty Gosse and her friend Anne, the piper's mother, who cannot know her son has abandoned her and taken all the other Rogerses with him, that the only neighbour here today is Walter Thirsk, who's skulking in the shadows with a bruise across his face?

I can't deny it's cowardly, but, now that the horses have been taken off my hands, I am free to edge along the slice of shadow, doing what I can not to catch anybody's eye again, and find some refuge in the open lane. My Master Kent has had the same idea. He does not want to take part in the packing for departure, the tying and the stirruping. I find him dressed for travel in his high hat and long topcoat, staring out across the fields, with his back pressed against a maiden elm, its warped feet bright with lichen and its craggy trunk already warm with light. I've seen him in this place a hundred times, a pipe in hand, belonging here. We all have somewhere private hereabouts where we can press our backs. Today — such is the light, and such the sap green of his coat — he looks as if he's part of it, a man of wood and leaf.

'This land,' he says, gesturing, 'has always been much older than ourselves.'

I do not take his meaning straight away. I nod respectfully, expecting him to say more, when he's found the words.

'So much older than ourselves,' he repeats in a whisper, shaking his head. 'Not any more.'

I understand his meaning now: this ancient place would soon be new, he wants to say. We're used to looking out and seeing what's preceded us, and what will also outlive us. Now we have to contemplate a land bare of both. Those woods that linked us to eternity will be removed by spring, if Master Jordan's saws and axes have their way. That grizzled oak which we believe is so old it must have come from Eden to our fields will be felled and rooted out. That drystone wall, put up before our grandpas' time and now breached in a hundred places, will be brought down entirely and replaced either with an upstart thorn or with some plain fence, beyond which flocks will chomp back on the past until there is no trace of it. We'll look across these fields and say, 'This land is so much younger than ourselves.'

My master takes his leave from me. We have embraced already this morning, in the orchard, beneath the apples and the hawks, and we are wise enough to let that parting serve. We could not better it. He does not even offer me his hand, but only puts a finger on my arm, and fixes me with the briefest show of eyes, as wide and white as they can be — he means me to remember this look; he means me to decipher it — before he turns towards his house, *the* house, his cousin's house, and for the first time in a dozen years prepares to ride a horse other than Willowjack.

I find that I am running up the incline of the common fields towards the top end of our land, the one place where it is high enough to gain a pinched view of other parishes, that little clovered hillock which on Mr Quill's rough map marks the nose of the brawny-headed man which I now know to be our village from above. It's just as well that I am on the move because I have an excuse to count my tear-filled eyes as proof of nothing more than my exertion. I am a man not used to moving fast. I can't recall running for such a distance since I came to this village. There never was a need to hurry here. We value effort over haste. I half expect to hear my neighbours calling out, 'What's bitten your backside, Walt?' or 'Where's the fire?' or 'Who the devil's chasing you, for doing what?' They'd wonder at my weeping eyes.

I'm glad to sit and rest my lungs and legs on Clover Hill — now there's a name that Mr Quill might like — until the travellers pass by. I've climbed up here because I know there is a stretch of lane where for, say, fifty paces, there are no hedges, trees or walls to curtain it from my view. I used to come here often years ago, before I settled in — yes, *settled* in; yes, *fitted* in; I can't honestly say *belonged* — hoping I suppose to be the first to spot a visitor, some enterprising carter, say, a tinker with his coloured and deceitful wares, a relative of Master Kent, perhaps (How could I know what that might mean for us?), some minstrel with a bag of songs and news of towns and palaces. But no one ever came to stay more than a day, of course. Not till this week, that is.

Now, I rest my arms across my knees, put my chin on to my wrists and allow the sun to dry me out. I am expecting cousin Jordan's party soon. Until it comes, my master's leaving, fixing stare is coaxing me. It shows wide and white again in my mind's eye. I've not seen his face like that before, so mimed and meaningful. It was an accusation of a sort, I fear. A plea, as well. Yet it was fond, in its own way. My Cecily would sometimes bulb her eyes like that. Hers was a wifely nudge that meant there was a duty to be carried out, by me. Or else it was a warning that I had said too much, or gone too far, or not gone far enough. The eyes speak louder than the lips, it's said — and they gather whispers better than the ears. My master's final, whispered words — 'Not any more' — are coaxing too. His voice is quivered like a dove's in this morning's sun-stoked breeze, as if, far off, he's cooing out to me. His voice is billowy, a sobbing parley in the wind, vabap-vabap. I catch only a gust or two. But I can tell it is a call to arms. It says that there are duties to be done. It says I haven't yet gone far enough.

The cousins are riding at each other's shoulders when they pass. I almost pick up their conversations. Even from this distance I can tell they are not ordinary men. I suppose their hats betray their standing. A working man would never wear or even need to own a tall and heavy hat, or one with so deep a brim. Such hats belong to gentlemen who rarely need to bend their heads or swing a tool. A working man could not afford to pass his day with so straight a back and so erect a head. It is as if these first two riders are suspended from their hats. All their wearers have to be is pendulous.

It's disappointing to see how cousinly they are, my twin masters now. It would have made me happier, it would have helped my quandary, to see them riding far apart, not ear to ear. They are

189

as close as two cloaks hanging from a pair of pegs. I cannot bear to think that they are friends or that there could be any liking between them. Blood is thicker than water, of course, and families are bound to observe truces which would not be kept outside the ties of kin. But the only blood these two have shared in common is Lucy Kent's. The thread that links them is a flimsy one. Their seeming fellowship this afternoon is baffling.

I want to believe Master Kent has a stratagem. His accommodations are a plot, a *subterfuge;* that word I didn't know before is proving its worth of late. But equally I fear the evidence of my own eyes — and my ears. There's laughter, even, from the riders. Their high hats are not shaking but their shoulders are. In that meagre distance between the courtyard of the manor house and this open stretch of lane, it could be that, flank on flank and simply with a shared click of the spurs, an allegiance has been forged between these two men, one that recognises their joint interests, an acknowledgement of how their futures will be shaped, the benefits and moieties. I cannot truly blame my Master Kent for that. He has to live. He has to have a roof. He's lately done his best to intercede on behalf of our two women and our girl. He has secured, I must suppose, a living for me too. And now he's thinking of himself. Perhaps that was all he meant by his briefest, widest show of eyes when he took leave of me at the maiden elm earlier today. Not a plea or an accusation after all. He was asking for my understanding, warning me of his defeat, showing me how wise it is to toe the line. I study him as he rides off. I'm almost tempted to call out. I want to say, 'Not any more.' But as it happens there's no need. Perhaps he's guessed I'm watching him. He knows my fondness for this clover tump. He might have even seen me sitting here. What's certain is that as these two mounted gentlemen almost disappear behind a screen of elders and a rising wall, my master — the slightly shorter, less round-shouldered one — lifts his right arm as if he's reaching up for fruit and twists his hand. It isn't quite a wave. It's not a farewell either. It's more like a dancer's curlicue, an unexpected gaiety, and not the gesture of a beaten man.

I'm standing up by the time the other horses and the other travellers come into view, at last. I do not waste my farewell waves on them. I don't suppose they're looking at the village hills. Their heads are down. They do not have the benefit of weighty hats to hang their bodies from. And they're more laden than the masters. The wounded groom is the first to pass. He sets the pace for all the rest, and it is slow and torturous. He tries his best to sit upright, but every step is juddering. He lifts a bottle to his lips. I'm sure it will be Master Kent's strongest cut-throat ale, or even better — quicker, that's to say — some stupefying barley blaze. A few mouthfuls of that every now and then should dull the pain; too many and he'll topple from his saddle. Two loaded horses follow, though I'm glad to see that little Lizzie Carr is sat on one of them, secured amongst the luggage like a market goose, a fancy goose in a green cloth wrap. I hope she makes it to a cosy place before our apples bring these horses to their knees. The widow Gosse and Anne Rogers walk at her side, tethered to the panniers with rope. And then the sidemen follow on, again dressed like foot soldiers in matching breeches, jerkins and brimless caps. They are not happy to be walking I am sure, not happy to have lost their usual mounts to their master's cousin and the devil's girl. One of them steps forward every few paces to switch the horses' flanks. I do not see it now, during this short stretch, but I'm sure he'll switch the women's flanks as well. Another carries a long stave. He's stolen it from us. I recognise its cut. It's too heavy for a walking stick. I do not want to think what it's intended for.

My master is too far ahead to know what's going on behind his back amongst his charges. Am I to be the only one to witness and know it all, the only one to wonder what this mounted pageant represents? Is that why I've been left behind? To watch this spectacle? It's like a costumed enactment at a fair, a mummers' show. I used to love them as a boy. I'd want to be the first to name the parts and identify the players from their garb. Today, I'm seeing Privilege, in its high hat. Then comes Suffering: the Guilty and the Innocent, including beasts. Then Malice follows, wielding its great stick. And, afterwards, invisibly, Despair is riding its lame horse.

The lane is empty once again. This hilltop is a friendless place, and capped in cloud. I've brought the end-of-summer sorrows on myself.

They spread their great black wings and cast their peckish shadows over me. The sun's still shining in the valley but its warmth's no longer reaching me. It is the middle of the afternoon, late harvest-time. I should be as dry and ripe as barleycorn. Instead, I feel as chilly as a worm. I feel no prouder than a worm. I am almost tempted to run down the hill to that now empty way and join the pageant as it heads off for a town. I'm panicking, not only for myself, but also for the prisoners, and the departed villagers, every one, and for Mr Quill as well. I have to fight the nightmares. I can't imagine living here for the coming seasons without someone to love or like, or any neighbour to share my troubles with. I can imagine living there, where they will be, above those smelling, busy, crowd-warmed streets, with Kitty Gosse as my hands-on-belly second wife. I can imagine bringing Lizzie Carr into our rooms and taking care of her. I'd be as loving as her uncle John, until the day that uncle John himself arrives. I can imagine being Master Kent's town man again, like in those lively days when he was still a bachelor. The prospect is not frightening. It wouldn't take me long to catch up with that mummers' show. I could tag on at the end and follow Despair and his dejected mount as . . . Shame, perhaps. As Servitude. I'd put up with their switches and their staves, so long as I could be with them and not beset by cloud.

Instead, I hold my nerve and let them go forward without me, without the afterthought of Servitude or the extra burden of my Shame. I hurry along the cattle path and down the far side of the hill, into the sunshine again. Here, in warmer light, I dare to slow my step. I want to bide my time and make the most of what remains of this upsetting day. I am not ready to face the choices I must make or even guess what they might be. I do not want to see the manor house or any of the cottages. I do not want to face the pillory. My eyes are not entirely dry just yet. My mood is tumbling again. I'm suffering what Cecily used to call my wilts. But it is a mood that will pass, in my experience, with every step I take into the open and deserted fields. These poisonous and leaden squalls are familiar to me, as bewildering in their coming as they are swift in their going, though lately the wilts have become more frequent. Cecily's parting is to blame. Without her love, I am an empty pod. I'm mourning her in tiny episodes, and will do, I suppose, until the mourning is complete. That day will never come, I think — and hope. There's solace in the thought that I will never finish missing her. And I suppose there's solace in the certainty that I will never finish missing here. I know I will not, cannot, must not, stay.

So I let the grieving have its way, as I escape from Clover Hill. I can allow myself to wallow like a village pig in the mud of my self-pity for a few more steps. I'm prone to that. I'm prone to feeling sorry for myself and feeling all the better for the indulgence. I allow my sadness to run its course, before I raise my head and, forging through a blizzard of thistledown which is falling up from the ground and supported by a breeze too soft for me to feel, I will myself to recognise what country folk are born to recognise, the amity in everything. Our fields are medicine. All days prove good to those that love the open air.

I pass our crest of great shade oaks, their first acorns and their summer leaf-fall cracking underfoot, and reach our flatter and more open ground, hard-working land, as flinty, thin and grizzled as a labourer. Here are pippin-jays to keep me silent company. The four or five I see this afternoon are too busy defacing pears and crabs to speak or even notice me. And there are finches in the quicksets as I walk. For the time being, at least, they're not short of anything to eat. They have the pick and peck of filberts, berries, hips and seeds. The hedges are heavy laden and grinning red with spoils, as if some puck has laid his magic wand upon their branches and ordered them to gem. This is the age of mushrooms too. It's a mistake to think that, just because the barley's in, the land has lost its open-handedness. Each weed and tree enjoys a harvest of its own.

Yet every plant and creature also knows that summer's in retreat. The wayside dandelions have whitened slightly in the last few days. They're growing pale with age. The year is leaving us. As are the swallows. A dozen or so are already vit-vitting overhead, preparing for their chinless journeys south. They always feel the chilling and the thinning of the air before we do, and understand when it is time to leave. I should not mind their parting. They've taken all the summer flies they can. They've kept our cattle company enough. They need to look elsewhere.

Somewhere better, I suppose. For all its warmth, the sunlight is slanting lower than it was a day ago. What sky is blue is more thinly so this afternoon. The woodland canopies, viewed from this sloping field, are sere or just a little pinched with rust, the first signs of the approaching slumber of the trees. Come, maids and sons of summer, get ready for the winter ice. Your day is shortening. The air is nipping at your cheek; the cold is tugging at your wrist. The glinting spider's thread will turn in a little while to glinting frost. It's time for you to fill your pies with fruit, because quite soon the winds will strip the livings from the trees and thunder through the orchards to give the plums and apples there a rough and ready pruning, and you will have to wait indoors throughout the season of suspense while weather roars and bends outside. The dead leaves fly. They're cropped and gathered to the rich barn of the earth.

14

Now there are only four of us. I hope that there are four of us. Mistress Beldam herself cannot be anywhere but near. Tonight will be her husband's fifth in the pillory. Mr Quill is missing still, of course. Tomorrow I will search for him, or what remains of him. My greatest wish is that I'll discover nothing of the man — my map-maker, my one-time greatest hope. Let's trust that someone from the manor house went out on the night of confessions when Mr Quill was elsewhere, on a rescue mission of his own, to warn him never to return, to let him know he is named as the master sorcerer, the witches' ringleader; that his ill-shaped, flimsy life is swinging on a thread of gossamer, and could soon be swinging from a sturdy noose. But who might that saviour have been? Not any of the sidemen, that's for sure. Or the groom. They wouldn't have taken the risk, they wouldn't have cared enough. The steward Baynham is a possibility. His educated conscience might have troubled him. I cannot say the man is bad, from what I've seen. He's just a spaniel, sluggish, loyal, obedient. As am I, so far.

I suppose some of my neighbours might have been the good Samaritans, unwittingly. That's easy to imagine. Catching Mr Quill on his way home late that night, they would not have resisted the opportunity to chastise him for the troubles he brought upon them, nor the chance to let him know what Mr Baynham blurted out at the manor door before suggesting they collect faggots for a public burning at the stake: 'I hear that there is witchery about. Three of your she-devils are in our custody.' I cannot, though, imagine Mr Quill running off at that. I cannot see him scurrying away. He's proved himself a brave, outspoken man before, unheeding of the dangers in his path, or insensible to them, an heroic innocent. Instead I see him striding even more speedily and erratically towards the manor house to have his say. He would have pulled that daughter and those women free. No, that is not the answer I am hoping for.

Master Kent, of course, was privy to those goings on. He would have done his best to warn his chart-maker and house guest of the dangers. Who knows, he could have pulled his topcoat on over his night chemise and gone out on the hunt. He could have had the fortune to discover Mr Quill on his way home. They would have startled one another in the lane, and then exchanged their whispers and their hugs. At the very least he might have marked a warning on a piece of chart and left it in the porch for Mr Quill to find. But surely Master Kent would have told me if he'd helped the man escape or, at the very least, persuaded him to stay away. He knows I have become an intimate. Yet, now I think of it, something was left unspoken the morning he came into my home with all that grim news to impart. 'And what occurred when Mr Quill returned last night?' I'd asked. And Master Kent had put his hand across his mouth with some embarrassment — as if to hide a lie, perhaps — and said, 'He has not come back to the house, not yet. He will have slept elsewhere . . . ' That *elsewhere* takes on a better shape than it has done before. I'd only thought *elsewhere* was Mistress Beldam's arms. I think now that possibly it was my master's hint to me that our good friend was safe. *Elsewhere* was not within our parish bounds.

But still I'm troubled by the waking nightmares I've had on my way down from Clover Hill. In these, my friend is wrapped up in a vellum shift, and colourless. Or he is melting in the flames, his flesh running off his bones like candle wax. The sidemen have discovered him and made a makeshift gibbet; the sidemen have discovered him and left him bleeding on the forest floor; our pigs have finished him. Or else my neighbours catch him in their lanes. They're not unwitting good Samaritans on this occasion. It's late and dark. There's no one there to witness them or to blame them for their violence. They treat him like they will treat the groom on the next afternoon. He's kicked and bruised. He might survive, but someone has a pruning knife and Mr Quill is coppiced and he's pollarded. There's not a limb remaining on his trunk. And once again the pigs have finished him.

And if Mr Quill has been discovered and dispatched, why not Mistress Beldam? We've not found any sign of either of them for two days now. So why not Mistress Beldam too? I see her sprouting head pushed and nuzzled like a turnip on the ground, a sweet and tiny dainty for the pigs. I see her spread out with the Chart-Maker amongst the carcasses at Turd and Turf. But then another, likely fear envelops me, a less than sweet and dainty one, but more believable, given what we know of her already, her grief and anger at her father's death. The woman who might well have slaughtered Willowjack, the woman who must still be looking for revenge, has run off through the sore-hocks with Mr Quill a dozen midnight steps behind. He thinks he's chasing her and will then have the chance to rescue her. But she is luring him. She means him to follow her. She even slows enough to give this halting man the chance to almost reach her back. Another twenty paces and she's his, he thinks. She's at his fingertips. If only she had longer hair instead of meagre fur, he could grab hold of her. They reach the open ground where the open fire was built, the day that they arrived. They reach the corridors of trees, behind. The darkness closes in on them; it pulls on its mantle and closes out the moon. She turns and faces him. 'I've come to warn you, sister,' Mr Quill begins to say. He does not see the length of wood come swinging at his head. He feels only the first of fifty blows. But I feel every one of them, a thorough pounding in my head that will not end until I know if this is fantasy or truth. Tomorrow, yes, tomorrow, I will have to go to search for them, the living or the dead. But now I need to find some peace in sleep. Today has been the second hardest in my life.

Despite convention and civility, I spend the

night, the first for many years, in the manor. I am its current master, after all, or at least the highest in ascendancy that still inhabits this discarded place. After me the bats can call it home. Again, I have my choice of beds, I have my choice of unmade beds. It is clear where the damaged groom has slept. He's left a crusty tracery of blood. And then there is a dormitory of sorts: straw is spread out deeply across the boards in a chamber off the musty upper gallery above my harking master's bed-parlour, where the sidemen passed their time — the torture room. It stinks of men and suffering.

Master Jordan himself has left his traces in his room, mostly the smell of rosewater from his casting-bottle and the soiled embroidered linen smock that he was wearing when he came to shake his fist at everybody in the threshing barn and in which, I must suppose, he's slept. I take his bed. He's made it comfortable, or at least ordered it to be made comfortable by one of his serving men. He's evidently turned down anything from Master Kent's supply of chaff mattresses and rough, hap-harlot coverlets, and made instead a cushioning of carpets, cloth and arrases that he has covered with one of Lucy Kent's old riding-capes. It is not quite up to the flock that he is used to. This is hardship for the man. He's had no spaniels sleeping at his feet or any supper tray of dainties on the side. But I am finding his bed unusually comfortable.

At first I do not recognise what Master Jordan has folded up and lately used as a pillow for his head. The room is dark. But when I put my own head down, I suspect the pillow by its texture. I can't have ever pressed my cheek into a velvet shawl before, although I've dreamt of it recently. At first I think I've put my face on mole. I've caught moles, hares and rabbits in my time. I've felt the thick pile of them, brushed my lips and skin with them. There's nothing living that's more silky than a mole. But mole will never smell as good as this. Behind the slightly breaded flavour of Master Jordan and his splash of rose-water, I pick up — despite its recent washing out of blood, horse blood, perhaps, its stain of Willowjack — the warm and musty scent of her. I lift it and I turn it in the half-dark hoping to confirm it is the Beldam shawl. It seems too dull and colourless. I try to make the cloth show mauve. It will not oblige. But there are moonlit, silver threads for sure, glistening almost wetly like snail tracks. The first time I saw this in its full finery was at the ending of our feast and dance. She had it round her shoulders then, at the entrance to the barn, and she was looking Turkish underneath its weighty, lordly weave. The last time I saw the velvet cloth it was heavy with blood and thrown across a fence in the cottage lane below the Saxton derelict. 'Give me her name,' my latest master demanded of me. 'By all my heart, I truly do not know her name,' I'd said.

So I am satisfied that this is the woman's shawl. I have to confess I try to sleep with it and her. I try to summon her to me by whispering into her velvet pelt. I stroke myself with it and her. I press it close up to my nose and nuzzle her. Her recovering hair would feel like this, I think. And can I say I take some strength from her? For while these lengthy hours pass, while I am sunk into these lonely furrows of the night, I think I find or dream or have delivered to me by the spirits of the shawl a sense of what I ought to do before King Edmund, as Mr Quill and I once christened him, vassals me entirely. I wake to a chilling clarity, as if my body has been swept with frost. Frost and furrows. That's the prompt. I know my duty now. I have to put the earth to plough. The time has come to put the earth to plough, no matter what the Jordans say. The frost will finish what the plough begins. Winter will provide the spring.

I am too cold and clear to sleep a moment more. So I stand up naked from my bed, pull on my boots and the abandoned Jordan smock for warmth, wrap myself inside the Beldam shawl and make my way outside. I mean, I think, to lay a trap for her. Or at least to test if she is living still, if she is walking out at night to tend her man and see on whom else she might exact continuing revenge for her father's death. I have to say the thought of that, the thought of her out in the night with a piece of stone gripped in one hand as her mallet and a spike of metal in the other, plus the image that I already have of Mistress Beldam luring Mr Quill into the woods and the sudden sweeping of her length of wood, the bloody compost of the forest floor, makes me as nervous of the dark as any foolish townsman ever was.

The sky is clear but it is too early for the moon to have fully crested the trees. I am determined to go down to the pillory. I'll hang the shawl close to the husband, but beyond his reach. She'll not miss it if she comes. Even in the flattest darkness its silver threads will glint and give away its place. But now that I am shivering outdoors and reminded by the deep-brewed quiet how neighbourless I am, I lose my nerve. I am not ready yet to face the husband. I don't want to chance the black and empty lanes tonight. So I only spread the velvet shawl out on the stone bench in the manor porch, exactly where her father has been spread, though I don't believe Mistress Beldam knows that detail. I touch its nap. I say farewell. I do not think that she will come at once.

I suppose she must have come at once. Because I've hardly regained Master Jordan's bed and laid my still-bruised head along the pillow of my arms, too tense and worried for sudden sleep, when I catch sounds that must be animal. The weather and the trees are random in their calls and songs. They are not rhythmic but unarranged and stray. These padding feet and footsteps are spaced and patterned. What I can hear is something on the outside of the house, something careful, something delicate and small. I do not dare to move inside my bed. I'll give away my sleeping place. The manor boards are loose and squeakier than mice. But by the time I've reached cautiously across the bed to pick up a candle holder in case I need to defend myself, should I need to hold her off, should I need to capture her, the sounds or footsteps have retired. The manor house is mine alone again. And finally I dare to sleep, though I am nervous what I'll dream or what I'll find when I wake up.

At dawn, I find the velvet shawl has gone. I cannot tell what that means to me because I do not know myself. Of course, it shows the woman is alive, unless some fox or badger has a taste for velvet shawls. But equally it indicates the chilling, thrilling probability that while the world around her sleeps, Mistress Beldam has been roaming like a living ghost throughout our lanes and corridors. She never sleeps. She's haunting us. She is patrolling every part of us. And now that all my neighbours have departed, and Mr Quill, perhaps, is sleeping with the cadavers, I am the only one who's left for her. Last evening she must have seen my coming home, my shoulders down. She will have seen where I decided to sleep. Last night, I must suppose, she will have watched the manor house and seen me standing, fearful as a child, at the porch door, dressed in Master Jordan's embroidered smock, every bit the gentleman, and wrapped in the beyond-her-station shawl. She will have seen me spread out her shawl on the stone porch bench. And when I closed the door on her I cannot think it rested in its place for any longer than a breath. She has been cold these last few nights. She has her purple velvet back again.

This is not what I expected when I agreed at Master Kent's prompting to serve as a Jordan man. I thought that though I would be troubled by my compromise, I would nevertheless find it comfortable to pass a little extra time in his employ amongst the places I have known and loved, indeed amongst the places where I have been known and loved myself. It would be a luxury, in fact. I'd have some privacy in which to grieve. Some autumn peace. But, standing here this morning in the deep shade of the manor porch, looking down on to the bench's cold and naked stone, I feel nothing but alarm, the rising, clenching fear of death. I was a fool to stay behind. I've had my chances to escape. I should have run down yesterday from Clover Hill and joined the pageant on its way to town. Perhaps, I should have left the village with the Carrs the other afternoon or with any other neighbours who could tolerate my company. Here's the truth of it: I should have got out of here as soon as Cecily died. I never could prove brave or blond enough to stay.

It's tempting even now to pack up and leave at once. I'm not indentured to this place, after all. I have no witnesses who'll care if I depart ahead of time. I've given Master Jordan my reluctant nod. But we hardly touched when we shook hands on it. My fingers only clacked against his rings. In the end it's not the nod or the clacking that are bound to keep me here. It's Master Kent's wide-stretched eyes of yesterday, and what I came to understand last night that they mean to me, what it is I have to do, what I should start, before I go, the folds and trenches I must leave behind. And so I dress, and arm myself with the old short sword with which the first Edmund Jordan is reputed to have felled a cattle thief more than thirty years ago and which, from the brown-stained point, I suspect has been used again more recently. Then I search the manor house for the master's chain of mostly unused keys. Mistress Beldam's husband need not serve his sentence out, so long as he agrees to help me with the plough.

I can only guess what he's thinking as I approach the pillory. I know that he will recognise at once how uneasy and shamefaced I am. There is no hiding it. My body feels as tense and knotted as a yew. I want to smile at him, to show I mean him well and that the blood-tipped sword I'm carrying need not be a cause for alarm, so long as he does not make it so himself. But the muscles in my face are not relaxed enough. My smile of greeting is fixed and artificial. I'm feeling sick to the stomach, actually. With apprehension, I suppose. But at least I've had a comfortable bed for the night and nearly enough sleep and I am thinking clearly. I know how I intend to spend the day. I cannot do it on my own.

If he is feeling any fear of me, my frozen face, the sword, my troubled bustle of intent, he does not have the strength to show it. I haven't thought how weakened he will be from staying still and doing nothing for so many days. We thought his and his father-in-law's punishment was mild when we sent them to the pillory for only seven days. That and the snapping of their bows, the clipping of their heads. 'Count yourselves as fortunate,' they were told. In other places, less hospitable than here, they might have expected a beating and a hanging. But, now that I am looking at him in the light — our past encounters have been largely in the dark — I can see how summer has sapped out of him, how he has paled, how he's hanging drily from the cross of wood. His arms were thick and oaky when they cuffed him there. I cannot say that they have become thin exactly, but they are certainly not muscular. They're drained of blood and energy. His wrists and throat are still bruised purple from when he has attempted to pull himself free. His eyes are hollowed out, from lack of proper sleep, perhaps. His lips are crusted; orange funguses, dry cracks. And his neck is swollen with insect bites and red with sores where he's tried to itch them on the wood.

'I have the key,' I say to the crown of his head, blackened now with new thick growth. He will not look at me. 'I've stolen it.' His forehead furrows. He might mean, So what? Or, Not before time. Or, My itchy neck is ready for your sword. Take off my head, and let's be done with it.

'I've stolen it,' I say again. He needs to know I'm taking risks for him. 'I have been instructed not to let you go until you've served every moment of a week. But I think you know, I'm the only friend you've had about these parts. I've never wished you any harm . . . ' His forehead furrows for a second time: So what? 'I'm free to walk away, if you prefer.'

'Do what you will.'

'What is your name?' I need to make a friend of him.

'It's mine to keep,' he says.

I'm tempted — momentarily convulsed by the impulse, in fact — to bring the sword down sharply on his neck. He is enraging me. I do not feel I've earned his disrespect. Instead, I only lay it flat across his infuriating forehead, and slowly tell him with my mouth no distance from his ear what his situation is: 'There's no one else can help you now. There's no one left excepting me. And, as you see' — I rattle them — 'I am the master of the keys.'

'Say what you want from me.'

'I want a little help with farming. For a day.' This time he nods. A day of farming is a task he understands. 'And there are other recompenses . . . for the time you've spent . . . with us.' I tell him briefly that the villagers have gone. The masters and the sidemen too. So he is free, as soon as we have finished with the field, to walk amongst our cottages and help himself to anything he wants. There're animals that he can take. And winter food. And if he chooses he can fill a wagon with our produce and our implements and draw them to the nearest marketplace. 'I'll make the pair of you' — he lifts his eyes, to mark my slantwise mention of his wife — 'quite rich. For just a single day of labour in my field.' *My* field, indeed. My true and only field. 'What do you say?'

'I say you are the man who holds the sword. I say you are the master of the keys.'

I hope to be less clumsy with the keys, but I

can't tell without testing them one at a time which will shoot the lock. My hand is shaking. I have to drop the sword down on the ground, so that I can use both hands. I put my foot on to the shaft, so that he cannot snatch it up as soon as he's released. Of course, he's in no state to snatch at anything. He sinks down to his knees the moment that I lift off the topmost beam. I've freed him to collapse. I let him sit and rub his legs and arms, while I stand back deciding if it's safe to trust the man. I think I've bought him with my promises of wealth. In all honesty, he could freely rub the blood back into his limbs, then club me to the ground and still be free to help himself to anything he wants, including my short sword. But there has been something in his manner that I trust. A scheming man would not have treated me with such disdain. He'd not have told me, Do what you will. A scheming man would have been more eager to offer help and quick to let me know his name. A scheming man would have lied, and he'd have made promises to break.

I take a chance and leave him recovering in the grass while I walk back along the lane towards the manor house. I mean to fetch him water and a little bread and cheese. I pick up windfalls for the man on my way back. I'm half expecting him to have fled, or armed himself with one of the church-yard stones, the sort his wife used if she murdered Willowjack, and used again on Mr Quill last night, in dreams. But he is still sitting by the pillory. His back is resting on its shaft. His legs are stretched out across the ground that he has scuffed for the past few days. He evidently still has pins and needles in his feet and arms. He is flexing his shoulders, and in pain. But I can tell that, not so long ago, he'd been a tough and worthy man. He's cut a bit of barley in his time. He looks much like a weary harvester, glad to have his apple, bread and cheese.

I tell him I'll return when he has eaten and is stronger. That frown again. But this time it's a frown that gives me confidence. The meal I've brought to him and he's accepted signifies a truce. He's broken bread with me. I do not think he's had such hospitality from any other villager or either of the masters. I take a further chance, and put the short sword at his feet. 'Defend yourself if anybody comes,' I say, though it doesn't make any sense for me to take that risk. No one will come. No one except his wife, perhaps, or Mr Quill, unlikely though that seems. But I've shown I trust him, and hold his future welfare close to me. Laying down my sword has made a comrade out of him, a fellow victim of the world. I am the scheming one, it seems. If Mistress Beldam's watching us, and I suspect she is, she will see that I'm a friend. I even whistle as I walk away to show how confident I am in him, and her.

But as soon as I'm out of earshot I let my whistling stop. Now I am talking to myself, drawing up a list of things to do. At first it feels like any other day at summer's end. There's fuel to cut and stack. There's field keeping and hedge trimming that must be done. There're falling walls and damaged barns to fix. This is the season of repair. It also is the season of prepare, when we make ready for the coming spring. I know that I will need some oxen for my task. We have a team of four allowed to pasture on the fallow fields and in the commons. They are sweet-natured animals, despite their crescent horns and deep bullish dewlaps. They have only to rest and eat all day and contend with nothing but the flies. The one thing they have to bother them is work, and that's sporadic hereabouts. It saves them from the butcher, though. So long as they are strong, they'll not end up as beef or leather. We'll not make cups out of their horns, or fashion bobbins, toys and dice out of their bones, or even boil down their hoofs for glue, until their natural deaths. Our oxen lead an easy life.

I can't remember exactly where we have tethered them, and so I have to go from gate to gate until I catch sight of their white snout patches and the insides of their comical pink ears. Their bodies — donkey-grey and mottled — blend in with the undergrowth. There're only two of them today. The smallest of the four. My neighbour families have taken the other two with them, first to draw their carts of family goods and then, perhaps, to trade them at the next village they reach. I rope the remaining pair, lead them on their strong, bone-weary legs down the lane and tie them at our tool-barn, where they're content to graze on fence weeds by the door. Oxen do not have the reasoning of horses and so they tend to be more pliable and patient. They're steadier; their winter keep is cheaper too. A horse will smell the saddle in another room or hear the pulling on of riding boots and start to kick in protest. An ox won't know he's needed for draught work until the moment that he has to pull — and even then he can't be bothered to protest.

I've always loved this little barn. It's ramshackle. It never mattered if the light got in, or rats, or rain: we didn't keep anything edible inside. We let the martins and the swallows nest in it, the robins too. We didn't mind if nettles set up house. When I was a greenhorn here and working none too usefully with the Saxtons on the land, I used to be the one they'd send — their big, slow-witted child — to collect and return their working tools. I think they had a lot of fun with me, demanding things they knew I could not recognise by name. Bring us some seed-lips and the suffingales, they'd say. We need some hog-yokes and a beetle wedge. Even when I'd learnt exactly what they meant, I'd still persevere with bringing back the least required of implements — a mould spear when they meant a cradle scythe; a weed hook when they wanted one for reaping — just for the pleasure of their laughter. And also for the pleasure of having to visit the tool-barn once again.

Today, the tool-barn is sweating in the heat, a heat that promises a storm. I need — we need, my volunteer and I — to get to work. The swing plough is the lighter of the two and nearest the barn door, but I know that with just two oxen instead of the usual team of four and only two pairs of hands to manage it, I need a set of wheels to support the beam at its fore-end. To plough today without a set of wheels would be too difficult and punishing. I'd not get any depth of furrow. The implement would throw its weight against the stilts and handles, and nothing we could do would tame it. So, I pull the swing plough to the side, and in the slanting shafts of light, busy with the dust that I am throwing up, I find the parts of the second plough, the one with wheels. I pull them clear and start to line them up outside the barn.

I do not need to go back to the pillory for my help. He is standing with the oxen, watching me. All three of them are watching me. He must have heard the clatter of the tools, and understood that he should come. He's ready for the labour. I cannot say he seems a happy man, but at least he looks more upright than he did this morning. And his colour has improved, no longer donkey-grey and as mottled as the beasts. He's brought the sword with him, I see. But that seems sensible. He will not offer any help until I say he should. He doesn't even greet me. I am the elder man and might expect at least a nod. He does speak, though. 'Nose before ear,' he says, without any warmth or flavour to his voice.

I stand and nod at him, surprised. How has he understood so much? It's not a phrase I've heard for quite a while. Possibly he only means it plainly. He thinks I'm not a practised country man. He wants me to remember that when I put the plough parts together, the coulter knife that opens up the soil — the nose — must go before the share, the wider blade. And that giant's arrow-head which cuts the furrow must go before the mouldboard — the ear — that throws the ridge. Only a fool or a townsman — me, he thinks, perhaps — would attempt anything different. Without the coulter at the front, the earth will not give way. Without the mouldboard at the rear, the earth will not be sufficiently turned.

But there is a greater meaning to the phrase. It is a warning — amongst country folk, at least — that life should be allowed to proceed in its natural and logical order. In other words, you do not eat before you cook, you do not weave before you shear, you do not attempt to light the fire until you have the kindling, and — to the point — you cannot reap your corn until you've ploughed and sown seed. He's obviously guessed what this day of work will be. He understands its greater meaning too: that ploughing is our sacrament, our solemn oath, the way we grace and consecrate our land. Not to mark our futures in the soil before the winter comes is to say there's no next year. I cannot admit to that. The coming spring must be defended. So, we'll put the nose before the ear. And then we'll plough.

'Come help me, then,' I say.

As he moves towards me, I can tell he must have been a ploughman in the past, before he was a newcomer. His skew is very slightly whiffed, another country phrase. You can always spot a ploughman from his uneven legs, they say: the long one's for the furrow and the short one's for the ridge. So I let him do the assembly work. I steady the share-beam while my new associate secures the blades, the mouldboard and the yoke. And then we set off for the barley stub, a pair of willing oxen and a pair of working men, intending to stir and loosen soil one final time.

The barley field has lost much of its spruce since harvesting. It takes only a few days of neglect for weeds and tares to settle in. Already there are newcomers, a tough-leafed smear of green where there was rusty gold. But still the marks my neighbours made are there to read for anyone that knows them well. That *knew* them well, I ought to say. The stubble has preserved their signatures. Here is our proof we brought the harvest in ourselves. I can tell where neighbour Carr and men like him — thorough, puritanical — have swept their scythes. The cut is low, the stubble short, no longer than a thumb. They haven't missed a blade of straw, and I am sure they won't have missed much barley either. Gleaners shouldn't step in neighbour Carr's unstinting wake, unless they don't want any ale for the winter evenings. The wavy cut is Brooker Higgs's best work. He's always busy talking when he reaps. His head is raised. His circles are too large. The more he reaches out, the more of the corn he misses. The tallest stub, up to the knee in places, is eager children's work, or the best that Willy Kip with his bad back can do. His portion looks as if the field was the victim of a massacre. Some horsemen came and, leaning from their saddles, felled the barley with their swords.

It seems an age since I was here with Mr Quill and Master Kent. We'd named our Gleaning

Queen and the master had said what he always says about 'this noble day', how in order of their station everyone and everything would benefit from gleaning — the families who worked so hard, the thoughtless cattle and the thankless geese, and finally the hogs. He had not said that hogs precede the oxen and the plough. He had not reminded us that this once-was barley field was set aside for winter-planted wheat. He had not promised that bread would follow beer. I remember thinking, bitterly, So our master's dreams for us do not include another crop. Our final harvest must have come and gone. I remember Master Jordan's words: 'You'll never need the plough again.' We'll see.

Mistress Beldam's husband has taken charge. I'm left to lead the animals and urge them on, flicking their pink ears. He grasps the plough handles and plants his feet into the soil, leaning back in expectation of the pull. He has to find a leverage that takes account of cattle, beam and soil, and finding it ennobles him: I've not seen his face so passionate up till now, or so full of consequence. He knows what ploughing is. If anyone is watching — and I hope Mistress Beldam is — it will look as if he's pulling against the oxen rather than working with them, that he's the strongest of the three. Just for today, he's walking on a field in heaven rather than on earth, he's ploughing up the lands of time, marking out the ridges and the furrows of a trying life. I can tell he has debts to settle of his own. Did not Mr Quill say that these newcomers were fugitives from sheep themselves, exiles from their own commons? That would explain the man's evident keenness to commence. We've broken bread together. Now he wants to break the earth with me. We'll liberate the spirits of the soil. We'll let the little devils breathe.

The key to ploughing is to hold a steady line, to be symmetrical, a skill I never quite mastered. I point down the field at a tapered oak which stands high above the hedgerow in the dell. That is the headland we will be aiming for with our first cut, I say. I fancy that even the oxen lift their heads and take a line on it. They place it in the middle of their horns. The oak is known for being still. It will not duck its head or lean, no matter what the winds might try. An oak is trustworthy. It wants the plough to find a true, straight way, then it can preside all year over a pattern that is pleasing to its eye.

The field seems limitless from where we stand, and beyond our mastery. It would normally take twelve days to plough its stubble under, even if we had our usual team of four oxen, and twenty brawny men to help and take their turns. But we are only two, and we do not mean to make a meal of it. We mean to make only a day of it. A narrow scar is all we have in mind: a field length down, the headland turn, a field length back. We will, though, do our best to make a noble and an honest scar. It will be straight and proud if good fortune labours at our sides. The single central ridge will be a proper height, the pair of furrows deep. 'This will be . . . to all of our advantages,' I tell my helpmate, hoping to provoke a conversation. But he stays silent. He loops the reins over his head, with a practised hand and a fitting nonchalance, and holds them taut round his right shoulder and under his left arm. I flick the oxen. We begin. Three steps, and already we are opening a top and putting up a high-backed slice of soil.

It is not long before he's whistling. His ridge and furrow channel the tune as we delve across the field. A ploughman's whistle has the strength to soften clods and break up stones. A ploughman's whistle warns the soil a blade is on its way. I am so satisfied I cannot stop myself from chattering. I'm telling him about the many, endless troubles of the week. I talk of Cecily, and Charles Kent, my boyhood friend. I tell him what a brave and decent man Mr Quill has proved himself to be. Oxen are noble creatures, I say. They work. But sheep 'from what I've heard' — what's his experience? — are helpless beasts: 'We'll have to wait on them like slaves on lords, come spring. Like fools.' I can't be sure if he is listening. He will not cease his whistling. But we both have busy lips this afternoon, and we are intimate through toil. Anything that's shared across the backs of oxen is intimate. We make our way towards the dell, and make our way back to the top-end gate. Now our wheels are clogged with mud. I have to free them every twenty paces with a heavy kick and, when that fails, with my bare hands. The rooks and starlings pick the furrows in the damp wake of the plough.

I make my ploughman stand away this afternoon when we have cleaned the blades and put the plough back in its place, and let the oxen roam off where they will. This is a task I want to finish without his help. I barrow in a bag of wheat seed for winter planting and use a casting shovel and some sacking in the corner of the field to select the heaviest grain for my baskets. I know I ought to let the strip of turned soil lie and mellow for a week or so, or at least let it be broken down by the rain, which has already begun to lay its own seed on the ground. But there's no time. Good practice must be sacrificed. I leave Beldam's husband resting in the corner of the remaining scrub, and sweep my seeded hands across the land, the richest of all scatterings. The farmer in me — yes, I can boast of that — knows that the best cruel nurture for this early crop is that after a week or two of growth its green ribbons are crushed by rolling. That way, the ground is firmed. The plants can take a steady grip. Wheat — like men and women — benefits from being crushed. Crushing makes it fit to stand up all the better. But there is only this afternoon for making good, for marking my revenge, my countryman's revenge, on Edmund Jordan and his sheep. This narrow sweep of wheat will be my farewell gift. So I walk the furrow for the final time, in the strengthening drizzle, taking it as a blessing that the seed corn is being watered the instant that it leaves my palm.

It is on my way up from the dell, with perhaps little more than a hundred paces and fifty sweepings of my hand remaining, that the light begins to fail. I turn to look, beyond the hedgerows and the pyramidal oak, at the dark horizon rearing deep and solid with grey-on-purple clouds. The few remaining scraps of blue blink barely brighter than an eye. What sunlight there is hardly makes a mark upon our field, though on the wood end of our land its best surviving ray is broad and strong enough to radiate and rim the beeches' pale bare branches, the grasping talons of the ash, and the high-veined frettings of the elms. Then it falls and slowly beams from common ground to field, as if searching for something. It is reluctant to depart. It even catches smoke pots and roofs before it lifts again to paste its silver on the clouds. For a moment, they are faced with light. Our field is black. It's shiny, suddenly. And then the day is gone. Its candle has been snuffed, or drenched. That is the end of it.

Dusk has deepened now. If it wasn't for the rain, I could be walking through the steep-domed, unlit chamber of a great cathedral, roofed by coal-black vaults of cloud. This downpour has not got the force to last. But for the moment it takes hold. The clouds carried too much weight before they reached this place. I can almost hear them sigh with relief as they let go their load. The furrows in our barley field are already brimming and draining off like streams in flood. The clouds intend every single seed I've spread to have its year's supply of drink in one delivery. The earth turns sticky. It clings heavily to my feet, and lards my legs with every step I take. It's hard work even walking in it now. I look up to the corner of the field, and wave at where I last saw Mistress Beldam's husband. I call out even, although my words are washed away. But anyway I think the man has gone already. He will have had his fill of late of being out in all weathers. He will have gone into the cottages or taken shelter in the barn. For an instant I imagine him in Mistress Beldam's arms amongst the field and pasture tools, amongst the nettles in the dark. She is getting wet and cold as she clings on to him.

I am excused, I think, for wondering if I am the only one alive this afternoon with no other living soul who wants to cling to me, no other soul who'll let me dampen her. The day has ended and the light is snuffed. I'm left to trudge into the final evening with nobody to loop their soaking hand through mine. And no one there to lift their hats, as our traditions say they must, when brought on by chaff and damp I cannot help but sneeze, an unintended blessing for the field. But I'd be lying if I said I felt as dark and gloomy as the clouds. I think I'm thrilled in some strange way. The ploughing's done. The seed is spread. The weather is reminding me that, rain or shine, the earth abides, the land endures, the soil will persevere for ever and a day. Its smell is pungent and high-seasoned. This is happiness.

15

My ploughman's happiness did not survive the night. Once it was safely dark and the storm had very nearly passed, I stepped out of Kitty Gosse's home hoping to catch a wink of candle-light or hear the knot and knit of voices — the Beldam couple reunited thanks only to my own leniency and maybe ready now to show some gratitude. I could not imagine they'd be hard to find. They surely would have slept indoors, somewhere in our row of cottages and within earshot of my own refuge. Why would they not have slept indoors? They must have known that here was now an abandoned spot and it was safe to help themselves to any bed they found. I'd sniff them out. I would be truly neighbourly, and call on them. Surely I deserved their company.

What moonlight found passage through the clouds misled me once or twice with its glints of silver catching on the puddles or in the rain damps on the roofs. I took them briefly as a sign of life. But candle-light is warmer and more intimate than any moonlight. It will not send a shiver down your spine as these cold glisters did. Orange was the colour I was looking for. I ventured for fifty steps or so along the muddied lane, hoping but not quite expecting to discover the Beldams. But, even though I harked my neck and ears about as alertly as any hunting owl, I could not make out any whispered words or catch the night-time mutter of a lovers' busy bed.

I was both sorry and relieved to find no ducking candle-light. What would I have done if, when I discovered the glow of household flame or caught the cloying whiff of melting wax, I also heard her crying out with ... let me call it gladness? I do not want to think I would have crept up like a cat outside the chicken coop and spied on them. I'd rather imagine myself as their good friend, their warm-hearted visitor, wanting nothing from them but some friendliness. So I hope I would have stood a respectful distance from their door and simply called out my name, declared myself to them. 'It's only Walter, come to talk.' It's only Walter come to make amends. It's only Walter come to share your oval den of candle-light and breathe the warm air of your room. I sorely needed fellowship.

I found no fellowship. I couldn't see or hear a trace of them. A leather pot would be my only bedmate for the night. Kitty Gosse always had a good supply of greenish barley ale. 'I find it beneficial,' she explained. Certainly, she slept on it and woke on it whenever I spent the night with her, and must have done the same when I wasn't there. It dampened down the sorrows of her widowhood, she claimed, though if anything she was more dampened down by it when Fowler Gosse was still alive. She's always had a loyal thirst, that woman. A single pot has usually been enough for me. I am reluctant to get drunk. I wasn't born to it. But last night, after I failed to find my only neighbours, I chased off my own sorrows with enough ale, as we say, to drown a bag of puppies in. For whom should I stay sober, and for what?

The first two pots were cheering companions, though not as fortifying as I'd wanted. I think I expected to take extra courage from the ale, a courage greater than a ploughman's, anyway. I was hoping that my animal response would not be goat's, or pig's, or dog's. I don't need drink to make me lecherous, or obdurate, or even barking mad. No, I wanted to be as drunk as a bull and ready for a brawl, ready to be strong and reckless. Ready for today. I persevered, heroically, with widow Gosse's ale. I do not think I much enjoyed the taste, or the leaden feeling in my arms and legs that it produced so rapidly, but I did enjoy the loosening of my anxieties. The next two pots of ale left me more spirited, as I'd hoped, but also more bemused and fanciful. I conjured up some company for myself. I invented visitors. They came up to the cottage door and knocked. I welcomed them, out loud, the fulsome host. But then, of late, I've done that often, when I haven't had even a sniff of ale. A widower will first talk to himself, then — tired of that — he'll have a noisy conversation with a candle flame or with the shifting shadows in his room, which he persuades himself are family.

Last night, the flames and shadows were those few men and women I most wanted to embrace. I imagined taking this reverie of friends down to the plough-scarred field at first light so that they could inspect my labours, and the evidence of my boldness and my disobedience. I lined them up, my seven sober witnesses. I stood them at the end of Kitty Gosse's bed. Mr Quill was soundless, shadowy. He was the bravest of us all. I'd prove to him that I could be daring too. The widow herself was there, of course. She always said she thought I was a cautious man. She counted me a civil owl, too quick to hoot, too scared to show my talons to the world. Well, she would see my talons soon and how I'd scratched a trench into the soil. Beside her, looking down at the back of his stubby, how-to hands, still avoiding my glance, was neighbour John. I'll not forget him pulling back away from me the last time he came to my cottage door. I flush even to think of it. 'Lord help you, Walt, if you're deceiving us,' he'd said. 'Lord help you, John, if you believe I would,' was my reply. Now he would see how defiant I could be on his behalf. Then came Master Kent, my milk cousin. Again he fixed me with the briefest show of eyes, as wide and white as eyes can be. They were asking, 'Have you made the land ours again?' The Beldams nodded their encouragement. They trusted me. 'You are the man who holds the sword,' the husband said. The woman pulled aside the velvet shawl and showed her wide-cheeked, thin-lipped face, her button nose, her bella-donna eyes. Nothing ever frightened her. And finally my thrush was there, my Cecily, full-throated and alive again. I had forgotten what a plump and honeyed creature she could be and how light a voice she had. 'Walter, Walter, make me proud of you,' she said.

226

I lifted my fifth pot and toasted all of them. We were the best of friends. I should have stopped the drinking there, while I had friends, while there was still some singing in the ale. Two further pots provided only tears — and anger too. The final pot was like a cudgel to the head. I would have dropped asleep at once if I hadn't had to go outside to clear both my bladder and my gut. That sobered me a bit. The night air helped. I cannot say, though, that my head had cleared or that my feet were no longer tangled. But I was soon unruffled enough to listen once again, between the heaving spasms of my drunkenness, for any human sounds, other than the voices I'd just invented for myself and the usual mouthings of the stars. There were none, of course. Whatever courage I'd discovered briefly in drink had by now been almost entirely gagged and pissed into the once sweet-smelling garden, and I no longer could pretend to be the hero of the field. I was too wretched for a hero of the field. I could hardly stand, indeed, and either had to sleep amongst the ghosts of Fowler Gosse's double-marigolds and thyme or take my spinning head back to its pillow in the room. Now my seven witnesses crowding at the far end of the bed were mocking me. Is that the only stand you'll take against the Jordans and their sheep, they asked. Is that your fiercest riot and unrest, to put a pair of dumb beasts to the plough and mark your outrage on a field? Our enemies will quake at that, your knee-deep furrow and your knee-high ridge. Those armies will retreat at that. What next? Will you perhaps cut back some weeds or fix a fence to spread more fear into the hearts of those who do not wish our village to survive? Only a townsman could be so timid, Walter Thirsk, and still mistake it for rebellion.

Then I slept, though poundingly and fitfully. My dreams were punishing. I knocked on doors in them — but no matter what I did or said, no one would let me join them in their candle-light. Then my audience of friends and witnesses were standing at the bottom of the bed again, hard-faced. Mistress Beldam hurried forward, light-footed as a little deer, and pushed her velvet shawl into my mouth, to stop my cries of pain. She placed her tethering prong against my head above my ear. I could feel the metal in my dented skin. She hit it once. Then all the others took their turns in striking it home, double-handed, with the square and heavy stone that had killed Willowjack. Even Cecily. She was the cruellest of them all. She said, 'It's not enough. The ridge and furrow are not enough. You've really haven't done enough.'

What was soon clear, once I'd woken late this morning with a drumming head, not feeling brave at all, and gone outside to sober up on air again, was that the Beldams had spent the night in the best rooms of the manor. I was surprised by their audacity. I was not pleased, to tell the truth, though I suppose a couple as young and poor as them will have always wondered about the insides of a master's house. If they'd ever hoped to sleep in airy space and any opulence, no matter how shabby, this might have been their only chance. I can imagine that they took Master Jordan's bed, exactly as I had done the night before. I only chose the widow Gosse's bed last night, rather than returning to the manor, because my evening there had seemed improper, afterwards — though I am the manor-keeper for the moment. So if it was improper for me to wrap myself in Lucy Kent's old riding-cape and fall down in the cushioning of carpets, cloths and arrases, surely it was more so for these two passers-by. I'd thought that only bats would have it after me, at least until and if one of the masters came back in the spring. The Beldams are not bats.

I shamed myself by standing in the cottage lane as grey-faced and disapproving as a piece of slate and shaking my ale-sodden head at the mauvish scarf of smoke that was being woven from the lower chimney stack. They must have lit the oven in the scullery. I did not want to guess what they used for fuel, what furniture, what parchments, deeds or books. Or what it was they cooked for their first meals together since the dovecote fire. Or, come to that, what might have happened underneath her velvet shawl last night. I was resolved to hold my tongue. I'd keep away from them, and not only because I felt too ill for conversations of any kind. They were not my business any more. If only I could find the courage and recover from my seven pots, then there were things to do for Cecily. I knew I hadn't done enough for her.

I found my courage in the woods, by chance. I wanted to give dear Mr Quill a final opportunity to show his face, to bare his waxy, trowel-shaped beard again. I'd call his name and let the echo seek him out. I took the lane towards the place where the Beldams first set up their den and followed round the outer edge of Turd and Turf, so silent then and glistening with last night's rains. The storm had quelled the usual stench to some extent. The carcass domes were mostly hidden by the water. Had there been anybody there to follow me, I'd appear a halting figure with legs as weary as any oxen's and shoulders as tucked as any goose's. I could not help but stagger on the rougher ground. For once I felt like Mr Quill must have felt since his sudden palsy as a child, wooden from the shoulder to the ribs, a man who was not fitted for outdoors. But still I did my best to not look to my left, despite the raucous foraging of our abandoned pigs, happy to be free and in the mire. I was in no hurry to discover evidence of Willowjack or what little remained of the short man from the pillory. Nor did I want just yet to risk discovering the body of my Mr Quill. I'd rather believe for a few moments more what was most likely true. He had been warned. He ran away — or lurched away, I ought to say. He was already safe. But I had to be sure, or surer anyway, before I could feel free to lurch away myself.

The longpurples were beaten down by rain. You wouldn't name it Blossom Marsh today. The major colours were the greyish-greens of goat-willows and the purple-browns of beech — but there was no sun to liven them or paint reflections in the flood. I found a raft of almost solid ground, then dared to look across the bog. There was an oblong monument of piled stones I hadn't seen before. The Beldam daughter had been dutiful and loving, unobserved by us. She couldn't let her father rest without a stone memorial. There wasn't any sign of Mr Quill's distorted frame. Not above the surface anyway. So I spread my legs and cupped my hands and called his name, despite the head pain that the calling out intensified. I summoned 'Mr Quill' and 'Mr Earle', until the two names caught the booming echo in the dell and merged to make a distant liquid *L*. The pigs were not disturbed at all. Shouting doesn't bother them. But I was loud enough to set some rooks and pigeons in the air, and cause some crashing through the undergrowth. A deer. If Mr Quill was in the woods or hiding somewhere underneath a roof, he would have heard — and recognised, I hope — my voice. I listened then. I half expected his reply. Nothing answered other than the echo, and the muffled sneezing of a skulking snipe. I must have tried a dozen times before I started swaying back towards the open fields.

I found the fairy caps growing in an oval ring between two exposed root arms under the goat-willow hedge which we have sometimes coppiced for fencing. At least, I think they were fairy caps. It is the time of year for fairy caps. I've seen some picked ones recently and believe I'd recognise their pointed parasols and purple gills. It seems a lifetime ago but it is hardly seven days since the Derby twins and Brooker Higgs jaunted along the lane in front of my cottage with their bloating faces and their bloated sack of toadstools. 'Had any luck?' I'd asked them. Oh, what bitter luck indeed. I can still almost smell their forest spoils, the caps, the shawls, the giant moonball beneath their dampening of leaves and the smoky cloud of yellow spores. I think it's reasonable to say that if it were not for their foraging, there would not have been that fire in the dovecote and the loft. There would have been no men in the pillory. There would have been no slaughtering of Willowjack, or anything that followed on from that. I would not have drunk so much or suffered this throbbing headache. The fairy caps must take the blame for everything. It makes less sense to say there would have been no pasturing of sheep before next spring, that Master Jordan has been conjured up, like a demon, by the young men's flames, that without their flames he would have stayed where he belonged. In town. But I still feel the truth of it. The tinder of the giant moonball has brought misfortune to our land. The fairy caps have set our lives alight.

I think if I had not been wearied by the night and growing weary of myself, I might simply have passed those mushrooms by. But my body was still full of ale. I could smell it in my sweat and I could see it in my piss every time I stopped — and that was often, this morning — to relieve myself. My throat was sore from being sick. My head was, surely, just as tender as if it really had been hammered with a lump of stone and pierced with a metal prong. How else should I explain the deep crevice of pain behind my eyes?

232

I had been split and ruptured by that half-imagined prong.

Of course, I was a novice in the arts of drinking heavily. I was not prepared for such harsh penalties. I was ashamed to be so vulnerable, but also — like all drunkards on the dawn; I'd seen this in my neighbours many times — I was just a bit pleased with myself, pleased at my capacity, pleased that I had lived to tell the tale, pleased to know the innards of a pot at last. I wished that at least some of my old friends could witness me today, especially the ones who'd always been suspicious of my level-headedness, my reluctance to make myself insensible, no matter what the feast or celebration, no matter what misfortune had occurred. 'You do not truly love the barley, Walt,' they said, a terrible rebuke, and more evidence of my timidity. 'There's no fermenting you.'

I suppose it might have been partly this wanting to prove myself to them again and partly my ale-soaked lack of judgement — I'd loved the barley far too much last night and so could not be sound of mind — that made me bend and look more closely at the fairy caps. I only brushed them with my fingertips. All mushrooms are a fearsome sight and even worse to touch. These were as cold and high and clammy as a week-old corpse. But I suppose my brushing with my fingertips was enough for them to work their sorcery on me. I became their carrion at once. I'd given them a brief taste of my skin. Looking back from the more clear-headed safety of this afternoon, I can't explain my madness or their sudden taking hold of me. But if I recall it correctly — though good recall isn't something that has survived undamaged from this morning's loss and doubling of senses — that timid brushing with my fingertips provided me the courage I had sought and lost so quickly drinking ale. I half remember reaching out and cupping mushrooms in my palms. I pinched them firmly at their stems. Against all reason, I wanted to discover what or who they tasted of.

Firstly, though, my country wisdom halted me. I had to make sure these were fairy caps. I picked a single one, the one least touched, the one least bruised, by the brushing, cupping, pinching of my hands, and pressed it to my nose. It's said that if a fungus is harmful to eat, you'll sneeze on smelling it. Its spores will warn you they're not safe. I did not sneeze. I smelt the forest and the earth, the dampness of a fast-retreating year, the acridness of leaf mould, and a kitchen odour which I could have taken for yeast but yeast that was soured from neglect. I can only think that I was insanely hungry, or more damaged than I'd thought possible by Kitty Gosse's ale and the nightmares that followed it, or suicidal, even, because I did not hesitate. The man who always hesitates did not, on this occasion, hesitate. He popped the mushroom in his mouth and started to chomp down on it. It did not taste as he expected it to.

The one and only time I tasted fairy caps before, with John Carr when we were younger men, we'd soaked them first in honey. I remember they were sweet and sinewy. I don't remember tasting this reasty mix of horse's hoofs, burnt hair and candle wax, nor the leather chewiness. All I could do was break and tear the mushroom with my teeth and swallow the pieces whole. I ought to have stopped after the first piece and let the mushroom declare itself. If there was any poison in its flesh and now in mine, then let it poison me in no great quantity. But he who dithers is a mouse, I heard my neighbours say. I would not allow myself to be a mouse. Only a townsman would be that timid. I finished that first fairy cap but, for an age, it produced nothing in me but a belch — and the certain knowledge, coming to me from thin air, that the one was 'not enough', that only three of them would bring the courage I required. I did not know what voice had whispered that number to me, but I was sure that three would do the trick. One for Brooker and one each for the twins. I would be as mad as they were on the day they played with fire. I wanted their immodest fits of laughter. So I picked another pair of fairy caps. I knew better than to chew this time. I swallowed them whole so quickly that I almost choked and coughed them up. I had to sit on the grass bank, amongst the willow roots, and catch my breath. What living fairy caps remained were growing in between my knees. I snapped and picked the surviving twenty or so, the ones I did not mean to eat, and tossed them towards Turd and Turf, waxy titbits for our happy pigs. And then I waited. I do remember that I stretched out on the still-damp ground and waited. Simply lingering.

I must have been expecting to experience again what has been beyond forgetting all these years: the dancing lights and merriment that John Carr and I encountered when we first tasted fairy caps, the melting trails that haloed everything. We were like sun-drenched butterflies and then we were like moon-struck moths. It was a blissful afternoon and night. I've not regretted it. What I hoped for most was the enormous fearlessness I'd felt, beneath that long-lost moon that went from pale to blue to red. But what came first this morning, before any melting haloes or oblivion, was a stretch of paralysing dread. I feared that what I'd eaten were not fairy caps at all, but something much more poisonous and wrathful. I was alarmed. And with good cause. I hadn't even been born, let alone become a villager, when it happened, but I have heard the tale so many times: one of the Kips' great-grandmothers picked by mistake some red-top toadstools thinking they were edible. She baked them with a rabbit she had snared. She poisoned both her husband and a son. She would have died herself except, as was the habit in those days, the men dined first; the women had their suppers cold.

I could not help but think this morning of the dying Kips and how they would have felt at first, like me, heavy and unsteady, sick. And how quickly — certainly before their pie had gone quite cold enough for the woman to come to table — they would have begun to cry out with the pain. Already I had stomach cramps, as if I'd eaten palsied meat and it was sitting in my gut

236

just biding time. Just killing time, perhaps, before it started killing me. My time was up. Certainly the fairy caps were keen to keep me on the ground. They would prefer it if I sank into the grass, if I became as rooted to the soil as them. Though stand I must. If I wanted to survive the day, I had to stand and rest my arms against the flat trunk of a beech so that my stomach could heave enough — yet again — to bring up these mushrooms. Yet, no matter what I tried to do, my body was both too slow and too fast to offer any balance when I attempted to get to my feet. The fairy caps would have their wish granted unless I could reclaim all the bones in my legs and arms, which were as spongy as the mushrooms themselves; I lay out flat again, spread myself across the ground, and waited to sleep or die or send down roots and put out leaves. But at last I succeeded in raising myself high enough off the ground to rest on my arms and knees, like the commonest and most wretched of beasts. I gagged and coughed but nothing came, except a skein of spittle and the overwhelming stink of barley ale. And then I flattened out again.

I was lucky, though. I must have been. I have survived to tell the tale, although there's not much of a tale to tell. Most of the day is robbed from me. Anything could have happened. What might not have happened? I'm aching, though. Whatever it is I've done was strenuous. What I recall is hugging animals, and finding gorgeous horrors on the grinning bark of trees, and endless tumbling. Everything was newborn and familiar.

My heart beats wildly at the memory. One picture haunts me. I was pinioned to the ground, just weighted to the ground, a seed, expecting only to be wheat and wanting only to be wheat and hoping only for the spring. The plough was heading for my back. Its blade was close. Its blade would bury me. I heard the rattle of the beam and the gritty churning of the furrow. That was the worst and best of it.

After that the fairy caps began to let me go. I had a twin, a standing twin, who came to rescue me. This other one who had my face, who looked like me and smelt like me and sounded like me, had got me by my shoulders and I was being pulled. I was being gleaned by him. My head came up and back. My bones solidified at last. My sudden twin put me on my feet and made me sensible again. Then, as far as I remember it, I walked the bounds once more towards midday, saying my farewells and making good, freeing any animal that was still tethered or penned, closing all the cottage doors, bolting every shed and barn, shutting gates. I stood and stared across each field, recalling in my reverie how tended and how tilled our years had been, how finely grained our lives. I know I passed the church ground where we never had a church and never will. I know I spent some moments standing on the turf where Cecily still rests, and Lucy Kent as well. My feet were heavy, not with soil, but with a leaden weariness. I think I felt like oxen might feel, if they weren't so innocent. Yoked to the troubles of the world. But then again, in parallel perhaps, I had a sense that I was flying for a while. At least, I seemed to see our land as Mr Quill has seen it with his brushes and his pens, his charcoal and his paints — just patterns and patchworks, as beautiful as embroidered cloth, not real in any way, but far below and not quite reachable. Time and distance seemed to play no part. Colour was the master. And then I was most like a dove, its cote destroyed by fire, circling in plumes of smoke, without the prospect of a roof at night.

But now my quest, my heady pilgrimage, my madcap, stupored odyssey, is either coming to its end or resuming on a calmer note, and I am standing in the courtyard of the manor house alone. I cannot tell you how it came about. I don't recall the final steps I must have taken to arrive, or how long I have been standing within a few paces of the porch, just staring, childlike, at the door, but I am here and it is me. I've never been this certain of a truth or more determined to proceed. Someone has packed two bags for me — that sudden twin, perhaps. I can't remember doing it myself. But I see that I have been equipped with everything a man who travels on his own two feet through empty lands must have with him. There's water in a leather pouch. There's dried bacon, biscuit, cheese. There is my brimless working cap, my jerkin and my rain-cape. I see the silver spoon, our wedding gift, tucked into one of Cecily's handkerchiefs. Someone has pulled off my thin shoes and given me my walking boots. I have a sturdy stick. My arms are folded at my back like wings. I swear that they feel feathery.

16

What strikes me in the manor house is how the smell has altered from when I slept here two nights ago. It hasn't smelt like this for many months, not since lady Lucy died. I will not say the odour is less manly, although of course this has been, all too recently, the lodging of at least six men apart from Master Kent. Master Jordan himself brought in the odours of a pomander and his casting bottle, so there was a hint, in his room at least, of what is womanly and superior. But the manor smells more homely this afternoon. There is the scent of family, of cooking for a family. Even from the hallway by the great front door I can smell fresh bread and a cooling grate, and other odours that belong to washing and to roasted meat, other odours that don't belong to recent times. Mistress Beldam has evidently marked the liberation and return of her husband by setting up home in our finest premises and helping herself to the manor's storeroom and its larder. She has been loving him.

The downstairs parlour door beyond which Master Kent used to sleep is closed. I hesitate. I am expecting to find them on the other side, despite the silence of the room, despite the stillness of the house. My instant image has the husband sitting on a bench, naked, wrapped up in her velvet shawl. The clothes he wore and muddied at the pillory and laboured in yesterday at the back end of our plough are freshly washed and draped at his side; bitter with lye, they are drying at a dancing, open fire. The trestle table there — the oaken table where I last took break-fast, with both the masters on the morning of their departure — is provisioned for eating. Three places have been set. I am anticipated there. The bread, still warm, is cut in wedges. A steaming pot contains a meaty stew . . . and Mistress Beldam holds the wooden serving spoon. Well, what I'm seeing, what in fact I'm hoping for, is the domes-tic scene that everybody wants to discover when finally they're home: the meal, the woman and the fire.

There is no proof, but I have determined it was the Beldams who made me ready for the journey, packing everything from water to the spoon. I am pleased to believe it was their way of thanking me. I try to count away the days. Is this the sixth or seventh day? I'm not quite sure, but I know the husband would without my clemency still be in the pillory this afternoon. It's possible they found me in my stupor, walking on unsteady legs, my chin and chest damp and crusty from my vomiting, and gave me some tonic or some salve to rescue me from mush-rooms and from ale. Then they packed these bags for me and placed me in the courtyard, to let the breeze clear out my head and lungs, while they went in and made a meal for us. I can't be sure of anything. But I would like to think it so. I would like to think they carried me, my arms around their shoulders, the husband's and the wife's, and made me safe and ready for the roads. Now they will feed me, and I will leave this village in their company. So, I am feeling ravenous, and long to plunge my black and shiny beak into some food.

All they've left behind for me are smells. Whatever was cooked this morning has been eaten, drop and speck. The only hint of new-baked bread is a wooden board, a carving knife and crumbs. The only evidence of meat and stew is unwashed platters, licked clean of everything, it seems, except for a scrap of bacon rind and smears both of gravy and of sugared blackberries. The only sign of washing hanging on the bench to dry is a salty lustre on the wood. The fire is open but it's dying back. Whatever homely times took place in the manor's parlour overnight and this morning ended long ago. In fact, it looks as if the room has been stripped of all its comforts and any remaining provisions. Two pairs of practised hands have rummaged everything. The master's coffer where he stores his papers and his documents has been tumbled over on to its lid. The mattress on his wainscot bed in the corner of the room has been dragged across the floor and slit open with a blade. Someone was hoping to find hidden silver, or some jewellery. Lucy Kent's small loom, one of the two reminders of his wife that my master kept in this parlour, is missing. Her hairbrush too. He always kept it on the mantelshelf, still twined with her long hairs.

I cross to the far side of the parlour and step over the gutted mattress into the scullery. The doors of the crockery cupboard are hanging open, and most of the familiar jugs and dishes from Lucy Kent's dowry are missing. The remains of one cracked cup, its handle snapped, is resting on its side and rocking slightly. The little larder too seems empty, though maybe it was emptied by the Jordan men while they were staying here. I know that there were winter hams inside, and salt and suet, and a row of different preserves. Someone has tipped over the master's honey jar and left it dripping on the floor. My walking boots are sweet with honey.

I hurry to discover what mayhem has been inflicted on the rest of the manor, though hoping that the damage is restricted to the parlour rooms and service corridor. But what I find is damage everywhere. A fury has swept through the place, a fury that reserved its wrath for mostly worthless things. In the downstairs rooms, there's not a table or chair that's resting on its own four legs. There's not a piece of cloth in place or any matting where it ought to be. Every floor is strewn with debris, including the shattered remains of Mr Quill's sweet-hearted fiddle. What isn't broken isn't breakable. What's in one piece has proved too tough to tear or snap. The disorder in each room is worse than any I witnessed on the day the sidemen pulled apart our village homes. I suppose that is because my master has so much more to disarrange than any of us, but also because the sidemen's searching was detached to some degree, impersonal, and so not quite as spiteful or as thorough. Master Jordan had required it done, and they were dutiful. But here the work has been completed by an enthusiast. And a pilferer. I am in too great a haste to carry out a leisurely inspection. This is no inventory, but I have become familiar enough over the many years to know where there should be tapestries and curtains in this house, where there once were table drawers and cupboards with valuables, where the pair of silver cups which Master Kent was given as a wedding gift by the cousin-in-law he was yet to meet had stood, where there was both costly furniture and the freely given hand-carved stool that Fowler Gosse's father made. The Beldams will find a market trader in the town or some eager tinker who'll happily exchange some food or money for these seized family goods. They'll sell the richer spoils. The Beldams have suffered at our hands. That is not deniable. But they've been feeding off us too. I think I feel betrayed by her, her keenness to punish everyone and everything for her calamities. I cannot say that I am being logical, or calm. Especially when I discover on an otherwise stripped-bare mantelshelf the bloody piece of square stone that was used to murder Willowjack. This is the house where horrors are preserved. This is the house where Kitty Gosse was tortured and abused, and Lizzie Carr, our little Gleaning Queen, has left her stain of tears.

It is no different in the gallery upstairs. The walls have been stripped. The fittings have been thrown aside. Even the side room where Master Jordan made his den and where I and possibly the Beldams spent a night has been plundered of every piece of cloth, each coverlet, each cushion and arras. Lucy Kent's old riding-cape has gone. Again, the heavy mattressing has been slashed.

I can't imagine that the man played much of a part in all of this. Such anger at the trimmings and the trappings of a house not worth the salvaging is woman's work, I think. A man takes vengeance on the flesh; a woman lashes out at anything that cannot bleed — unless it is an animal of course, a Willowjack, let's say. Many times I've listened to the tantrums and the arguments of married neighbours in our cottages. The men were woundless come the dawn, though their best breeches or favourite jugs, or possibly their dinners, had been thrown out along the lane with terrifying force. But many of the wives appeared next day nursing their twisted wrists or showing bruises on their faces, or even on one occasion — the Kips again — a scorch mark where William had snubbed out a burning candle in the centre of his wife's forehead. He'd branded her, he boasted. While he was out, she snapped his smoking pipe in half and stamped on all the pieces.

I find myself for the first time in many months in the lobby room at the far end of the long gallery. The spiral staircase here leads up to the attic and the turret, the hideaway where I once made my nest in my first season, before I met my Cecily and moved into the village. Or at least it would lead to that lonely suite of sloping lofts if the supporting timbers had not collapsed into the well with age and rot, and from disuse. The middle section has no treads or flights at all these days. The lower steps are treacherous. There are very few dependable balusters. Only last year at Master Kent's bidding I roped off the access, just in case any visitor was tempted to ascend — and then found himself descending rapidly, head first. Today I see that someone with a knife or sword has cut the rope away. The fibres have not been neatly severed but hacked aggressively. I imagine it will be the work of one of the sidemen, bored perhaps at being stuck in this dull house or, possibly, just trying out his blade after a tedious session with his whetting stone. I would not want to chance those stairs myself but it is clear that someone has, and recently. One of the treads is freshly splintered and I can see where hands have gripped the newel for support leaving traces, of what? Blood, or gravy, or even some of those preserves that have gone missing from the larder downstairs. I reach and touch. I cannot say that the traces are still damp, but they are sticky certainly. I hold my fingers to my nose. The smell is neither sweet nor savoury.

I stand in silence, or at least in as much silence as these creaking floorboards will allow. It's hard to isolate the sounds, to separate the ones coming from my own weight on the boards from those caused by the house itself. A timber house of several storeys such as this is seldom absolutely quiet. The building shrugs and breathes. It's like an old man shifting his hips to make his back more comfortable. A creak might denote not a footstep in the room above but the shifting of the roof frame or the settling of the wood.

246

Still, it's too late for such sensible opinions. I have already alarmed myself with several possibilities, the main one being that the Beldams have not left the manor yet as I thought but have heard me entering their door and — fearful that the masters have returned — taken refuge in the highest rooms. They've left the smudges of their hurriedly abandoned meal on the column of the unsafe stairs. I call out just as I imagined calling out last night when I was hunting for their company, 'It's only Walter, Walter Thirsk . . . ' But of course they do not reply. They would have gone beyond the attic and up the wall ladder into the turret, too far away perhaps to hear my shouts. They will be huddled in the corner of that space and fearful for their very lives.

If I was feeling fitter and less damaged by the only food and drink I've had all night and day — the pots of ale, the fairy caps; I haven't had a crumb besides — I might make a quicker and less noisy job of climbing up these stairs. At least, I could be less fearful. But as it is I feel nothing but foolhardy. If I fall or if the wood gives way, who's to hear me tumbling and who's to run down to my aid? And if my clumsy efforts are heard above, what's to stop the Beldams mistaking me for someone other than myself and standing in the shadows at the top of the stairwell until my head comes into view clearly enough to invite the welcome of a well-aimed kick or a blow from a length of wood? Nevertheless I climb, using the treads and strings at the edges of the stairs as my supports, and always gripping the central newel with at least one hand. I keep on talking too, as I go up, repeating my name, promising that I mean nothing but to forge my peace with them, to thank them even — if they truly were responsible — for getting ready my possessions for the journey out.

The worst part of the stair is the blind stretch reached neither by the downstairs lobby window light nor by the sharper attic light. I have to test each footing with my toes, searching for the most solid timber and then chancing my full weight on it. Only once does my footing fail me. My ankle's caught in splintered, wormy wood. I hear a piece of it clatter through the maze of stairs below. But after that either the going is easier or, having scared myself enough, I find the courage to proceed with more resolution. The pair of attic rooms is entirely empty except for some of Master Kent's abandoned junk: a broken chair, broken not by the Beldams but by the weight of Master Kent himself, as I remember, and long ago; some leather riding tack; the great, long travel chest in which I once stored my clothes; the painted child's cot which sadly was never put to use; a rusty brewing pan. Unlike in the downstairs rooms, however, these items have been left in peace. No one has upturned them, or thrown them about the place.

I turn at once towards the ladder mounted on the wall and climb the twenty rungs up to the trapdoor which will allow me entrance to the turret space. I half expect the trapdoor to be resistant to my push, weighted possibly on its upper side by Mistress Beldam and her husband standing on its boards, opposing me. But it swings open easily and showers me in dust. My eyes, once I have rubbed away the grit, are flooded with the full daylight of the unshuttered turret windows. I pull myself on to my feet, a little breathlessly. The floor is covered with the usual fallen scuff of under-roofs and with the undisturbed remains of bird nests and a waspery. It's obvious that no one other than myself has been up here for years. The view is mostly chimney pots and roofs. I cannot see into the courtyard, as I intended, to check that my stick and the two travel bags with my glinting silver spoon are safe and where I left them. But I can see out to the orchard and the unbuilt church beyond, and I can see our village roofs and fields.

★　★　★

What starts with fire will end with fire, I've heard it said. At first I do not spot the plume of smoke which, reluctant to rise on this almost windless day, has gathered on the tool-barn roof. I think at first it could be just a cloud of blackened dust — but dust does not behave as if it's weightless, dust does not billow or form up in rounded shapes such as those that are now lifting from the roof. Another plume of smoke has started up a little further down the lane towards the cottages, this time from the whitehouse roof. I am as yet not able to make out the unsteady burst and blaze of actual flames or even, from this high vantage point, hear their crack. Now the first of our twenty or so inhabited — let's say recently inhabited — cottages begins to offer up its smoke. It is the pretty home where Thomas Rogers played his pipe and Anne, his mother, raised her finchy voice. So far the smoke is so thin and undramatic that, if this was only chimney smoke, I might have taken it for nothing more than what was normal for tea-time in our village lane, with cooking and a row of blazing hearths. But by the time the fourth and fifth cottages have been set afire, the tool-barn and the whitehouse are leaping with orange light, and flames are running up their sides, blackening the wood. And by the time the fourth and fifth cottages are doing the same, the widow Gosse's home is breathing black and mine is coughing smoke.

I do not need to guess who's setting fire to us. Indeed, I see the evidence all too clearly. The Beldams have found themselves a cart and the pair of oxen that we used to plough our final mark into this summer's barley field. The husband has evidently taken me at my word. 'I'll make the pair of you rich,' I'd promised, and, so far as I can tell, looking down at their great load where they have left it in the clearing by the pillory, they have pillaged us exceedingly and have assembled quite a cargo for themselves, both from the village homes and from the manor house. I recognise my master's tapestries, his better chairs, his wife's old loom. I can even make out the several parts of the plough we assembled together yesterday. Was that just yesterday? I only shrug. Their father's death has paid for this, it must be said.

For the moment I can see and hear only the husband. He is sizing up the pillory, the great unwieldy cross of wood where he has spent the most part of a week. He proves himself to be as clever with an axe as he has been with a plough. His first strike is a little high. The oak of the upright is too hard for him, but lower down, where the timbers have been dampened and the surface worn away a bit by weather and by time, his axe bite takes a mouthful at first try. He cuts out the chip with a sideways blow, and then addresses his old resting place from the other side, until even I can see the hollow where the axe has landed. I hear his every strike. I do not think it takes him more than thirty, but I am no longer watching him. I have caught sight of the Mistress herself, my eyes drawn to her by the skittering of a narrow thread of smoke, the burning faggot she is holding as she hurries in and out of the final cottages, checking there is nothing left to steal and then setting fire to anything that is dry. Her head and shoulders are wrapped in velvet, to protect her from the smoke, I guess. She has my short-bladed sword in her free hand. I have forgotten how small she is. Her smoky trail is like a moth's, erratic, wilful, spirited.

I know I have to drag myself away from this high window. I do not believe that Mistress Beldam intends to part from here leaving the manor intact. When she reaches the last house of the village and has satisfied herself that everything is beyond rescue, she is bound to scamper down the lane, together with whatever livestock has been panicked by the blaze, to where her husband is now resting from his exertions, with the pillory as dead as mutton at his feet. Then they will continue through the orchard's apple strew to finish off the manor farm buildings left by Brooker Higgs, the Derby twins and their moonball. If there's to be a fire started in the dry wood of the downstairs rooms, I could not be in a worse place — in the high turret of a timber house with a wooden ladder, a collapsed staircase and a wide stairway to hurry down before I even reach the flames. Indeed, I wonder if this has been her plan all along, to lure me, through some sorcery beyond my understanding, to this upper space and then to bake me here.

I do not know what makes me pause when I reach the attic rooms. I do know that going down into the lobby should be speedier and less dangerous than coming up. Descents are not as weighty as ascents. I can simply slip and slide and keep my fingers crossed. I'll reach the safety of the courtyard very quickly. Then I'll gather up my things and be on my way before the woman catches me. All neighbourly and more-than-neighbourly feelings I've ever had for her are gone. She frightens me. She only frightens me. That woman carries blade and fire. But pause I do. I'm anxious suddenly, alarmed, and not by the prospect of a manor fire. Something else has caught my eye so thinly that, when I stop to check, I don't at first know where to look. Then I spot it for a second time. The oblong of dark that first I took to be a wedge of shadow under the great, long travel chest is looking now more like a seeping spill of blood.

He's lying face down, covered only with the chest's loose lining. But I do not need to turn his face to verify his name. I recognise his finer clothes. He's wearing what he wore the last time I laid eyes on him, hurtling in pursuit of Mistress Beldam at the midnight pillory. Here are his gentlemanly boots, his decorated jerkin, his townsman's breeches and his plain, unfeathered cap. His fingers and his knuckles are still blue and green with paint. I recognise his wealthy beard and see how waxed and shaped it is, a trowel-shaped wedge of hair. I even think I can see some proof of his enduring smile from the creases on the back of his neck. I can't believe he would be parted from his smile, even in death. The body is crunched up, of course. Full stretched, it would be longer than the chest. But this is not a body I have ever seen full stretched. This is a body that appears as I'd expect it to, lop-sided, stiff and out of line. He's died exactly as he stands, off-kilter as if he has been struck by lightning. The heavens opened and a tongue of light gave him the body of an old gnarled tree. I have no doubt that this is him, the stumbler, the Chart-Maker, the man who was too oddly brave to turn his back on us.

So far as I can tell from my brief examination of the body before I close the lid on him and tumble downstairs to run along the gallery, more fearful for myself than I have ever been before, his wounds were inflicted by a sword, the same one, I presume, that cut the ropes away at the access to the stairwell. He has been run though with great force and commitment. The blade has entered at the front a dozen times and exited behind his back, piercing his main organs and his chest. The blood has blackened and stiffened in his clothes. I do not know enough about a corpse to tell how long it has been here, or when his killing took place. It could have been last night, or equally it could have happened on the night of torture when the women named him. What's probable, given the poor repair of the attic stairs, is that his killing took place in the upper rooms and close enough to the travel chest for the victim to be toppled in before he bled too much. Who should I hold responsible? Apart from the Beldams or the Jordan men? I have to say that for a moment I hold myself responsible. I feel that I have failed the man. I feel that I am failing him again, because I have to leave him here. By rights I ought to carry him to Turd and Turf to join the other corpses of the week, and mark his grave with a proper monument of piled stones and within sight of his beloved longpurples. He liked it there. He liked the blossoms and the light. He liked its solitude. He would have liked to listen to the juking of the birds until the end of time. But I cannot carry him, not on my own, not down those stairs, not with the fire-maiden pressing down on us with her revenging flame.

The odd thing is, she does not come. Perhaps her husband has decided that she's burnt enough or he is impatient to depart before the evening and the darkness close in. He knows it's wise to get away, to pass beyond our parish bounds before they're stopped by someone coming back or asked for their account of where the oxen were acquired and why their cart is so loaded down with property beyond their station. Perhaps she's tired of it herself. Her grief and anger have been spent. What is the point of taking down the manor house? What is the point of burning it with Mr Quill inside to haunt its attics and its roofs? Maybe she has no idea that he is there, and she's not the murderer. Whatever is the truth of it, it's clear that I will never know. I step out of the courtyard with my bags, and there I glimpse the back of them and their great haul of plunder disappearing down the lane. The husband leads the oxen from the front, and she sits riding on the cart, her skirts pulled up to her thighs, the short sword resting on her knees and her bare legs swinging over the back. Her shoulders are draped in velvet, naturally. She's getting even smaller now as they retreat behind the hedges and the walls, as they retreat into another world.

I'll follow those Beldams, of course, but now only in dreams and without the emboldening of fairy caps or ale. I see myself trailing them by fifty paces, say, a neighbour in their wake, and free to close the gap only when she calls out to me and says that I am welcome to travel at their sides, that it is safe to bridge the space between us, that she does not wish me any harm. We can be reconciled. But I don't want to dream of them just yet. I want to watch the manor burn. What starts with fire will end with ash; it has to end with ash if I am to give Mr Quill an honourable cremation rather than abandon him in the chest for woodworms, rats and attic birds to feed upon. Is this at last the courage that I sought this morning and last night and which I intended, at the very least (and at the very worst), to invest in redeeming mischief of some kind? Will this hot-headed deed make it too unsafe for me to stay on here as Master Jordan's trusted winter man? Will this satisfy my seven witnesses? Will I be satisfied? Apart from wanting that one day behind the plough, I genuinely have not had a plan till now, but I have come to understand that I should finish what the Beldams have begun. I have a sudden, dutiful desire to set some further timbers cracking in the heat and to watch the ginger cats of flame, which have already put an end to all the other village homes, licking at the milky air of the manor house, licking through the many rooms and treading lightly up the several flights of stairs. I want to see the turret flaring like a beacon with flames higher than the pinnacle of any steeple.

It isn't hard to coax some flame back into the ashes of the parlour fire and light a candle that I can carry from the hearth to some deeper place. I need kindling but there's plenty at hand. The parlour floor is strewn with the documents spilling from my master's overturned coffer, his titles, muniments and deeds. They are as dry and brittle as barley husk. I'll only have to touch them with this candle flame and they will leap with fire.

17

So I have reached our village bounds. On this main lane, our outer limits are marked on one side by a merestone, about waist high and vivid with its orange overcoat of lichen. It is dressed for travelling. I've not been this close to the edge for several years. It has always seemed too precarious a place; on our side of the stone there can be no trespassing, as Master Kent has told us many times: 'If we stay within our bounds, there are no bounds to stay us.' One further step beyond, however, and everything you have is left behind. You are disowned.

I snap off a stalk of grass from our side of the limits, tasting our own fodder with an ox's mouth. I grasp the merestone in both hands and bump my head against it, beating in the bounds just as we have beaten the bounds into every village child as soon as they were big enough to stray. I am that boy who needs reminding where he does and does not fit. I bump the stone three times, just hard enough to break the skin and lay the groundings of a bruise, just hard enough to make me admit to pain.

Now there's nothing to detain me here or to encumber my escape. I have my four mementos of these seven days, all marked in skin or made from skin. There is the forehead I've just bloodied on the stone; there is the shiny pink scorch mark in the middle of my palm, still slightly stiff; there is the kick-wound on my brow and cheek, faintly sore but it will mend, and disappear; and, finally, tied in a scroll with hogging string, the piece of calfskin vellum I crafted myself in the manor's scullery and which I almost used as kindling along with Mr Quill's two preparatory charts. I burnt them both: the one that's decorated with our commons and our fields and lanes, the fabric of our village lives marked down in colours and in lines; and the other, busy one, proposing future pastures. I burnt them with the man that painted them. But I have kept the flap of calf. My vellum is an unmarked sheet. It could be anywhere.

I'm resting for a moment with my hip against the stone, and facing inwards towards the village of my choice for what I know will be the final time. It's silent there. I cannot hear the clacking of a single tool. Or any animals. It's simply quiet and undisturbed, attending to itself, an Eden with no Adam and no Eve. My winter wheat is swelling, unobserved. It won't be many days before that single furrow where the barley grew this year will imp with greenery. Earth and seeds are soundless labourers. Even the manor house has ceased its cracking, though its pall of smoke is still stretching out across our blackened roofs and browning canopies, with Mr Quill amongst its residues. There is a story I can tell, if ever I am caught by any of the Jordans of this world and asked to give an account of why I failed to save the manor house. The orphaned witch caressed its timbers with her fiery breath. That Mistress Beldam — not content to have spent her venom on the doves and Willowjack, not yet satisfied by Philip Earle's thin blood or the damage to the groom's face that she encouraged with her sorcery, not sated by the fires in all our homes — was determined to destroy the Kent and Jordan property as well. That was the meanest act of all. Watch out for her. She has a cart, I'll say. She has the blackest eyes and hair. She's bearing sin and mischief to the corners of the earth. I will not say she's also bearing me away.

It's time. I have to finish my farewells — though actually there's not much of a view. From here, the prospects are hemmed in and limited: a lane, some stone-built walls, a well-attended hedge. Even the brambles and the traveller's joy have been cut back by some attentive hand, some sickled villager who must by now be far away, and safe, and bewildered. Apart from the lichen cladding on the stone, the only colour comes from scarlet haws, deep in the pruned-backed thorns.

If anything, the views ahead, beyond our bounds, are more rewarding to the eye. They are more savage, certainly. And more formless and more void. The hedges there have not been cut and trimmed for many years, if ever. They spread across the lane with their great arms as if to send all travellers back, or at best to make their passage forward troublesome. I can see where the Beldams' cart has churned its muddy wheel ruts in the track and where its loaded sides have snapped back twigs on a pair of hazel trees, heavy with some timely nuts. The lane is telling me I should not fear the futures that it holds. I'll not go hungry anyway. Once I tire of hazels, I can blacken my tongue with bramble berries and rouge my lips with elders and with sloes. I can fill my mouth with fruits and nuts at every step I take. The countryside will provide its seeded surplus of infinity for long enough for me to find another place where I can rest.

An unwary, solitary mouse, intent on foraging in daylight, against its custom, and too short-sighted either to spot or to be alarmed by me, pokes its tender head into the lane. I watch its fussy searching for a few moments before I let it know I'm close; I kick a loose curl of earth against its hedge. Take care. The mouse freezes for an instant, then scurries over rock and moss to disappear into its crevice home. If it is wise, it will stay there until tonight. I am left to gather up my bags of modest assets and removables, my sturdy stick, my roll of unmarked vellum chart, my silver and my bulky burdens of remorse and memory. This is my heavy labour now. I have to leave behind these common fields. I have to take this first step out of bounds. I have to carry on alone until I reach wherever is awaiting me, until I gain wherever is awaiting us.

I have enjoyed a fortunate career in books and publishing.

I want to thank Pam Turton, Tom Crace and Lauren Crace for letting me get on with the anti-social habit of writing in a happy, stimulating and loving household.

I am immensely grateful to David Godwin, who has been, in turn, my editor, publisher, agent and friend since my first published short story. I have been lucky to work over several years with (amongst many others) John Glusman and Nan Talese in the USA and Tony Lacey and Kate Harvey in the UK.

We do hope that you have enjoyed reading this large print book.

Did you know that all of our titles are available for purchase?

We publish a wide range of high quality large print books including:
Romances, Mysteries, Classics
General Fiction
Non Fiction and Westerns

Special interest titles available in large print are:
The Little Oxford Dictionary
Music Book
Song Book
Hymn Book
Service Book

Also available from us courtesy of Oxford University Press:
Young Readers' Dictionary
(large print edition)
Young Readers' Thesaurus
(large print edition)

For further information or a free brochure, please contact us at:
Ulverscroft Large Print Books Ltd.,
The Green, Bradgate Road, Anstey,
Leicester, LE7 7FU, England.
Tel: (00 44) 0116 236 4325
Fax: (00 44) 0116 234 0205

Other titles published by
The House of Ulverscroft:

ALL THAT FOLLOWS

Jim Crace

Leonard Lessing is a jazzman taking a break. His glory days behind him, his body letting him down, he relives old gigs and feeds his media addiction during solitary days at home. Increasingly estranged from his wife Francine, who is herself mourning the sudden absence of her only daughter, Leonard has found his own safe, suburban groove. But then a news bulletin comes that threatens to change everything. A gunman has seized hostages a short drive from Lennie's house. His face leaps out of the evening news — and out of Leonard's own past . . . Leonard has a choice to make.

REGENERATION

Pat Barker

Craiglockhart War Hospital, 1917, where army psychiatrist William Rivers is treating shell-shocked soldiers. Under his care are the poets Siegfried Sassoon and Wilfred Owen, as well as mute Billy Prior, who is only able to communicate by means of pencil and paper. Rivers' job is to make the men in his charge healthy enough to fight. Yet the closer he gets to mending his patients' minds, the harder becomes every decision to send them back to the horrors of the front . . . *Regeneration* is the classic exploration of how the traumas of war brutalized a generation of young men.